THE CHINESE WESTERN

SHORT FICTION FROM TODAY'S CHINA

Cover design by Bill Toth
Book design by Iris Bass

THE CHINESE WESTERN

SHORT FICTION FROM TODAY'S CHINA

Translated by

ZHU HONG

AVAILABLE
PRESS

BALLANTINE BOOKS • NEW YORK

An Available Press Book
Published by Ballantine Books

Copyright © 1988 by Zhu Hong

All rights reserved under International and Pan-American Copyright
Conventions. Published in the United States of America by Ballantine
Books, a division of Random House, Inc., New York, and simultaneously
in Canada by Random House of Canada Limited, Toronto.

Grateful acknowledgment is made to the individual writers for permission
to translate and publish their Chinese Western short stories.

Library of Congress Catalog Card Number: 87-91880

ISBN 0-345-35140-1

Manufactured in the United States of America

First Edition: August 1988

Contents

The Chinese Western
An Introduction

Chinese literature of the last dozen years, generally known as the "literature of the new age," is mainly a reaction to the Cultural Revolution (1966–1976) and has evoked interest both inside and outside the country.

This new fiction has branched out into various "schools" according to subject matter and literary mode, falling into such phases as "literature of the wounded generation," "literature of retrospect and examination," "literature about reform-related problems," and, in the last few years, "literature seeking cultural roots."

One independent trend emerging from this new wave is the so-called Chinese Western—prose and (to a lesser extent) poetry from and about China's outlying regions in the West and Northwest: Xinjiang, Gansu, Qinghai, Ningxia, Shaanxi, and Tibet. These regions, approximately one-fifth of China's land surface, are inhabited by a great number of China's national minorities. Here is the meeting place of three great religions: the Muslims of Xinjiang, the Lamaists of Tibet, and the Buddhist Hans of Shaanxi.

Historically, the Northwest is where the silk road passed. It was a thriving political center during the Tang dynasty. But when trade was carried on by sea route, and the imperial capital moved eastward, the region deteriorated economically. The Northwest has since been regarded as one of the most backward parts of the country, entrenched in tradition, closed to the outside world.

The Northwest of China is not a frontier in the geographical sense, but inevitably it is on this vast soil that the current policies of reform and opening up to the outside world will invariably create the biggest impact. Here too are amplified all the problems China faces in her drive for modernization.

There is no need to make arbitrary comparisons between the Chinese and American Western, or to look for influences and imitations. But there are striking affinities—emerging out of vastly different situations. Both are national genres—in epic dimensions—that register a moment of change in historic significance, and both ponder the meaning of that change.

Interestingly, it was a young writer of Hassack nationality from Xinjiang—Akbair Mijiti—who first made a specific analogy between the American Western and its Chinese counterpart. In his article "The West! The West!" he refers enthusiastically to James Fenimore Cooper, Willa Cather, and Owen Wister, and stresses that in spite of differences, there is much to be learned from the American Western. Another rising young writer, Zhang Rei (from Gansu), contends that the Chinese Western should benefit from imitating not merely the American Western but also Latin American fiction and Soviet literature.

It was in 1984 that Zhong Dienfei, a veteran film critic, first used the term *Western* in connection with films. (A new movie genre was born, which subsequently produced many prize-winning works.) The following year, two special conferences, one in Xinjiang and the other in Gansu, were held to discuss the emergence of this new literary phenomenon, and articles have continued to appear hailing new works and emerging writers.

Western Fiction in China, a literary magazine, commands a growing readership, while other influential journals such as *Trends in Modern Literary Thought* carry special columns devoted to the Western. A magazine called *Western Film* has also been launched. Many other projects are being developed to promote the Chinese Western, foremost among these a fiction series to be issued by Xinjiang Youth Publishing House.

Writers of the Western fall into two groups: local writers who know the region and mainstream writers sent to the area for "reform through manual labor." The latter, in temporary or permanent political disgrace, write about the region through "foreign" eyes. (An example is Wang Meng's series of stories and sketches about Xinjiang.)

Recently, because of the popularity of this school of writing, established authors have made special trips to the Northwest (especially to the exotic Xinjiang) for research purposes. Mainstream novelist Bao Chang made the journey to collect material for his *The Vagabonds,* too long for inclusion in the present volume.

As one of the most compelling schools of contemporary fiction in China, the Western presents a truthful description of the region—its bleakness and barbarity on one hand, its native strength and unsullied beauty on the other. The genre resurrects all the conflicts that are raised by the new changes—and it depicts the Chinese themselves differently. Charged with melancholy and the burden of history, the stories portray vital, resilient men and women, committed to survival.

The eight stories in *The Chinese Western* have been selected on the basis of intrinsic merit, but I have also attempted to highlight the variety of themes and subject matter that appeal to Western readers. Clearly, these writers wish to combine a sense of tradition with

a modern consciousness. That's another common de-
nominator in all the tales.

Most of these stories are concerned with the peasant, for whom life is first and foremost a matter of
survival. The writers break away from the romanti-
cized stereotypes and unbridled sentimentality that
marred many basically good stories of earlier periods.
These eight selections rely heavily on irony to illus-
trate not only the misery of the peasant's situation, but
the irrationality, even absurdity, of the rules and regulations imposed by bureaucracy—rules that will ostensibly save the peasant, but which are actually alien
to the culture and destructive of the economy.

Zhu Xiaoping's "Chronicle of Mulberry Tree Village" raises the question: Who is taking the food out
of the peasants' mouths? Answer: (as the peasants interpret the matter) The students. But when we see the
land "assessors" casually name figures for the amount
of grain to be handed to the state, as they sit over
their "indispensable" dinners, we are in no doubt as
to who is exploiting the peasant. Not the students.

A further consideration is: Who is offering the peasant help and leadership in the struggle for survival?
In the student-narrator's eyes, Li Jindo, the team leader
of Mulberry Tree Village, is a tyrant ruling by pa-
triarchal right—a typical situation in a rural community. But as the story unfolds, it is Jindo, not the
"cadres" sent from on high, who secures the peasants
their yearly allowance of grain, even if he has to re-
sort to cheating.

Into this stagnant region and these preposterous situations, the winds of change begin to blow. The vast
rural areas of the Northwest, like the rest of the country, have been (as were Sherwood Anderson's people in "The Egg") "seized by a passion for getting up
in the world."

It is in this manner that, in China, the clash between tradition and innovation began. This confrontation has been manifested between town and country, between astute city residents and naive country folk, or between clever peasants who want to get ahead and peasants who want to honor the old ways. The innocence-vs.-experience clash is also reflected in differing attitudes to the soil, to morals, marriage, family, and community. Writers are not sure whether the changes are all for the good. As Jia Pingwua says, "It is traditional virtue matched with modern beauty, as well as traditional evil matched with modern vice."

A tragic irony lies in the fact that the peasants consider "getting rich by the flood" (see "How Much Can a Man Bear?" and "Daughter of the Yellow River") perfectly acceptable, while they distrust making money through business acumen. In "Family Chronicle of a Wooden Bowl Maker," the "upstart" young Huang is looked upon as something of a magician by his neighbors, when he has only profited by market information. Huang's neighbors feel that business success is somehow innately evil. That is why when the young man's bus is wrongly confiscated, his neighbors think he has been fittingly punished. They have become accustomed to, even bask in, their poverty.

The old father in "Family Chronicle of a Wooden Bowl Maker" exclaims, "What are we anyway, that our sons should make so much money in the twinkling of an eye! It is not right!" This points to an even more basic problem: the peasants' assessment of their own dignity and worth. When the poor struggle tooth and nail for survival, they become oblivious to their value as human beings.

In "How Much Can a Man Bear?" whole sections of the local population are unjustly convicted of belonging to a nonexistent "antirevolutionary" unit, some being sentenced to as long as fifteen years. After the Cultural Revolution, the case is reversed and the prisoners are released and paid several hundred *yuan* each, according to the length of their incarceration. The peasants are grateful, considering themselves lucky, because as one of them states, "The government is good! . . . Because of my imprisonment, I have been able to buy grain and clothes. And I plan to repair my house. Of course the suffering was hard, but I have been reimbursed very well for those years."

   All the stories in this collection are concerned in one way or another with the individual's thwarted search for a fuller life. In "Daughter of the Yellow River" by Wang Jiada, the heroine's search for love is cut short by a combination of feudal ideology and contemporary law-enforcement authorities, both inimical to women who want to emerge from poverty and a lifetime of frustration.

   In "The Progress of the Military Patrol Car" by Tang Dong, the young protagonist, the son of a "class enemy," pays dearly for the satisfaction of being accepted by his betters. Another story, Wang Meng's "Anecdotes of Chairman Maimaiti," derives irony from the hero's realization of his dream of becoming a writer—only by having himself labeled "demon and monster," a figurative delineation for all class enemies during the Cultural Revolution.

   The Chinese Western has also created a new kind of hero, one who breaks away from the stereotype of the positive socialist hero of yore. This new pioneering protagonist combines traditional virtues with new expertise, and he truly benefits the people—though he often bends rules to do so. In fact, what instantly strikes the reader is the hero's challenge to established authority. China is a country whose citizens live constantly by rules and regulations: residence permits, grain coupons, cooking oil coupons, gate entrance certificates, work certificates, union cards, identification cards, certificates for medical aid, and—for Party members— membership cards. By all these cards and certificates, people are abundantly supplied with identity—and are kept organized in one area, one unit, one family. And any change requires not only authorization but new certificates!

In the vast uncultivated spaces of the West and Northwest, one can afford to flout all this bureaucracy. The writers of the Chinese Western celebrate this sense of freedom from petty restrictions. The far west, especially locations like Xinjiang, is so vast it takes in everybody, with or without ID card.

These regions are so removed geographically from the center of authority and the excesses of various campaigns that more room arises for individual initiative. In two representative narratives—*The Vagabonds,* mentioned earlier, and "Shorblac: A Driver's Story" by Zhang Xianliang—it is precisely the outlaws who migrated west with no official certificates who have helped to build Xinjiang. They are outlaws in the official code, but they are intended (and readers will recognize them) as heroes. Here the emphasis is on strength, resourcefulness, decency, loyalty, and the ability to survive. The hero in "Shorblac" says, "If it were not for this liberal policy in hiring labor, if people in charge here still insisted on looking at a piece of paper and not at the man himself, why, Xinjiang would have been nowhere." This young man, after witnessing all the chaos of the Cultural Revolution (including his own "reeducation" in the countryside), finally settles in Xinjiang and marries a Shanghai girl, herself a victim of physical and mental cruelty.

Underlying "Shorblac," underlying all these Chinese Western stories, is the conviction of a people—individuals who have suffered injustices and cruelties but who, with unsuspected wellsprings of fortitude, survive and prevail.

—Zhu Hong
February 1988

HOW MUCH CAN A MAN BEAR?

by Jia Pingwua

JIA PINGWUA *(1958–   ) is a prize-winning novelist and short-story writer. A native of Shaanxi, he has over ten volumes of fiction to his credit. He is the deputy chairman of the Writers' Union of Xian. "How Much Can a Man Bear?" was originally published in 1985 in the Shanghai literary magazine* Encounter Monthly.

It is an old custom in Shangzhou County that good friends are called "close relations." When two men become especially friendly and their wives give birth at about the same time—one to a son and the other to a daughter—then the children will be married when they grow up. This custom is quite barbarous, particularly nowadays, but according to the mountain people, those who grow up to do their own courting are never assured of marital bliss, while those who are betrothed while still in their mothers' wombs might just have a chance at happiness.

Guangzi, of the southern part of the county, was betrothed twenty years ago in this manner to a family in Lonan County. Unfortunately, his intended bride turned out at birth to be a male child—Lamao, by name. Though Guangzi and Lamao could not marry, they still believed that fate had joined them together. So they became bond-brothers, living with each other year in and year out.

During the first two years of the Cultural Revolution, the world was in chaos, and Guangzi came and settled in his bond-brother's home in Lonan. The two were never seen apart. In time, their parents died and the young men relied on one another even more. They learned the art of castrating pigs and made a living around the countryside as itinerant craftsmen.

By this time the Cultural Revolution had ushered in various "campaigns" to purge the country of liberal elements. In 1969, the third year of the Revolution, one such campaign was termed "investigating and eliminating bad elements," and with a lot of pomp and circumstance, one serious case was brought to light: the so-called clandestine Liu Defense Brigade. Liu refers to Liu Shaoqi, and defending him was, of course, a heinous crime and many were implicated. After the campaign had run its course, over a hundred people were jailed or executed. Guangzi, terrified by this state of affairs, wanted to go back to his native Shangnan.

But Lamao persuaded him to remain in Lonan. "Look here," Lamao explained, "our ancestors have taught us that prosperous times are good for running around, but in periods of upheaval, folks should stick together. You've always been able to rely on your craft to make a living, so we have nothing to fear. Let's stay through the summer and think of going back in winter."

And so Guangzi stayed on.

A month later, the weather suddenly turned cold. It was said that there were heavy rains upstream on the Lo River. One morning, after the two brothers had finished castrating a batch of piglets in the southern mountain region, they sat drinking a bottle of wine. Suddenly distant rumblings were heard. At first they thought it must be thunder, but then noticed that the old sow did not come indoors to bed down in the hay, as she had in past thunderstorms.

They kept on drinking. Suddenly there was the sound of rushing footsteps. Then voices were shouting: "The flood is coming! The flood is coming!" The thundering sounds intensified. The two rushed out and saw the villagers running toward the river carrying nets and baskets.

"Quick!" Lamao said. "Let's go and get rich!"

The Lo, in fact, was a big river. And it flooded every year. Firewood, building material, and other valuables would be washed away, and the people downstream would seize the chance to secure them. Every year, then, the citizens of Lonan prospered under the misfortune of the peasants upstream.

When the two brothers reached the shore, the setting sun had begun to cast its rays over the turgid waters, and every conceivable kind of object could be seen borne by the crest of the flood. The villagers occupied all the prominent spots along the shore that afforded any firm foothold. They were all naked, with long-handled nets ready for the catch.

"Let's go farther up," Lamao said. "It's harder to get footing there, so there will be fewer people and we can catch more."

When they reached a spot farther upstream, they also stripped naked. They warmed up their chests and bellies with their own urine and then plastered their groins and genitals with mud. Thus armored, Lamao fixed his eyes on a floating log. He whipped out his tiger-claw rake, landed its claws onto one end of the log, and pulled. With Guangzi's help, he lugged it on shore. Very pleased with themselves, they sat down for a smoke.

By this time the sun had set, the water was dark, and apart from the sound of the river, everything was wrapped in silence. While they were calculating the price that the log would fetch, the wind suddenly rustled eerily and the sounds of snapping reeds floated up behind a bend in the river. As the sound came nearer, the willows sweeping the water were disturbed. A black object appeared, bobbing up and down as it was carried by the flood. Before the brothers could collect their wits, the object struck a jutting rock and was hurled back. Guangzi saw that it was a tree stump and cried out to Lamao. Lamao hurled his tiger-claw rake and started pulling. But the stump was caught in the reeds and nearly dragged Lamao into the water.

Lamao said, "Oh, brother, it must be the water spirits. Otherwise I'd be able to dislodge it."

"It's just the reeds," Guangzi replied. "Let me go and find out."

Guangzi was perfectly at home in water and, holding a cutting knife between his teeth, he slipped down into the river. He was at the tree stump in a twinkling. He ducked below the surface in an instant. When he reappeared, he looked scared.

"Is it caught in the reeds, or in the willows?" Lamao asked.

"How strange!" Guangzi replied. "It's soft. It feels like flesh."

Lamao was in a great fright. "A body! It must be a corpse. Come up quick! Don't let it weigh you down. It's dead anyway," Lamao shouted after him. "Why don't you cut off the hands, to get them off the stump?"

Guangzi resurfaced for a third time, a ragged piece of printed cotton held aloft in his hand. "It's a woman," he shouted. "Her hands are around the tree stump, but her body is entangled by the reeds."

Lamao then saw a bundle of reeds disentangled, then

a human form being placed on a tree stump. Guangzi's head appeared.

"Pull! Pull!" he cried.

The tree stump with the human form on it approached, and Guangzi carried the body ashore.

"The river is flooded regularly and every year people are drowned," Lamao complained. "What is the
sense of bringing up a corpse?"

But Guangzi said, "She is young and there is some
warmth on her breast. Even if she is dead, her family might look for her body downstream. We could
be performing a good deed."

So they put the young woman under a tree and
looked at her in earnest. She seemed to be alive. They
started to move her limbs so she would regurgitate the
water she had swallowed. Her eyes were closed, but
her nostrils at last began to move.

Guangzi and Lamao looked at each other in silence.
Then Guangzi murmured, "This woman's life force
is strong. She is recovering."

Lamao agreed. "She is destined to be saved by us."

They carried her back to their hut. Within minutes,
the villagers heard the news and came to have a look.
Some versed in medicinal practice washed out the woman's mouth, cleaned her ears of clinging mud, rubbed
her chest with alcohol, and applied mint to her forehead and upper lip. Then everybody dispersed.

Night fell. The brothers sat in the middle room of
their hut, drinking under the shade of a lamp, waiting for the woman to wake up.

At the first crow of the cock, there was a rustling
in the inner room. The two brothers looked at each
other uneasily and decided to enter the room. Just then,
the curtain over the door lifted and the woman appeared, leaning against the door frame. Her hair was
in disorder, but with expressive eyes, she was ap-

pealing in her delicate state. She was a vision of beauty hitherto unknown to the brothers.

Guangzi gathered himself together and said, "So you are awake. You're even strong enough to stand."

The woman looked at them mutely as she slid to a kneeling position. The lamp illuminated two streams of tears running down her cheeks.

"Respected elder brothers, you have saved my life!" she exclaimed.

Lamao helped her to a chair and offered her wine. The woman did not refuse the libation; she accepted simply and drank it down.

"You should have some soup," Guangzi insisted.

The two brothers lighted the fire and started cooking. The woman, after slowly sipping the soup, was gradually revived.

Guangzi and Lamao kept drinking until their eyes were blurred. They plied the woman with questions and learned that her name was Liangliang and that she was originally from Jichuan. She was passing by the Lo River when the floods poured down and washed her away. When asked about her family, she refused to talk and just let the tears fall. By then, the pot of wine was drained. Lamao got up to fetch more, his eyes riveted on the woman. The woman herself sensed his interest and cast down her eyes.

Lamao blubbered, "Liangliang, it's us brothers who saved your life, right? Are you aware? While your hands still clasped the tree stump, there was no breath in your body." He chuckled uncontrollably. Patting Guangzi on the shoulder, he continued: "Brother, our ancestors have said saving one life exceeds erecting a seven-story ladder to heaven."

Guangzi realized that Lamao was in one of his drunken fits and tried to stop him, but Lamao stumbled to the floor and remained prostrate like a lump of clay.

"Respected elder brother," Liangliang said, "I will always remember you with gratitude. At the moment I have nothing to repay you with, but the day will come when I will be able to express my gratitude." So saying, she rose to leave.

"But where are you going?" Guangzi asked. Liangliang answered that she had no fixed destination.

"What!" Guangzi remonstrated. "You, a woman, alone and just snatched from death! Where can you go? Come, we brothers are rough peasants, but our hearts are in the right place. We have saved you and that's that. No need to talk of repayment. Tonight you sleep in the inner bedroom. Tomorrow you can leave. As for him," he said, looking at Lamao, "I'll haul him over to the loft in the cowshed."

Liangliang protested, but Guangzi had already left with Lamao on his back.

The next morning Guangzi woke up when it was barely daylight. He remembered he had promised to castrate pigs at several households in the town. "Lamao, brother," he shouted, "time to get up!" But Lamao continued to sleep in a drunken stupor. Saliva drooled from the corner of his mouth.

Guangzi laughed in exasperation. "Oh you, go on with your death of a sleep!" He covered Lamao with a blanket.

During the night, lying in the hayloft over the cowshed, they had shared a blanket. Guangzi now saw that they were both covered with flea bites. That's what comes of drinking, he mused. He shook the wisps of straw out of his hair and climbed from the loft. The door to the main rooms was still shut. He called out once. When there was no reply, he felt it was not appropriate for him to enter.

He thought to himself: *the woman will leave at dawn;*

there is no chance to say goodbye anyway. And so he set off.

The town was not far. The main street was usually quiet and deserted. But today firewood salvaged from the flood was stacked before many doorways.

One housewife sat in the doorway on one side of the street, her work basket by her feet. She was sewing the sole of a shoe as she chatted with another housewife sitting across the street. This one was at her weaving machine, and with every tap of the foot and wave of the hand, her shuttle flew back and forth, while her tongue was busy recalling the previous day's happenings at the riverside.

"What a big flood!" she said. "The Lius round the corner have the advantage of a big family. They fished up ten beams."

"I heard that many died," said the other woman. "My husband saw with his own eyes a woman floating in a tub. She screamed for help and then disappeared under a wave."

Her neighbor added, "I heard that the pig castrator Lamao and his brother rescued a woman. They took her home with them."

Guangzi appeared and all the idle chatter stopped. But from every doorway faces peered out, smiling at him with significant nods and winks.

Guangzi, unaware of anything unusual, went straight to the house of his host. The master of the house was ready with wine. Guangzi drank until his face was flushed. Then he stood up to go to work. He drew a piglet from the sty, squatted down, one foot holding down its hind legs. He felt for the knife at his belt behind his back, and with one twirl of the shining blade, he made an incision in the piglet's hindquarters. His fingers delved inside and fished out the bloody knot of flesh and cut it free.

"There," he exclaimed, "this is it. The organ that makes him restless." Saying this, he threw the mass of flesh to the cat, who devoured it at once.

"Guangzi, you be damned!" said a bystander. "Isn't that bit of flesh the only thing that brings some joy to living?"

Guangzi laughed. "Joy, yes, but also sorrow and disaster."

The onlookers laughed while a woman cried, "You lowbred rascal, say what you will, but why don't you castrate yourself? Look at all the people drowned in the Lo River. How is it you rescued this one woman and no other?"

He hastily sewed up the incision and let the piglet go. Then he washed his hands and sat down to more wine.

When he was three quarters done, his host said, "Guangzi, I heard them say that the woman you saved was white and tender looking?"

"Yes, her looks were well above ordinary, and she does not seem to be of peasant stock. We asked about her family, but she would divulge nothing."

"That's strange," the host said. "Perhaps she's from far away. That's possible, the times are so restless. You know, you're not getting younger. It's time you take a woman to yourself. Since it fell upon you to save her, it means that you two are bound together from a former life."

Guangzi was quite insulted. "What do you take us for? My brother and I did not rescue this woman to make her a wife. Anyway, by now she has already left us."

There was an embarrassed silence, and the party broke up.

Guangzi finished his work with a heavy heart. He could not understand how people could interpret the situation so calculatedly. What had the world come to! How filthy the villagers' minds were! This came of the evil times.

Guangzi's own mind worked in extremes, and for the moment he wanted to wash his hands of these people. His only solace was in the bottle. He spent all his earnings at the wine shop. Hours later, he wobbled homeward. When he reached Lamao's house, the door was shut but not bolted. He pushed at it and fell inside, throwing up all he had imbibed. At the same time, he heard an exclamation of alarm from within the room.

"Brother Lamao!" he cried, but there was no reply.

The window frame shuddered as if someone had jumped from it. Guangzi was full of apprehension. Had a thief been here? To his surprise, Liangliang emerged from the room, her hair in disorder, her face flushed.

"What!" Guangzi was amazed. "You are not gone?"

Frightened, Liangliang was speechless as Guangzi continued to peer at her.

"Where is my brother? Who is in the room there?"

Guangzi strode in and found the bed in great disorder; on the ground in front of the bed was a pair of Lamao's straw sandals, while his pipe was still in a niche in the wall. Guangzi scrutinized Liangliang as she trembled.

Without waiting for Guangzi to ask, she knelt down and cried, "It was all my fault. Don't blame Lamao. He saved me, so when he asked for this favor, I gave it to him out of gratitude."

Guangzi was at first struck dumb. Then, with one slap he flung Liangliang to the floor and rushed out for Lamao. But Lamao, whose footprints were left on the windowsill, was nowhere to be seen. Guangzi came back into the room and, with all the force he could muster, he struck a flour jar from the top of the cupboard. Broken pieces of the jar cut him. Although blood flowed from his hands, he stood there like a man of stone.

At the time, Lamao was actually hiding in the cowshed, half buried in the straw and dung, full of shame for what he had done. He listened for half a day to Guangzi's ranting and to all the destruction going on in the room. When the noise quieted down, he came out dejectedly and saw words written with ashes on the door board. He went over and read the message—"Lower than cur or swine"—but he did not see any sign of Guangzi. He guessed that his bond-brother must have returned to his native Shangnan in anger.

The next day, Lamao took the bus for Shangnan. He arrived there three days later.

As Lamao expected, Guangzi was back in his own house. Lamao knelt in front of him in the dust and pleaded for forgiveness, but Guangzi would not speak to him. He went mutely to the kitchen. When he returned, he placed a bowlful of noodles on the floor in front of Lamao.

Lamao took up the bowl, thinking to himself: *my brother has forgiven me*. He began to eat the food eagerly.

When he was half through, he found raw beans and hay beneath the noodles. He now understood what Guangzi was insinuating—that he was no better than a beast; hence he was being served with the feed for the mules and donkeys.

Lamao stood up. Taking a length of rope, he went out of the house—and hanged himself on a persimmon tree.

When Guangzi heard the news, he rushed to the tree. But Lamao's corpse was already stiff. Guangzi was struck down with sorrow, and cried till he fainted from grief.

He removed the body to his own courtyard, set up a pavilion and platform to honor his friend, and spent a large sum of money for his coffin and funeral clothes. He had Lamao buried in a field behind the house in Shangnan. In uncontrollable sorrow he prepared three meals a day to the spirit of Lamao and wandered about dazed and absentminded. All this went on for three years.

Guangzi refused all matchmakers' proposals, never went near women, never troubled to wash or take care of his own person. In short, he went around looking like a starved ghost, and everybody in the village said he was out of his mind.

The following year Shangzhou suffered a great drought. The surface of the soil was as cracked as the back of a turtle; the crops were poor; and many peasants deserted their homes to go out begging. Guangzi had only one mouth to feed and so was better off than others. At mealtimes, all the ragged children of the village would sit on his doorstep and stare as he ate. Guangzi would scold, "You are sent by your parents, you rascals!" But he would still scoop up a ladleful of oats for them to share.

One day Guangzi took out his pan and dry-stirred a handful of wheat over the fire and added some dried *jao* roots. Then he stirred half a jarful of oats and placed the combined mixture into the mill to make cooked flour, which could be eaten mixed with water.
The millstone was heavy. He labored at it until the sweat coursed down his face. As he continued to push with head down, the weight of the millstone was suddenly lightened. Guangzi looked up and saw a woman

pushing on the other side. It was a stranger with a
sad-looking face. Guangzi was struck with amazement.

The woman smiled sadly and said, "Respected elder
brother, I hope you are not offended at my being
here."

"Who are you?" asked Guangzi. "Where do you
come from?"

"I am from South Mountain," the woman said simply. "I am running away from starvation. If I help
you push the millstone, could you give me a handful
of dry-stirred flour?"

There was nothing on earth so alarming to Guangzi
as women. He became uneasy and said hastily, "No
need to trouble yourself. Take a bowlful of the flour
and get on your way."

He scooped out a half-gourd ladle of the mixture and
poured it down the woman's bag. He then resumed
his work.

But the woman stayed to help at the mill, then helped
Guangzi sift the mixture. She had a copper thimble
on the middle finger of her left hand; it would knock
against the side of the sifter as she worked and it made
a pretty sound.

Guangzi stopped working long enough to study the
stranger. She had a large face, with high cheekbones.
Her eyebrows were thin and she had a black mole under her left ear. Guangzi felt attracted in spite of himself. Suddenly he remembered Lamao, and his face
burned. He took back his sieve and ordered the
woman to depart.

The woman stood up in a daze. "Respected elder
brother," she said, "do not suspect me. I have been
in Shangnan for over ten days and have helped at all
the households around here. I am an honest woman."
With that, she left.

Later Guangzi learned that the woman was called

Baishui and had indeed labored in the village in exchange for food. At night she slept in an abandoned temple at the southern end of the village. The temple was famous because it once housed a clay figure of a legendary god. After the harvests, the production brigade would store its grain there.

Some vagabonds had in the past slept in the temple, and in the small hours of the morning had heard a pit-pat sound going from one end of the roof beam to the other. And then everything went silent. When the strange sound was repeated night after night, the place was believed to be haunted. Thereafter nobody was foolhardy enough to pass the night there. Later on, the clay god was toppled. Although the figure had been shattered, its two eyes, cast in glaze, were thereupon set in the wall of the temple. Now the windows were broken and the two boards of the door flapped and creaked in the wind. Guangzi could not imagine how a woman like Baishui could spend the night in such a place.

One day a fellow in the village nicknamed Baldpate strolled over to Guangzi's for a chat.

"Heh, Guangzi, what about a quick trip to the temple?" he asked, winking lewdly.

"But why should I go to the temple?"

"Oh come on," Baldpate said. "Don't tell me you haven't been going. All the other men have. There's a fairy god in that temple."

"What fairy god?" Guangzi retorted. "You'd better keep a check on your tongue! If the revolutionaries hear you, why, you'll be labeled a remnant of feudalism."

Baldpate snorted, "It's precisely the revolutionaries themselves who are saying these things. And the fairy god is none other than Baishui!"

Guangzi cursed him for a mischief maker, but Baldpate prattled on. "I hear that those who went on the first night didn't get anything for their pains. The woman snatched up a knife and nobody dared go near her. But the second night, we surprised her after midnight and held her down. . . ."

Guangzi pushed Baldpate out and closed the door after him, not wishing to hear any more vile slander, as he thought it was.

Soon afterward, it was whispered in the village that Baishui was doing her cooking in the temple and, falling short of firewood, she was collecting the bones of sheep and pigs, which sent off a disgusting smell in the neighborhood. It was also rumored that she would look for dead infants among the reeds and strip off their swaddling clothes. After washing the garments, she would sell them as cloth patches for making shoe soles. For this, it was said, the captain of the production brigade had whipped her soundly and ordered her away. Guangzi wondered if Baishui would stay on in the face of threats and physical dangers.

His apprehensions were fulfilled. Three days after Baishui's beating, Guangzi met the captain of the production brigade on the street. The captain, as it turned out, had also thrown in his lot with the revolutionaries.

Catching hold of Guangzi, he asked, "Guangzi, are you or are you not joining us to make revolution? Early-starter or latecomer makes no differences, you know."

"What if I do, and what if I don't?" Guangzi parried.

"Well, if you don't, it proves that you have no views of your own, which proves, in turn, that you have no soul. This is the teaching of our Great Leader. But if you decide to make revolution, join me tonight at the temple. The fact is, Baishui refuses to leave, and we suspect that she is a bad element hiding from the authorities. We are going to try her tonight."

"All right, I'll make revolution with you," Guangzi replied.

That same night, Guangzi and four companions walked toward the temple. But Guangzi wondered in his heart: *how can a beggar woman be a bad element? This is a rough crowd,* he thought, *and I have no business in their company.* He announced that he must go and relieve himself.

"Be sure you join us later," the captain called after him.

But Guangzi slipped into an alley and, reaching home in the dark, went straight to bed.

The next day the village was all excitement. It was bruited abroad that the night before four men had indeed crashed in on Baishui. They beat her first and then stripped and gang-raped her. Guangzi felt the blood rush to his temples and went to protest with the captain of the production brigade.

The captain defied him. "What proof do you have? And what if we *did* gang-bang her? She's from South Mountain and has no home or family around here. She had only that bit of you-know-what to earn her feed. She's gone now, and good riddance!"

Saying that, the captain gave Guangzi a resounding slap on the cheek. What could Guangzi do but swallow his anger and slink back? Still anxious on Baishui's behalf, he tried to find out about her fate after she left the village.

Some of the villagers said that she was eaten by wolves. Others maintained that after the night she was raped, she went begging in the Dragon Hollow of North Mountain, and that later her body was found eviscerated in the woods, evidently devoured by wolves, but that her head was intact, and the expression on her face with the high cheekbones was even smiling. At this news, Guangzi was devastated. He had a relapse of his old malady. Apart from tending to his crops, he would not concern himself with the outside world, and was more than ever cut off from people.

Harvest time came around. The crops were poor. The corn was only half grown, but had to be cut down anyway, stalk and all, and put to the mill. The ground mixture would be eaten in a thin gruel. The villagers' bellies were all distended, like bloated toads, from subsisting on their meager food.

Luckily for Guangzi, his private plot, sown with oats, thrived and was ripening fast on its stalks. Fearful that this treasure might be stolen, Guangzi put up a shed near his plot and began a nightly vigil. Finally the day came to harvest the crops; but by the time he completed the task, darkness had fallen. Guangzi decided to haul the crops back the next morning, so he sat down for a smoke.

As he finished his first pipe, the moon rose and shed its light over the rooftops. Guangzi suddenly remembered that it would be three days to Lamao's birthday. The past rushed back and Guangzi could not keep the tears from falling. Precisely at that moment, he heard a rustling sound. Looking up, he saw a figure at the end of the lane, moving stealthily toward his stack of oats.

A thief, Guangzi thought to himself, but did not make a sound.

He saw the thief take out a piece of string and tie together a sheaf of oats, and then spread a piece of clothing under it. Then the thief started pulling back the stalks one by one at the lower end so that the grains at the top would be squeezed out as the stalks were being drawn. As the sheaf got slighter, it would be tightened up again with the string and the drawing of stalks would go on. After a while, the grains of oats made a little pile on the cloth. Then the thief started to tie up his bundle. Just then Guangzi pounced on him, holding him down with one hand while he grabbed at his head with the other. Only then did he discover that the thief was a woman. She was startled, but did not try to escape even when Guangzi started slapping her face.

"Hit me," she cried. "I am a thief and deserve to be punished."

Guangzi looked closer and realized that she was Baishui! Now he was himself pulverized with fright.

"Baishui! But weren't you eaten by wolves?"

He was paralyzed, not knowing what to do. Then he bundled up the oats in the cloth and presented them to her.

"Go, go," he repeated, motioning her away.

Baishui did not refuse. She grabbed the bundle and dashed away. Before she disappeared, Guangzi noticed that her waist was quite thick, as if she had been eating well.

Returning to his shed, Guangzi wondered if he had seen a ghost. But the empty stalks shorn of their grain were quite real. Only then did he believe that Baishui was not dead and had turned to thieving. In the morning, he related what had happened to the villagers, and they were amazed.

The following night was very hot. Guangzi left his door open and lay down on a piece of matting on the threshold. At the first streak of dawn, he wanted to relieve himself. As he was hoisting himself up, his body touched something soft and warm. He opened his eyes and saw that it was Baishui.

He was dumbfounded. He wondered when and how she got there and tried to remember if anything had happened during the night. Baishui, seeing that he had awakened, also got up. She smiled sadly and disap-

peared. Guangzi was very frightened, but being embarrassed by things that he could not explain, he
lacked the courage to speak of the incident. The third
night, he dared not sleep in the doorway any longer;
he even barred both the front and back entrances.

The following day, coming back from the fields,
he saw his door ajar and the lock not in place. He
thought he had forgotten to lock the door and felt
for the key in its niche above the door frame, but the
key was not there either. He paled in fright. He
pushed the two boards of the door open and stepped
in. In the middle room a steaming hot dinner was
set on the little table, and beside it sat Baishui, waving a pair of straw sandals. Baishui was still in her
old clothes, but her face was washed, her hair combed,
and she presented an entirely different appearance.

She slid off her chair and cried, "Don't drive me out.
I won't leave you anyway. Please just say this one
word: stay."

Guangzi stammered, "Here? That is impossible. You
are free to stay anywhere, but not here with me."

Baishui knelt down and sobbed. "Where can I go?"
she wailed. "I have been wandering two years. Because I am a woman I have not starved. But I also dare
not remain alone anymore. You are a good man.
Please let me stay with you. I know that you have no
wife or child. I am not good for much, but I work
hard and I can bear children."

Before she finished speaking, Guangzi had already
pushed her out of the room.

Baishui held on to the door frame and exclaimed in
despair, "I am an evil woman. I deserve to die, but
the child is innocent. Do you want me to kill the
baby?"

"Baby?" Guangzi asked. "Where?" Only then did
he notice that her belly was full. "Whose child is it?"

"I don't know."

Guangzi was swept with revulsion. "You're shame-less! How dare you come to me!"

Trembling in anger, he pushed her out the door. He heard her steps moving away and then a sound like a muffled fall. Guangzi opened the door and saw Baishui on the ground, the tears coursing down her face. Guangzi felt the earth spin around him. He leaned against the door, completely unnerved.

After a long while, he caught his breath and said, "Baishui, go now. Go to the temple, and I will come to you later."

Baishui stood up and walked away wearily.

That whole night Guangzi tossed in bed, racked by indecision. *Isn't it strange,* he thought, *that I should come across these women in my life.* After the disaster of Lamao's death, he had lost all interest in women. He vowed to remain single and let his family tree die with him. And now this woman offered herself to him.

Baishui is not an honest woman, he thought to himself. An honest woman would rather die than live in this shameful manner. Baishui hated the villains who had defiled her, but she also loved the evil seed planted in her by these men. Is that what it meant to be a woman? Guangzi was not a creature of wood and stone, but how could he imagine himself married to such a woman? He knelt in front of the tablet dedicated to the soul of Lamao and vowed to his departed friend that he would never marry Baishui. Then he went inside to lie down. But the minute he closed his eyes, there before him was the image of Baishui with her protruding stomach.

Guangzi wished he could pull out his heart and throw it away, to be spared this conflict. The same night, he knocked on the door of Second Elder Uncle, the superior in the family line.

The elder, upon listening to his nephew's story, said, "Guangzi, look at this affair as building up your store of virtuous acts. The woman must be desperate if she continually offers herself to you. Take her in. This is not the same as what happened to Lamao. He tried to take advantage of a woman in distress, but in this case you are helping the woman."

Guangzi followed the elder's advice and went to fetch Baishui from the temple. He got a letter of certificate from the captain of the production brigade in order to register for marriage at the commune.

The captain snickered. "Ha, take this woman and you have a wife and child at the same time!" Guangzi said nothing in reply.

He brought Baishui back to his house, and that was all there was to the wedding. But now the bed held a pair of pillows, and at night Guangzi did not have to pee through a crack between the doorboards. The newlyweds bought a brand-new chamber pot.

During the last moon of the same year, Baishui gave birth to a chubby boy child, and Guangzi called him Tiger. Tiger was born with a stubborn nature. If he started crying, nothing would stop him. But he was a hearty baby. When he drank rice soup, his little mouth would clamp onto the rim of the bowl. He would keep his eyes on the soup, while the breath from his nostrils would make the surface of the soup erupt in ripples. Guangzi was fond of his little son and now had more pleasure in life.

Since Baishui had found a husband for herself, the color came back to her face, her cheeks filled out, and her complexion became clear and creamy. She actually looked much younger than other women her age, which was a marvel considering all she had gone through.

Often, when Guangzi returned from working in the

fields, he would see his wife with the child in her arms.

At the sight of Guangzi, she would say, "Tiger wants to ride his horse!" And she would deposit the child on Guangzi's shoulders.

Guangzi would place Tiger on his back and crawl around on all fours while the baby pulled his hair. In no time, something warm and moist would start trickling down Guangzi's neck.

"So what!" Baishui would say. "Baby boy's urine is a cure for many diseases."

Baishui was forever setting the table with hot food, lovingly prepared. Even her thin gruel, for drinking, was delicious. Guangzi had now come to realize the comforts of having a woman.

At dinner he would scoop out the first bowl and set it before the tablet of Lamao, saying, "It is my eternal regret that I have injured him!"

In the twinkling of an eye, Tiger was two years old. His birthday was on the fourteenth day of the last moon. Guangzi had been economizing the whole winter, and now had enough money to buy six *jin* of meat, fifty *jin* of white carrots, and thirty of red. He also took out the remaining sweet potato flour, all that remained of his household stock. He planned to make noodles to feed the guests the next day at Tiger's birthday party.

The next morning Guangzi was still dozing at the first crow of the cock. Baishui shook him awake. "Oh, father of our child," she cried, "I had an evil dream."

"What dream, to make you so frightened?" Guangzi asked.

"I dreamed that somebody came and killed you and Tiger and then burned down our house."

Guangzi, very superstitious himself, felt his insides

turn cold. He murmured, "What you brood on in daytime, you will dream about at night. Tell me, who was the villain in your nightmare?"

Baishui would not answer, but only bit at one end of the quilt and cried.

Guangzi assured her, "Forget about it. Why be scared by a dream? There's a saying that everything turns out the opposite of our dreams. Go back to sleep."

Later that morning, the couple rose, cleaned the house thoroughly, dressed Tiger in his new clothes, and painted a red spot between his eyebrows. When the guests arrived, firecrackers were set off.

One of the guests held Tiger aloft and said, "What a fine boy! Although he's not Guangzi's own flesh, he actually resembles him!" Guangzi stood nearby and laughed awkwardly.

Afterward, when Guangzi was out of earshot, some of the fellows from the village took hold of Tiger and said, "Call me Papa," whereupon Baishui angrily took the child from them and handed him over to Guangzi.

When all the guests were seated, Guangzi filled each cup with wine, the last one for himself. "Come," he said in a toast, "do not hold back and refuse my poor offering. Please drink."

Just then one of the neighbors helping with the party came and whispered, "Guangzi, there is another group at the gate and we don't know them."

"Anybody who comes is welcome to join," Guangzi replied.

The helper went outside and immediately strangers appeared in the courtyard, all arrogant and hostile.

One called out, "Which of you is Guangzi?"

At that moment, Baishui came out of the room. She gave one look and rushed back with an exclamation of alarm. But she had already been seen. Two of the intruders went up and, holding her wrists, they pushed her into the courtyard. The whole gathering was alarmed, including Guangzi, who, still holding his little son, dashed after Baishui.

A pockmarked man said, "This woman is my wife. She disappeared four years ago. I have been looking for her everywhere."

Guangzi paled. "Is this true?" he asked Baishui.

But Baishui only shrieked, "I won't go back! I won't go back!"

Then Pockmark sneered at Guangzi. "Now don't you see?" Then he hit Baishui in the face and cursed her. "Not go back?!" he ranted. "Is that what you said? Let me tell you: living, your body belongs to me, and dead, your ghost is mine!" He tried to lug her away.

Guangzi held her back, but Pockmark said, "Brother, she has served you as a wife for a while. Isn't it time to return her? If you don't see the light, I will take you to court for abducting my wife."

Everything went dark before Guangzi and he sank to his knees. The child screamed for his mother. Guangzi frantically held the infant to his bosom while crying, "Baishui, Baishui, mother of Tiger!"

As Baishui was being dragged through the gate of the courtyard, she worked the copper thimble off her finger and threw it to Guangzi. Then she was dragged away, wailing piteously.

Guangzi became seriously ill. At first he lay grief-stricken in bed, barely able to move. Tiger, who cried for his mother day and night, was taken care of by a neighbor.

After two weeks, Guangzi started moving about in the village, but people could hardly believe he was the old Guangzi. His hair and whiskers had turned gray almost overnight. He would never speak, but just shuffle around or lean against a wall. Sometimes he would thrust a hand under his belt and fumble around for a louse. When he got hold of the creature he would not crush it, but toss it up in midair.

Three years passed. Guangzi managed to bring up Tiger by being both father and mother, or rather, neither father nor mother. Their life was hard.

It was now the fall of the third year. Tiger, playing outside, fell into a fight with other boys. They called him bastard and he ran home crying for his mother. Guangzi felt his heart contract with pain.

He said, "My son, you do have a mother. She is far away, though. It seems we cannot stay here any longer. I'll take you to look for your mother."

That very day they locked the gate and set off.

They arrived in Lonan County and found the place where Baishui used to live. It was in a marshy valley, just a couple of cave-dwellings cut into the hillside. The entrance to the cave-dwelling was padlocked, and spiders had spun their webs over it. In the open ground in front of the cave, serving as a courtyard, wild grasses were knee-high. The minute father and son stepped into the grass, a swarm of black mosquitoes attacked them, leaving an instant mass of red boils on their skin.

Guangzi retreated and asked for information from the villagers. The answer was that after Baishui returned, she was like a woman demented, always muttering Tiger's name—and she would not sleep with Pockmark. The latter would bind and whip her. After months of abuse, she died.

Upon Baishui's death, Pockmark went further downhill and began holding gambling parties in his cave-dwelling. Then he ran into trouble and was taken away by the police, and was never heard of again. Guangzi, holding tight the copper thimble in his fingers, fell down in front of the cave and wept.

The villagers took pity on the father and son and
helped them settle in a discarded cave-house nearby.
The dwelling, held up by a log, acting as a pillar, was
on the point of collapse. Guangzi gathered some brushwood and wove a sort of gate. In the daytime he would
stroll the area with Tiger, doing odd jobs for food
and drink. At night the two would sleep in the cave.

The neighbors were sympathetic and tried to offer
advice. "Guangzi," one of them pleaded, "you can't
go on like this. Don't you have any other skill?"

Guangzi answered that he had learned the art of castrating pigs and donkeys in the old days, but had not
worked at it for many years.

The villager said, "That's good. Go ahead and get
yourself a set of tools and pick up your old trade. It
would be much better than your present life. You may
live anyhow, but think of the child! He cannot endure this!"

Guangzi saw that his friends were right. So he went
back to his old job. He made a living and even
managed to send Tiger to the village school.
He was grateful to the people in this area. Moreover,
he felt he could not return to his home village with
all the memory it carried. He continued to work hard,
was on good terms with everybody, and acquired
some degree of popularity. Gradually the villagers accepted him as one of themselves, and he managed to
get himself a certificate entitling him to be a regular
householder in the village.

Not long afterward, a great event altered life in the
village: the government reversed the verdict on the case
of the Liu Defense Brigade. Many people, formerly
sentenced to fifteen or twenty years in prison, were now
released. All the families rejoiced and the wine flowed
freely.

At one celebration, Guangzi asked a prisoner who had been pardoned, "What case was it that brought you a sentence of twenty years?"

"The Liu Defense Brigade," the man answered. "I never expected the truth could be brought to light! How unpredictable are the ways of the world! The Gang of Four is now down and Liu Shaoqi is a good man after all! And all the imprisoned are released!"

Guangzi recollected that he had heard about the same case in Lamao's village. He was amazed that so many innocent people were implicated and on so wide a scale. He looked out of the windows and saw firecrackers exploding and children shouting boisterously as they ran about.

"But even with rehabilitation, does it mean you were clapped into jail for nothing?" Guangzi asked.

He had no heart to go on drinking, but his host retorted, "How can you say for nothing! The government is good! When we were released, those sentenced over fifteen years were paid six hundred *yuan* in compensation; those sentenced over ten years got four hundred; and those under ten years got three hundred. Just think! How can peasants expect to make so much money? Because of my imprisonment, I have been able to buy grain and clothes. And I plan to repair my house. Of course the suffering was hard, but I have been reimbursed very well for those years."

Guangzi could say nothing more. He sipped some wine, found it harsh and unpalatable, and left.

Three days after the celebration, Guangzi made some extra money by castrating pigs. He brought back one *jin* of pork. Tiger was out collecting firewood. A strange man appeared at the front door of Guangzi's shack. He had a long thin face and a hairy black mole on his upper lip.

He smiled as he came in and said, "You are doing very well nowadays, even having pork."

"We have not touched meat for an eternity," Guangzi answered. "My son has been longing for pork. Stay and share with us."

The man did not refuse. As he crouched with Guangzi by the cooking pork, a curious smile spread across his face.

"What are you smiling at?" Guangzi asked.

Suddenly the man grasped Guangzi's head and gave his face a thorough scrutiny.

"Let me see if your eyebrow bone has turned white."

Guangzi laughed. "Can you tell fortunes?"

The man studied Guangzi's eyebrows and said, "White indeed! The time is ripe. It seems I well deserved this meal of pork, Guangzi." He then went on to explain: "I have come to make a match for you."

Silently, Guangzi went on with his cooking.

The man continued, "I have come on a matter of such importance, and you are not interested! Let me tell you, many people have their eyes on this woman, but I will not stir myself on their account. I am securing her for you."

"I'm afraid I'm not born for such good fortune," Guangzi retorted. "Anyone who marries me must share the lot of a beggar."

The matchmaker said, "The woman said she is not seeking a husband in high office with a fat salary. She wants only an honest man. She also vowed she will not marry any local man. So aren't you the perfect choice?"

Just then, Tiger came back with a load of firewood. He was soaked in dirt and sweat. As soon as he saw the pork, his face grew happy and he approached the cooking pot.

"Tiger, do you want a mother?" the man asked him.

"Yes," Tiger replied. "If I have a mother, I can have new clothes."

The man then turned to Guangzi. "A widow's life, without a man, is arduous, but a widower's life is even worse. Two baldpates running a house is impossible. There is nobody even to patch your quilt."

Guangzi was half persuaded. "What kind of woman is she?"

"You cannot ask for more," the other said. "A fine figure she has. In ordinary circumstances, a person like you could never aspire to her hand, no matter how much bridal money you pay! Actually she is just out of prison. She even has five hundred *yuan* rehabilitation fee in her possession!"

"Another of the Liu Defense Brigade?" Guangzi asked. "You mean they gave fifteen years to a woman?"

"Indeed, she has endured much! Her sufferings have made her mature. Guangzi, come, make up your mind. I'll bring her to you this afternoon and the two of you can talk."

By this time the pork was cooked, and the three finished the meal with great relish.

The same afternoon Guangzi sent Tiger away. As he waited for the woman, his heart was in a turmoil. Guangzi had no desire for women anymore; all his passions had been drenched in the icy waters of his vicissitudes. But he realized that Tiger was still young and had nobody to take care of him. If he went on living in this hand-to-hand way, half man, half beast, Tiger would never have a chance to go to school regularly. He surmised that if he married this woman, he would settle in his native Shangnan, make a regular home, and rear Tiger properly.

As Guangzi was weighing his thoughts, he heard footsteps outside. His heart beat wildly, but he sat unmoving.

The matchmaker cried, "Your guest is here." Only then did Guangzi go out to greet his visitors.

A woman stood outside the shack. With one look at each other, both she and Guangzi blanched.

The matchmaker was astounded. "So you know each other?"

Guangzi said simply, "Yes, we know each other." Then he spoke to the woman. "Liangliang, how is it you are here, and how did you get into jail?"

The tears cascaded down Liangliang's face before she could utter a word. Guangzi invited her inside, where she unfolded her story to the two men.

"All the tortuous paths of the earth I have trod, and all the people I gave up hope of meeting I have come to meet. But where is Elder Brother Lamao?"

"Dead. I trampled on him, and he hanged himself."

"Dead?" Liangliang exclaimed. "Well, perhaps he's better off that way."

They talked calmly about past events. Their recollections were drained of all emotion. Guangzi noticed that Liangliang was very much overweight, but not in a normal way. It was evident that she had the fat disease. Her character and behavior were also changed. If it were not for that familiar face, nobody would have known her for the old Liangliang.

After several hours the matchmaker got up to leave. "Since you two know each other, I am superfluous. I'll leave you together, but please let me know your decision by tomorrow."

Guangzi and Liangliang sat talking until dark. Tiger came back, and when Liangliang called to him, the child went to her joyfully, as if they had been linked together in a previous life. Liangliang lost her former reticence and revealed all she had gone through in those intervening years.

It turned out that she had been in the village of

Beichuan in Lonan County, where her father was once
a schoolteacher. Liangliang had no brothers, so she
stayed with her father and attended the middle school
where he taught. During the investigation of the case
of the Liu Defense Brigade, her father was implicated and beaten to death during the interrogation.
Liangliang went about trying to overturn the verdict
against him, so she too was convicted of being a member of the Brigade. She was in hiding in the Lonan
area when she fell into the Lo River and was rescued
by the two bond-brothers. She was grateful to them,
but dared not reveal her identity. That day, while she
was still asleep, Lamao broke into the room and demanded to have intercourse with her. She refused at
first, but then thinking that she owed him her life,
she submitted. After they were discovered, she was
deeply ashamed, and left the place. Unexpectedly, she
was pregnant from this encounter. Seven months later,
she gave birth to a girl. She took the infant back to
her home village, but the night she reached home, she
was discovered and arrested. Before being taken away,
she had to give up her infant to a stranger, only having time to tell him that the child's father was called
Lamao from a village in Lonan County. Since then, she
had been in jail, cut off from the world.

Before Liangliang could finish her story, Guangzi was
in tears of sorrow. He deeply regretted what he had
done to Lamao; if the two had been united, all this
might have been prevented.

"Guangzi, it is no use fretting over what's past and
gone!" Liangliang assured him.

"That is true. But all these years in prison, you must
have suffered much!"

"I expected to die there. I never dreamed that I could
come out alive! But now that I am, I have a great
task to accomplish!" She picked up a cigarette from

the table, lighted it, and, looking straight at Guangzi,
said, "Do you imagine that I have spent all these years
in prison for nothing! That my father was beaten to
death for nothing! That nobody is to pay?!"

"But didn't the government pay you?" Guangzi
asked.

Liangliang plucked a wad of banknotes from her bosom and slapped it down on the table. "Yes, they
paid us. But a put-up case like that, implicating hundreds of people . . . Now who was responsible in
the first place? You can't blame everything on the Gang
of Four, can you? The authorities in charge at the
time are still in office! They say they were right in making the arrests at the time, and equally right in re-
leasing us now! The fellow named Gung, head of the
Military Propaganda Team, has been demobilized and
is in the same job with a different title, head of the
department! The chief of public security is right there,
too! As a matter of fact, they did not want to reverse
the case at all, they just wanted to suppress the entire affair. But there were inquiries from above, so they
couldn't. But from the commune level right up to
the district, all the people who have conducted secret
trials and torture are fixtures. I can never believe that
in all these years, nobody has sought justice. Most of
the freed prisoners just want the money. But not me!
I am going to seek retribution!"

Guangzi listened and he smoked in silence.

That night Guangzi could not sleep. He stared at the
moonlight which crept through the opening in his
cave. Throughout the night, he listened to the chirp-
ings of the crickets inside and out. Tiger sat up at
one point and saw his father's eyes wide-awake.

"Father, you are also not sleepy?" he asked in a surprised voice.

"No," answered Guangzi. "You are also thinking of that aunty?"

Guangzi let his eyes rest for a long time on Tiger, his heart contracting. He asked, "Do you like that aunty?"

"Oh, yes," said Tiger, "I saw her before."

"Nonsense, child, how can you have seen her before? Go back to sleep."

After Tiger fell asleep, Guangzi's ruminations still kept him wide-awake. He pondered on how fate had played with him over those years! He sympathized deeply with Liangliang's sufferings but was afraid to marry her. He could not help thinking of the past. He had injured both Liangliang and Lamao very deeply, leading to Lamao's death. Those memories hung heavy on his heart. Besides what was he, anyway? A peasant and a most unlucky one. How could he aspire to the hand of a teacher's daughter? She could certainly find somebody better than himself. He could not face Liangliang and did not know how to explain his reasoning to the matchmaker. Before dawn he shook Tiger awake, gathered together all his belongings, and left the village.

On the way, Tiger asked, "Father, where are we going?"

"This is not a good place to settle in. I'm taking you back to my native country."

Tiger persisted. "But will aunty join us?"

"You have no aunty!" Guangzi snapped.

He led the child to Baishui's burial place. Father and son knelt in front of it and prayed. Then they headed straight east, making their way by castrating pigs and donkeys. They did not ask for cash payment, only food and board.

One day, several weeks later, they found themselves in a town in Lonan County. Father and son were

walking limply across the street when they saw a crowd
rush by. Guangzi did not understand what the excitement was; when he asked, he was told, "Come
watch the fun!"

"What fun?"

One of the townspeople answered, "There's a woman
who goes daily to the county party committee to ask
for justice. The party secretary has lost patience and
refuses to see her, and now will not even let her inside the reception room at the gate. She's there right
now, making a scene. A madwoman."

Guangzi did not inquire further, but went into a restaurant. Halfway through the meal, he discovered that
Tiger had sneaked away and was nowhere to be found.
Guangzi was in a great fright. But soon Tiger reappeared.

"Father, I know that madwoman," he said.

"Who is it?"

"It is aunty!"

Guangzi had never imagined that Liangliang would
go to such lengths, and she but a woman, and ill,
too! Where could she stay? To whom could she pour
out her grievances? Guangzi cursed himself for a
good-for-nothing.

Now, Guangzi, he thought to himself, whatever have
you done in this life of yours? Liangliang needs a
home to settle in so she can continue her petition for
justice. But you, you just left without a word. The
poor woman, persecuted all her life, what must she
have felt when she called the next day and found you
had abandoned her?

Guangzi's mind was made up. He said to Tiger,
"Come, take me to aunty!"

When they arrived at the scene, the crowd had dispersed. They asked the secretary at the reception desk
where Liangliang might be.

"That madwoman?" the secretary asked. "Who cares? Can you imagine a woman so shameless? Just out of prison, too! Back again soon, if she acts this way."

A bystander paused beside Guangzi. "I know where she is."

Guangzi respectfully asked to be informed.

"Nobody would take her in," the man said. "She went around trying to mobilize the other former prisoners. She wanted them to petition in a group, but all she got was abuse. They called her a troublemaker. Nobody would allow her to spend the night under their roof, for fear of being implicated. In the daytime she rushes about seeking an audience with leaders, and at night she sleeps in the night watchman's shed at the production brigade."

Guangzi thanked the man and went in haste to the dilapidated shed. There was no door. Inside was a ragged quilt, but Liangliang was not beneath it.

By now Guangzi's face was bathed in tears.

"Tiger," he asked, "what would you say if we took aunty with us?"

"Oh, yes."

"Would you be willing to call her mother?"

"But my mother is dead!"

"Your mother who gave you birth is dead," Guangzi explained. "Aunty could be your stepmother. Would you call her mother?"

"Oh, yes!"

Father and son sat for a while longer, then Guangzi left Tiger behind and went off to buy some pancakes. When he returned, Tiger was asleep with his head in Liangliang's lap. "Liangliang!" Guangzi called out to her. He ran to sit beside her.

The two looked at each other, embraced, and burst out crying as if their hearts were broken.

★　　★　　★

Father and son resumed their trek homeward with
Liangliang in their company. (Guangzi and Liangliang
did not go through the formalities of a marriage ceremony, but they were man and wife all the same.) En
route, Guangzi plied his old trade to earn them food
and board. A hard and strenuous trip, but they made
it together.

Time and again, Guangzi tried to dissuade Liangliang
from her mission. "It is absolutely useless for you to
go on petitioning in this way. You are appealing to
the very people who were instrumental in persecut-
ing you. You are just heading into the wolf's mouth.
Once we are settled at home, let me work with you.
We must petition to a higher authority. To the provincial government, and if that doesn't work, right
up to the Central Committee!"

Liangliang knew that he was right. "With you, I feel
more secure," she said. "A woman like me, all alone,
faced with this issue, sometimes I really lose my nerve.
There's nobody to care for me. I used to lie awake
all night in that shed, crying to myself. Now that you
take me for wife, everything is different. Do you
blame me for being insubordinate?"

"Such a notorious case of injustice!" Guangzi exclaimed. "I cannot dream of holding you back! Some
say you are mad, but I think you are stronger than most
men! I am just a poor peasant. That night, I left without a word because I knew I was not good enough for
you. But I never realized you were in such a plight!"

Liangliang was also in tears. "See how my sufferings have changed me," she cried. "I am just a cru-
sader, neither man nor woman. I am certain this case
can be thoroughly reversed and the villains punished.
When that day comes round, we will lead a more human life."

*   *   *

When the trio finally arrived in Shangnan, the whole village was astounded. One citizen exclaimed: "Guangzi made a journey to a distant region and has come across good fortune, even brought back a wife."

But the villagers soon discovered that Liangliang was different from any ordinary peasant woman. She was not good at any kind of work in the fields; she smoked; she flew into a temper at the slightest provocation; and she always had to have the last word in an argument. Altogether, the village decided that she was not like a woman. Later they found out that she was recently released from prison and was still running around making petitions. Then they looked at her with contempt. And prattled about her behind her back.

Guangzi did not bother himself with the gossip and never mentioned it to Liangliang. He bought many tablets of paper and Liangliang would spend night after night writing out their petition. Guangzi had very little schooling, and could not write properly. So he would sit next to Liangliang and weave straw sandals. The straw being drawn would make a wheezing sound, which often distracted Liangliang. When that happened, Guangzi would get up with a smile and do his weaving in the courtyard. Past midnight, Liangliang would call out to him, "Go to bed!"

When Liangliang's writing was done, she would read it aloud to Guangzi. Sometimes, when the diction was too harsh, Guangzi would suggest alternatives. "Don't phrase it that way. Officials are also human, and we must not imply that they are all bad. Just name a handful in the county government who are directly responsible. When their superiors come to investigate, we can go into more details."

And Liangliang would nod in agreement.

Time passed. All their petitions were sent off one after another to the provincial government. And all of them were cast in oblivion, like clay figures tossed into the seas.

Liangliang went back to her native Lonan County to inquire. The clerk explained the procedure. "Your petitions! Sure, they're right here with me. You send your petition to the Emperor of the Heavenly Kingdom, but it will be sent back to me to dispose of."

Liangliang wept in despair all the way home. Guangzi could not bear to see a woman in tears. He comforted her with words, but she would not be comforted and cried all the more.

"You were always a woman of iron," exclaimed Guangzi. "How can you give way in this manner?"

"I don't understand it myself. Before, I never cried, no matter how black things were. But since marrying you, there seems to be no end to my tears. But what am I to do now?"

Guangzi made a suggestion. "Since appealing to the provincial government does not work, we must go to the Central Committee!"

So, once every ten days, the couple started sending their petitions to Beijing.

By now Liangliang had been settled in the village five months. Despite all the bitterness of her disappointments, she did not lose weight. Instead, she grew fatter every day. One day, in the depths of a snowy winter, the couple cuddled in their warm bed. Suddenly Guangzi turned to Liangliang. "Do you feel anything unusual?"

Liangliang blushed and shook her head.

By and by she said, full of shame, "Guangzi, I know perfectly well that at your age you wish for an offspring. I have not been pregnant, and I am sure it's because of my disease."

"No, that's impossible. You will certainly have a

child." A few more months passed and Liangliang still betrayed no signs of pregnancy. On the fourteenth day of the seventh moon, melons and fruits were ripe to bursting. That night, Liangliang went to bed and felt something round and hard in her bedroll. She opened the blanket and saw a big melon.

"This is called stealing a baby!" Guangzi told her.

According to local custom, a childless woman places a melon in her blanket to increase her fertility during the seventh moon. When Liangliang heard the story, she laughed. Then suddenly she clasped the melon to her bosom and moaned, saying that her disease was to blame. Years before, she cried, when she *shouldn't* have given birth, she had a child by Lamao; now she was not able to conceive.

"I wonder if Lamao's child is still living?" Guangzi asked. "Poor child, born to such a dire fate."

After that, Liangliang was even more loving to Tiger, leaving him all the tasty bits for meals. Tiger, in turn, became even more affectionate.

A second spring came round, but still no results from the petitions. In desperation, Liangliang said, "I might as well take a trip to Beijing and make inquiries."

Guangzi gasped. "You're mad! You haven't the slightest idea in which direction Beijing lies!"

"I can always inquire. As the saying goes, the right path is under your own nose, hanging on your lips. And once in Beijing, I can surely find Tian An Men Square. And I'm sure people in Beijing would know where petitions are filed."

"It is a long journey. Let me go with you."

But Liangliang would not hear of it. "If things go wrong, I might be thrown into prison again. No, you must stay at home."

And now, the couple began in earnest to save money for the trip. When Guangzi was away working steadily, there was never a scrap of meat on the table. Thus they put aside over a hundred *yuan*. But how long can a hundred last on such a trip?

Guangzi went up into the mountains to cut brushwood for sale. He worked desperately. On most days he would carry down twice the normal load. By the time he was finished, it would be pitch dark.

Meanwhile, Liangliang and Tiger went to cut stones for the railway maintenance station. They would make a rim of bamboo, encircle the stones within, and pound steadily and evenly with a hammer until the stones were the right shape. Mother and son would start working before daylight and not stop until the stars were out.

The villagers approved. "Now this family has finally hit on the right path," one of them told Guangzi. "That's a proper way to run a household. If the two of you had worked like that earlier on, you would be rich by this time."

"Oh, we are making money to go to Beijing to seek justice," Guangzi explained.

When the news spread, the villagers were aghast. "Still seeking justice!" one neighbor exclaimed. "If you proceed this way, it is wreck and ruin for sure! One must behave, you know. We are but peasants after all. What more can we hope for? Is Liangliang still not satisfied with her five hundred?"

Guangzi could only sigh in despair. "You do not understand anything."

"So I don't understand anything, is that it? What is this wife of yours good for anyway? She can't bear children, and she doesn't work. All she does is drag you with her making petitions!"

People were more than ever convinced that Guangzi had lost his mind.

*   *   *

On the seventh moon when Tiger was already over six years old, the couple sent him to school. The child was very bright. He had learned to read at four and could recite figures up to a hundred. At five, with Liangliang as tutor, he could recite ten Tang poems by heart. So at school, he was far ahead of the class, a virtual prodigy.

In August the couple counted their savings and made ready for Liangliang's trip to Beijing. But just at that moment, she fell ill.

Guangzi cried, "I can't let you go alone while you're in such a condition! I might as well go instead."

"No, that wouldn't work," Liangliang objected. "All the ins and outs of this affair are stored in my head, not to mention the fact that you are ill at ease speaking in public. No, I'll never rest comfortably if you go alone."

They finally decided to go together. But Tiger was too small to bring along; besides his schooling would be interrupted. After much hesitation, they went to the teacher with their problem. The teacher—a young woman—had not known of their sad past and, hearing their story, she commiserated with them.

"If you think me trustworthy," she said, "let me take care of Tiger for the next few months." She then offered thirty *yuan* to help them on their way.

After much protestation, Liangliang was forced to accept the money. She knelt to the teacher. "I can never repay you enough for this kindness," she cried. "I will accept this thirty *yuan* as a loan and will repay you twice over when the time comes around."

Arrangements completed, the couple baked pebble bread, hoisted their bedding onto their backs, and started off. They did not stop at inns or eat in restaurants; when hungry, they would request some water and eat their pebble bread soaked in water.

Thus, Guangzi and Liangliang struggled toward Beijing. Whenever possible, they would stow away on a train. When there was no train, they would go back to walking. After two weeks had passed, they finally made it to Zhengzhou. Liangliang was completely exhausted. She sat down in the waiting room of the railway station, too tired to move.

The weather was stifling and the room crowded. Guangzi said, "I have found out that we are just halfway to Beijing. And you are so ill. We will never get there at this rate. Let's buy a ticket and go by train."

But the price of a ticket was over ten *yuan,* and Liangliang could not bear to part with so much money. "Our business does not end when we get to Beijing," she said. "I know that there are thousands in Beijing with petitions. We might have to wait for perhaps ten, twenty days or even more. If we run out of money, then what shall we do?"

Guangzi purchased two cups of water to go with their pebble bread.

"What a cursed place!" Liangliang exclaimed. "Everything costs money! To think of all that water in our village well, and here we are actually paying for a drink!"

The crowd in the waiting room also brought their own food, but theirs were mostly spoiled in the heat. They were curious about the pebble bread and asked when was it baked.

Everybody was amazed when Liangliang told them "Twenty days ago."

Liangliang offered them a taste. The bread was so delicious they whipped out their money and started buying.

The poor couple was staggered. Thirteen sheets of pebble bread actually sold for twenty-three *yuan.* They were overjoyed! And with the windfall they immediately bought two tickets for Beijing.

On the train, when she was certain she was unobserved, Liangliang laughed out loud. "Pebble bread is our savior! It is always said that city people cheat country folks, but now we have reversed the process. Let's save the rest of the pebble bread. It might fetch a good price later."

They arrived in Beijing later the same day. Once there, they inquired where to deliver petitions and were told the filing could be done in several locations—but that there was a special office for petitioners from the provinces.

Finally they found the appropriate office. The street in front of the office was packed with people, all from the provinces. Judging by their clothes, most of them were peasants. Guangzi felt at home and struck up a conversation with one of them. It turned out that most of the people waiting in line had been petitioning for justice for several years without result.

The stranger said, "Nowadays, if you want justice, you must appeal to Deng the Great himself!"

Guangzi did not understand. "Who's Deng the Great?"

"Deng Xiaoping, of course!"

There were many petitioners and the hours for receiving them were short. Guangzi and Liangliang stood in line from morning till night, but they never had their turn. The two dared not separate. They would eat plain noodles together, spend the night on a street corner, and rush over in the morning. But already a line had formed.

Liangliang said, "Rushing backward and forward in this way, we will never have a chance. No, one of us must stand here while the other goes for food. We must take turns."

Liangliang was fearful that Guangzi would get lost
on his way back and gave him endless directions before they parted. But Guangzi still managed to lose
himself. He walked through many streets, sweating
in fright. He spat on the sidewalk and was just about
to walk on when he found himself detained. Alarmed,
his hand shot to the valuable pack under his belt.

"What is it?" he asked.

"Fifty-*fen* fine for spitting!" a man in a uniform announced fiercely.

Guangzi could not believe his ears. "I was walking
peacefully, neither stealing nor robbing. Why should
I be fined?"

"Fifty *fen* for spitting!" The man was adamant.

Guangzi was completely mystified. "Yes, I spat.
What of spitting? Do you expect me to swallow it?"

By this time a crowd had collected and began to re-
buke Guangzi. Poor Guangzi was even more alarmed.
He said, "How strange it is in Beijing. You are not
even allowed to spit!"

But he resigned himself to the situation and paid the
exorbitant fine.

When Guangzi finally found his way back to the
Central Committee building, Liangliang, at first
relieved, scolded him roundly for his carelessness. Guangzi dared not mention the fine, but meekly accepted the
blame for losing his way.

After this incident, the couple were more fearful than
ever of being separated. For one whole day and one
night they went without food, guarding their place in
line. The following day their turn came round. After listening to them state the circumstances, the person in charge sent them to another department in
another street. The two wandered round a whole day
before they found their way to that particular office.

An official there accepted their petition and promised to evaluate it.

Liangliang asked, "When?"

The answer was, "You go back, the petition will be handed down. . . ."

"Handed down!" Liangliang cried. "Handed down level by level! Like a meatball thrown to a dog! Whoever expects to hear of it again?!" Suddenly she broke down and sobbed loudly.

"All right," the person in charge then said, "come here in three days. Then we'll give you an answer."

And the couple thanked heaven and earth.

When they came out of the building, Guangzi said, "How could you fall apart like that? Don't you know where you are?"

"Of course," Liangliang replied. "That's exactly what I wanted. I must rouse pity. There's so many people petitioning for justice, if you're not a special case for pity, when will your turn ever come?"

After three days they returned, as directed, and were asked to come again. Another three days passed, and still no results. Half a month passed. Their funds were being depleted and they were physically exhausted. Guangzi sat on a street corner and started to sell his remaining pebble bread. His business was good. Once people started buying, everybody wanted to sample it. Guangzi's special bread made quite a bit of money. Liangliang said, "How funny that people in Beijing love this stuff! After our case is reversed, let's come here and start a pebble bread business."

On the twentieth day Guangzi and Liangliang finally got a document confirming their petition. Attached to it was a note specifying that an identical document was being forwarded to the appropriate departmental head. They were advised to go straight to the provincial leadership. The two left in great haste for the provincial capital, spent seven days there, and finally got back home to Shangnan.

After another month, the case of Liu Defense Brigade was thoroughly investigated. Liangliang, as one of the most injured parties, was recalled to her native Lonan to give evidence. Soon afterward, the officials in charge at the time—those directly responsible for the trumped-up case—were punished in accordance with state laws and party discipline. Liangliang's father was exonerated posthumously, and Liangliang was granted urban residence rights and employed at her father's former teaching post.

The news exploded in Shangnan. The more than two hundred implicated and all their families were astonished, even ashamed. They were forced to acknowledge that Liangliang was a heroine.

Even before Liangliang returned from Lonan, the villagers began to stream into their home and praise Liangliang to the skies. They also contended that Guangzi's fate proved that an honest man would get an honest reward.

"Just think," one neighbor said ruefully, "he has actually got a wife drawing a government salary—and with an urban residence."

Even Tiger often found himself the object of admiration. People would say that they had been sure all along that he was born for better things than just being a peasant; some even called him "city boy."

But privately the villagers would change their tune. They thought it unlikely that Liangliang would stay married to Guangzi. Men could go out to work and women stay on the farm, they reasoned, but whoever heard of women going out to work while their men stayed home? It upsets the order of things.

Guangzi heard some of this chatter but did not concern himself with it. When Liangliang finally re-

turned, Guangzi put together several tables of meat and
drink to entertain their neighbors and acquaintances
in the village.

"Why waste money on that lot, the double-faced
hypocrites!" Liangliang objected. "Don't you remember when everything was against us? They were ready
to pounce on us. Now that we have come out on
top, they behave as if our families have been lifelong
friends!"

"This is the way things are done," Guangzi said.
"Having got to where we are, let them send in their
congratulations. We'll accept them for what they're
worth. No need to offend this lot."

The party was a grand success. By the time the last
guest left, the house was in a shambles, and after the
couple cleared up the mess, they were completely exhausted. They sat down in a daze.

Finally Tiger broke the silence. "Mother, are you
going to be a teacher?" Liangliang nodded. "Then it
is true you are going to leave us?"

Liangliang was surprised. "Where did you hear that?"

"Everybody in the village says that once you are a
teacher, I will be motherless again. Please, can't you
take me with you? Don't you want me anymore?"

Liangliang drew Tiger to her side while she looked
at Guangzi uncomprehendingly.

"Guangzi, how can people say that to the child? I'm
not without a conscience. Without you and Tiger, I
would get nowhere. Such a thought must never enter
your mind. I am your wife in life and in death."

Guangzi was embarrassed, as if caught out in something; he then laughed and said, "Why distress yourself with the child's chatter?" And the subject was
closed.

Four days later Guangzi and Tiger accompanied
Liangliang on her way to Lonan. They did not take

the highway, but cut through the mountains. Liangliang had her bedroll on her back, and also an umbrella. Guangzi carried a shoulder pole. Tiger snuggled into the bamboo basket at one end, while the other end was balanced with food and household necessities. They traveled in haste; the cock crowed as they neared Calf Ridge, and by the time the frost descended, they had reached Seven Fork River.

The group reached the school in good time for registration. After staying five days, Guangzi wanted to go and leave Tiger behind him.

Liangliang said, "Don't leave so soon. Stay a few days longer. Our happiness has been hard won. Stay and enjoy yourself some more." And so Guangzi stayed on.

The teachers of the school came over to inspect the husband of the new teacher.

That same night Guangzi confessed to Liangliang, "My being here just makes you lose face."

"Nonsense!" she said. "You stay on and hold high your head! So long as I am not ashamed of you, others have nothing to say."

In the daytime after breakfast, Liangliang would go to her class, Tiger to his school, and Guangzi would wander about outside the schoolyard. Or he would sit glumly in their room. Barely two weeks passed before Guangzi found himself riddled with boredom.

At last he said, "Liangliang, I am destined for the country, I just can't enjoy this easy life. Please let me go. After a while, I will return and see you both."

Liangliang accompanied him part of the way; after walking with him ten *li,* they parted. She stood and watched him go, waving all the time.

When Guangzi arrived in his home village, he found his house occupied by a neighbor. After a family argument, the neighbor had left his own home and, by

forcing the lock, had settled in Guangzi's quarters.
Upon seeing Guangzi, his distress was extreme.

"Oh, everybody knows you are flown to a higher
branch. Why are you back?"

Guangzi said, "With the half-dozen words that I can
read, what can I do out there?"

For the sake of companionship, Guangzi decided to
share his house. He gave his neighbor one-and-a-
half rooms while reserving the other one-and-a-half for
his own use.

Five years passed in a twinkling. The couple did
not need to write to each other. After every harvest,
Guangzi would make a trip or two to Lonan, while
Liangliang and Tiger would always come back for summer and winter holidays. Their days were smooth
and cozy. The family was the envy of the village.

Another autumn came by, and Tiger was promoted
to middle school. When Guangzi heard the news, he
wanted to go over immediately, but a big pear tree in
the middle of the courtyard was heavy with fruit. Day
in, day out Guangzi gazed at it longingly, waiting for
the pears to ripen that he might bring some to mother
and son.

When the pears were finally picked, Guangzi received a letter, notifying him that Liangliang was seriously ill and requesting his presence at once. Guangzi
nearly fainted with fright. He rushed to Lonan non-
stop, traveling day and night. But upon his arrival, he
learned that Liangliang had died the day before. She
had been so buffeted by her stormy life that soon after
the tension relaxed, she collapsed.

The night before her death, Tiger had lain down to
sleep. Liangliang was still at her desk, correcting
homework. In the morning Tiger woke up and saw
his mother bent over her desk.

"Mother, were you up all night?" he asked, but there was no answer. He came to look and found her dead.

Guangzi silently bathed Liangliang's body, dressed the corpse in new clothes, and bought a coffin. As he nailed down the coffin, the sound of the hammer was heavy and dull. All the teachers and students cried. Guangzi did not cry, however, not even a tear.

He hired laborers to carry the coffin back to his village, where he silently buried her. Everybody there was amazed that he didn't cry. Even though they were not married long and Liangliang did not give him a child, still they were husband and wife sharing the same bed, and he owed her a good cry. Tiger also resented his father's apparent heartlessness.

Guangzi urged him to transfer to a local school, but no, he would have nothing of it. He did not want to be with this coldhearted father. He wanted to stay on in his mother's school. He lived in the student commune and ate from the dormitory kitchen. Monthly, regular as clockwork, Guangzi mailed him money and grain coupons.

From then on, Guangzi never left Shangnan. He rarely spoke, and he never mentioned Liangliang. He was often asked why he was so hard-hearted, but he never bothered to reply. He tended to his crops and would go out to castrate pigs upon occasion, but always asked for the full price of his labor. Although on the first of every month, he would go to the post office and send money to Tiger, he would never enclose a word. The sum was invariably nineteen *yuan*, eighty *fen;* when the postage charge, twenty *fen*, was taken into account, the sum amounted to twenty *yuan*, not a *fen* more, nor a *fen* less. Tiger never wrote to his father either. After junior high school, he was accepted at the senior high school of Lonan.

*   *   *

Guangzi aged quickly. His hair and beard were one mass of white. He was not strong enough to castrate animals anymore, so he just worked on his private plot, wheat on one half, tomatoes on the other.

This season's tomatoes were exceptional, hanging heavily on their stalks. Guangzi would sit in his shed every evening after dark to keep watch over them. One evening the tomatoes on their props were immersed in the misty twilight. Guangzi pulled at his pipe in silence, his eyesight failing. Still, he continued to stare at the horizon. The clouds shifted and merged their colors into each other, sometimes gathering, sometimes dispersing, an ever-moving mass, until they finally were swallowed in the darkness. Suddenly Guangzi heard a rustle in the tomato patch. He assumed it was the sound of insects, but, turning his head, he thought he saw a shadow creeping under the tomato props. Guangzi was on the point of getting up and calling out when he saw that it was a child creeping forward. He sat back and resumed his smoking in silence.

The child picked three big tomatoes and then crept away stealthily. Guangzi inspected the ground after him and saw that his little hands and feet and belly left deep marks in the earth, showing the difficulty of crawling in and out. He was sorry for the little thief, so he picked some of his biggest and ripest tomatoes and put them by the side of the plot. But the days passed and the child did not show up.

Guangzi would wait for him by the side of the shed every evening, his heart empty and restless. He would watch through the night, under a canopy of stars; his vigil always continued until he heard the cock crow. Even then, he would keep his ears alert. But the only sounds were those of the insects. Finally, one day he packed a basketful of tomatoes and went to the county town to look for the boy, but there was no sign of him. The next day he went again, and again with no results.

One day he sat drinking moodily in a wine shop; when he was half drunk and his head hung heavily, he suddenly saw someone race by outside.

He thought the figure looked familiar; after consideration, it suddenly occurred to him. Why, it is Liangliang who once fell into the river! Or is it Lamao?

He ran out hastily. Rubbing his eyes, he ran along the street, but he did not catch up with the elusive figure. He stood there distractedly, laughed out loud, and shook his head. Then he walked away unsteadily.

That night, in a dreamlike trance, he saw a girl, the daughter of Lamao and Liangliang. She was already grown up; her foster-mother had explained that her father was called Lamao, from the county of Lonan. She had been to Lonan and told that her father had left for Shangnan, which explained her presence. The next morning Guangzi was sure that his dream was factual.

He then said to himself, "The girl is older than Tiger by a year or two. And so what? Isn't there a custom of taking an elder-sister wife? Isn't Baishui older than I am?"

In his obsession, he left his tomatoes unguarded and wandered to the neighboring villages and counties. Everywhere he went, he asked after this girl—Lamao and Liangliang's child. But no one had ever heard of her.

CHRONICLE OF
MULBERRY TREE VILLAGE

by Zhu Xiaoping

ZHU XIAOPING *(1952–   ) has only recently begun writing fiction. Born in Sichuan province, he was a 1982 graduate of the department of literature at the Central Institute of Drama in Beijing—
where he remained as a teacher until 1985. He was then reassigned
to the administrative staff of the All-China Writers' Union. "Chronicle of Mulberry Tree Village" was his first story to be published. Its
initial appearance was in the literary magazine* Zhong Shan.
A theatrical version of the story has been produced in Beijing.

On a business trip to Chengdu, I was held up by railway repairs on the Baoji–Chengdu line. I was stranded for the night in Baoji.

As evening descended, I walked through the streets
of the city, the biggest in west Shaanxi. The Qing
Mountains, grand and imposing, loomed in the distance, while the Wei River rippled eastward with a
merry sound. A wave of emotion swept over me. I
was actually quite near Mulberry Tree Village, where
I received much of my education.

Mulberry Tree Village, always in my thoughts, was
just a hundred *li* away. Yellow sandy slopes and yellow sandy cave dwellings; the sweet smell of golden
wheat wafting from the fields; the crystal-clear brook
with its shaded banks; on the slopes, giant poplars
stretching to the sky, their leaves forever rustling; in

53

the distance the crack of the herdsman's whip and the echo of his mountain song:

> "Go eastward, my lambs, where the grass is
> good for grazing,
> In the eastern slope, my lambs, a certain girl
> is waiting."

It was almost a dozen years since I left the village. I wondered: *what is it like now?* How I longed to see it again! Actually, the person I most wished to see was the production team leader Li Jindo.

Isn't it strange how a person can entangle himself in your very heartstrings, giving you no peace? Such a man was Li Jindo. Though I had spent two whole years with him, I still found him baffling.

The next morning, suffused with memories, I set out for Mulberry Tree Village.

My first encounter with the village—and with Li Jindo—came in 1968, when I was seventeen. A resident of Shanghai, I had been relocated to the countryside and was bused along with other students to the county of Linyou, one of the poorest counties of the Northwest. The bus left me off on the grounds of a dilapidated middle school forty *li* from Mulberry Tree Village. It was arranged that I would spend the evening at the local guest house. The next day I would be picked up by someone from Mulberry Tree Village.

The weather in March was still quite chilly. Even the sun hung listlessly in the sky. Lying in the clammy, stinky bedroom of the guest house, I hardly slept a wink that night. I was plagued by anxiety, overcome with nausea, and, finally, attacked by fleas. Gathering courage, I got up with the first light of dawn with the intention of sneaking back to Shanghai by hopping aboard the six-thirty train.

I pushed open the gate of the guest house, tripped over a dark bundle, and nearly tumbled down the steps. The bundle let out a cry of pain. It turned out to be a man, cowering under layers of posters torn from the walls. Evidently he had spent the night in the doorway of the guest house and had used the paper for warmth.

The hovering figure scrambled up and we scrutinized one another.

He was a man of about sixty (later I realized that I was a bad judge of faces, as people living in the hills age faster, and that he was only forty-six at the time). He had a dried-up, sallow face and a wisp of yellowish whiskers straggling on his chin. My first impression of his face was: this is not an honest fellow. Just look at his clothes! He was a mass of rags from head to foot. His pants and jacket were covered with patches in all the colors of the rainbow.

I had stepped on him and disturbed his sleep. I should, by all reason, apologize; but as he was just a street beggar, I turned and walked away.

"Are you a student from the province?" he called after me.

I stopped. "Yes."

"Are you going to Mulberry Tree Village?"

"Yes. What of it?"

"Oh, heavens, how I have looked for you all over the place! I have come to fetch you!" He reached out and grasped my hand. I made haste to extricate myself from his grasp. His palm was like a saw!

This peasant was none other than Li Jindo.

It turned out that he had been sent by district administrators to accompany me the rest of the way to Mulberry Tree Village.

"Why didn't you put up at the guest house?" I asked,

thinking that he would be the perfect customer for
such a miserable hole.

"Oh, that is not for people like me!"

"Then why didn't you go to an inn? It's so cold in
the open."

Evidently Jindo thought my last question not worth
answering. He took out his pipe, filled and lighted
it, and said: "You babies from the city don't know a
thing. I am lucky enough to spend the night here and
not be chased off." He pulled at his pipe silently. (Later,
when I had settled at Mulberry Tree Village, I learned
that three days' hard work in the fields would not earn
Li Jindo the price of one night on the common bed
at the county inn.)

Jindo squatted down and went on smoking. When I
considered that he had spent the cold night out in
the open, all for my sake, my sympathy toward him
began to grow.

"Come on, let's eat before we start off." I extended
an invitation to Jindo as compensation for his priva-
tions the night before.

"Oh, forget it. I brought my own steamed bread."

No matter how I urged him, Jindo would not budge.
Suddenly it occurred to me that this peasant did not
get my message. So I said point-blank: "I am paying,
I treat." It worked immediately. Jindo stood up with
alacrity, mumbling, "No need for youngsters to stand
on ceremony." He led the way to an eating-house.

We walked to a place that opened early. I took out
money and grain coupons to buy tickets for our meal,
but Jindo snatched the notes out of my hands, saying,
"You go find seats while I take care of this." So I
sat down, my mind assailed by conflicting emotions.

The house sold only one kind of food: the local
steamed bread soaked in mutton soup, five *jiao* a serving. It was served in a steaming bowl—broken bits of

bread saturated in soup with a few pieces of greasy meat floating on the surface.

I cast a glance in Jindo's direction and immediately saw something fishy was going on. He did not buy the steamed bread, after all, and he bought only one bowl of soup. He divided his own steamed bread in two and placed the portions in two bowls. He divided the one bowl of soup similarly. Thus he saved seven *jiao* and one grain coupon, which he quietly pocketed.

I fumed inwardly at this petty trick, but I didn't say anything. I realized that my impression of peasants had been derived from movies, magazines, and novels. And this flesh-and-blood Li Jindo had nothing in common with those imaginary peasants.

Jindo brought the two steaming bowls over. I closed my eyes and tried to swallow a few mouthfuls. Although the soup was thick and spicy, it could not disguise the smell of Jindo's musty bread. Jindo inhaled his food, almost burying his head in the bowl until it was empty. He then saw that I had put down my chopsticks and was sitting dejectedly.

"Why don't you eat? We have many *li* to travel!"

"I'm not hungry."

"You city people are so choosy. You don't even enjoy bread in boiled meat!" So saying, he finished off my bowl in a twinkling.

Having eaten, Jindo wiped his mouth with his hands and started to pull at his pipe, hiccoughing all the while. He was enjoying himself immensely.

I went back to the guest house to fetch my luggage, altogether seven pieces, a full two hundred *jin*. "My! My!" exclaimed Jindo. "Just a youngster and so many belongings, more than my whole household." He strapped the big bedrolls onto his back. It was impossible to take care of everything. "You store the rest somewhere," he said, "and I'll send somebody for them later."

Spring had arrived in the Linyou hills. On mountain slopes and terrace fields, on branches and treetops, specks of tender green wove together the bright hue of the season. The joyful tidings of spring swept away all my unease. The place was beautiful.

My luggage pack of a hundred *jin* was like a bundle of hay on Jindo's shoulders. His stride was long and firm and fast. I began to respect him in spite of myself.

We walked in silence for a few *li*. There's nothing as bad as silence when you walk in company. Jindo started to chat.

"What does a baby schoolboy want to do in this poor valley?"

"To be reeducated by poor and lower-class peasants!" I joked.

"Don't underestimate us poor and lower peasants. Don't we know that you've been up to all sorts of mischief in the city? You've obviously offended the powers-that-be; on the surface, they're not revenging themselves on you, but actually they're sending you here to suffer for your sins. And to take the food out of our mouths!"

Jindo had said his say, and was silent. So, I thought, that's how they think of us students!

We walked on in silence.

Before long we had worked up a sweat. But when we descended into a valley, a cool wind curled up and wrapped itself around us. It was wonderful. Evidently, Jindo could not bear the silence; he raised his voice and sang a tune from the *Qin Qiang* opera:

"The grass is green on the slopes, and the
        flowers are sweet.
Spring is stirring in my maiden's bosom.
Across the nine-arch bridge, a scholar is walk-
        ing toward me,
More handsome than Sung Yu or Pan An,
        stirring my desire."

Jindo's voice was hoarse and hollow, but he sang
in the singsong voice of the young lover. Looking at
his beggarly appearance and hearing his falsetto voice,
I could not help laughing. This Jindo is really quite a
character, I thought, the typical village idler and rascal.

And so, without realizing it, we cleared the forty *li*.
Once we crossed Beanpod Valley, the little village
of Mulberry Tree spread out in front of us.

The moment we entered the village, Li Jindo seemed
to change into another man. Never had I seen such
a strange metamorphosis.

As we walked through the village, a big strong peasant emerged. Li Jindo started to abuse him. "Guaiquan,
you mother-fucker, are you blind? Get over here and
give me a hand!" The man made haste to relieve Jindo
of my bedrolls. "Take these things to the western cave-
dwelling, and tell your aunt to fix dinner for this student baby." The man took his orders submissively and
went.

On our way to the western cave-dwelling, everybody we met greeted Jindo respectfully. "What have
you been doing with yourself the whole morning?" he
asked one fellow.

"Carting manure."

"How many carts?"

"A dozen."

"You lazy bastard! You stand there and tell me you
carted only a dozen in one morning?!"

"I also drove over a cart of cattle feed."

"Fuck your cattle feed! You finish carting all the manure this afternoon!"

Only then did I realize Jindo was leader of the production team.

The village was small, composed of about ten families; but Jindo lorded it over them in grand style. The entire population, man, woman, and child, all bowed to his orders.

I learned that the whole village, with one exception, was all branches of one family by the surname of Li. Except for his uncle and his cousin, Jindo was the eldest in the village.

My first two days in the village, I relaxed and put my lodging in order; the third morning I got up early—at the first stroke of the big bell calling the villagers to work.

Everyone was gathered under a big elm at the village entrance. Jindo was waiting there. One villager told me that ever since Mulberry Tree Village set up the cooperative, Jindo had personally struck the work bell—every single day, year in, year out, for ten years. After he struck the bell, he would light his pipe, and after smoking one pipeful, he would assign the work for the day. After he finished giving orders, he would go out into the fields and join in the work. He would never wait for late arrivals. If you did not turn up before his pipe went out, you were not given work and you lost work-points. Understandably, late arrivals were very rare in Mulberry Tree Village.

"What shall I do today, team leader?" I asked that morning after the assignments had been dispensed.

"Oh, you!" He looked in my direction. "You're still new; why don't you relax for a couple of days?"

I did not want to be idle. So, since Jindo did not assign me any work, I went off to seek work of my

own. I saw some villagers tilling the soil; I saw others
sowing corn.

But each time I tried to join a work group, I discovered that my enthusiasm was not appreciated. On
the contrary, the laborers shunned me, as if they dared
not tire me with work. They would either push me
out of the way or refuse to let me use their tools. I
could not understand this behavior, though I assumed
it was owing to Jindo's supreme authority in the village, as if allowing me to work would violate his
wishes and incur punishment on the offender.

There was nothing I could do. I borrowed a long-
handle hoe and joined a group of women and children in breaking up lumps of soil. Only then was I
allowed to work without interference.

After three days of pulverizing lumpy soil, I attended a regular meeting of the laborers.

According to regulations, the production team held
a meeting every three months to adjust the members' work-points—that is, to determine how many
points each member was worth according to physical strength and farming skill. Those who could perform hard tasks or were skilled at farming were
conceded "full labor." These laborers were usually allotted over nine work-points. According to this scale,
those under six points were granted "half labor." The
old or the very young usually fell in this category,
and they were really superfluous as far as real farming
was concerned.

As the village was small, the number of exceptional
farm hands came to about twenty. Everybody knew
how many work-points a man was worth, so the allo-
cation of work-points at the meeting was but a for-
mality. The procedure went this way: first the members
spoke up and gave their opinion as to who was worth
what; then Jindo would say, "That's not far from the

mark." Thus the tone was set and the matter settled. No one had the slightest objection to their alloted
points.

When my turn came, absolute silence reigned.

The women sewed. The men puffed their pipes. Nobody so much as opened his mouth. They were all
waiting for their cue.

"Come on, everybody," Jindo finally exclaimed,
"speak up your minds. Of course, the student comes
from a rich family and doesn't depend on a few mea-
sly work-points for food and drink. Still, he is now
a member of our team." Jindo raised his eyes and
looked over the gathering. Whenever his eyes fell on
them, the women would hastily stop sewing while the
men would also pretend to concentrate. Clearly Jindo
had set the tone: that I didn't care for a few beggarly
work-points. The members now started to speak up
in a babble of voices:

"The kid hasn't started work yet," said an old fellow. "Let's put it at five points for the moment, and
then see."

"Who said the kid didn't work? He has broken lumps
of soil for two days. Five and a half is fairer."

Soon everybody was babbling, but none of them suggested my work-point should exceed five and a half!
I was mortified! I had thought that I would get at least
eight points. All the women who worked with me
were evaluated at six and a half, and they only showed
up for work half the morning, sneaking back to cook
dinner before noon. Compared to them, I was a full
laborer.

In our group, there were but a few half-grown kids
like me who work full-time. Among them was
Jinsheng's son Fulian. We had wrestled with each other
several times during workbreaks, and every time he
lost to me. And Fulian had been granted eight points.

It's true I didn't care for the evaluation from the material side, but my honor was involved and I felt hurt.

"Fulian is worth eight work-points," I chimed in, "and I am much stronger than he is."

The whole assembly burst out in a loud guffaw.

Someone shouted, "Fulian is better at farm work than you; farming requires skill, you know."

With that, everybody started talking at once. I was at a loss for words. Suddenly Jindo struck the table with his pipe and there was immediate silence.

"That's not far off the mark," he said. "We should give the kid more credit. It's true he can't do hard work, and he has no skill, but he can learn. I suggest we add another half point. Let's give him a nice, round six."

Nobody raised any objections. My gratitude to Jindo was beyond bounds. He had spoken up on my behalf, asking people to give me more credit, and encouraged me to learn farming skills. From then on, I was a "half labor" at Mulberry Tree Village, worth six points.

The following day Jindo formally issued my assignment for the day: carting manure into the fields. One cart was given to each worker, and the worker was responsible for filling and transporting the cart. The distance from the animal shed to the fields was at least one *li*. The soil had just been turned and was soft and moist. As I pulled the cart through the field, every step was agony. Soon the cart rope left two deep blood-red welts on my shoulders, which burned with pain. Before half the morning was over, my whole body was one collective mass of pain. By afternoon, I sat on the shaft of the cart, unable to move.

The shepherd Old Li passed by me on his way back from the mountain slopes. He saw my misery and said, "Poor boy, you're still tender. You don't know

the harshness of farm work. Just look and see what
kind of people are here."

I raised my head and, sure enough, only the full la-
borers worth nine or ten points were doing this work.
I was the only half laborer present. What did it mean?
Why did Jindo give me this assignment?

"It's Jindo at his tricks again. You've been taken in."

Old Li had left the village when he was young and
only after liberation had he returned from Xinjiang.
He was virtually a newcomer and did not get along
well with the other villagers. Perhaps that was why
he was the only person who dared to stand up to Jindo,
and for this he was treated as an alien. Hearing Old
Li's remark, I began to see the work-point meeting in
a new light.

It was, I realized, a charade to take advantage of me,
a stranger. I felt cheated. In anger I stood up and
wanted to confront Jindo.

"Fuck him," I spat out. "I'm not working
tomorrow."

"Poor kid, if you don't, you won't even get six
points at the next evaluation. You'll never put one
over on wily Jindo."

"But what shall I do?"

"There's nothing to do. Just keep a cool head. It's
only the fool who babbles. Set your teeth and keep
working for three months and at the next evaluation,
Jindo will treat you better. Actually he's not a bad
man."

"Not bad! Then why did he deceive me?"

"It's not personal. When people are so poor, they'll
do anything for a bit of amusement. Who can blame
them?"

Six work-points! That meant that if I worked hard
for two whole days, I would earn the price of a pack

of Hai He cigarettes, the cheapest brand on the market. *When people are so poor . . . who can blame them?*

I suddenly remembered how Jindo had first cheated me of seven *jiao* at the eating-house. But then he had gladly shouldered my hundred-*jin* weight of luggage and walked a full forty *li*. This Jindo, I really didn't know what to think of him.

Old Li wanted to say something, then changed his mind. He made his way back to the village, the valley echoing with his song:

> "Dear maiden, your parting words I keep in
>   mind,
>   My way through the world is long and
>   arduous. . . ."

Soon it was dusk, but I still sat motionless on the shaft of the cart, my mind in a turmoil. I turned and looked at Mulberry Tree Village. Smoke was rising slowly from every chimney. The villagers had all returned to their homes.

Suddenly I saw a figure walking through the empty fields, stopping here and there as if looking for something on the ground. In the dusk the shadow looked like Jindo's. The last few days I had discovered that Jindo was always the last to return.

It was Jindo indeed. He appeared to have discovered something. He then walked to the edge of the fields and, facing the village, shouted in a loud voice. The village was so small he could be heard in every corner.

"Pao Wua, you dog-fucker, is this the way you spread manure? Who do you think you're cheating anyway? If this is how you farm, you'll never fill your fucking stomach."

After he had abused the careless Pao Wua to his

heart's content, he called out to the recorder of work-points, Li Fuquan. "Fuquan, do you hear me? Strike out Pao Wua's work-points for this morning!" He then saw me and said, "You must throw in the whole of body and soul just to be half fed. How dare anybody cheat the soil?" Then he hobbled away.

Again I recalled how he had cheated me at the work-point meeting. My anger dissolved. I smiled bitterly. This Jindo was really a riddle!

The wheat-cutting season arrived. The peasants had sweated and toiled for a whole year. This was the time they looked forward to; this was also the time they feared.

In that period of tumult and confusion, with few exceptions, everybody was suffering. But even in the worst years of the Cultural Revolution, the peasants dared not stop their labor. Nobody cared for their situation, but they had to work doubly hard to produce the grain to maintain the country through the turmoil. It seemed as if everybody was concerned for the future and destiny of China—except the peasants. As for them, their eyes were fixed on the soil. They were concerned only about the year's harvest.

The crops were really not bad that year. After the lunar month of May, the golden wheat stood thick and heavy in rows. From the fields, the rippling wheat sent out the sweet smell of harvest.

Old and young began to stir themselves to prepare for harvesting, but nobody was as busy as production team leader Jindo. He had to take care of every detail relating to the harvest. In a few days he was worn to a shadow. It seemed that only the skin on his lips had not wasted away. On the eve of cutting the wheat, Jindo made an announcement at the villagers' general meeting. To my surprise, he said that during the summer harvest, I was to be his personal aide.

I would work as his liaison, running back and forth and helping him with all the business related to harvesting.

I had not forgotten how Jindo had tricked me before. I had even gritted my teeth and kept at heavy farm work for three months. Now that the next evaluation meeting was approaching, I suspected Jindo was up to new tricks, probably shifting me to some light work in order to lower my work-points.

"No thank you," I said. "I've had to work like a dog!"

Jindo replied hastily: "No, no tricks, I promise. Let's settle this right away. From now on, your work-point is eight and a half."

I was bewildered. What did it mean, giving me eight and a half points just to be Jindo's assistant? The villagers all looked at me expectantly. I sought out Old Li sitting in a corner, and appealed to him with my eyes, for fear I'd be taken in again. Contrary to expectation, even Old Li, usually hostile to Jindo, supported this decision. "Go ahead, my lad," he said. "The important thing is for our production team not to suffer loss. Jindo will treat you right."

I agreed. The very next morning, the harvest evaluation team from the commune leadership made its way into Mulberry Tree Village.

Every year at that time the evaluation team would invade each village. Their job was to assess the size of the harvest, judging by the yet uncut crops in the fields. Like the farmers, these assessors were shrewd and quite accurate in their assessments. And according to their assessment, the leadership would hand down the figures for the amount of grain to be turned over to the state.

Hence, it is the assessors that are really the scourge of the peasants. The way the assessors casually let drop figures from their lips was a matter of life and death to the poor peasant; it meant either food and warmth or hunger and cold for the next twelve months.

Jindo made early preparations to receive these all-important officials. The production team killed two fat lambs, and every family contributed eggs and wine and cigarettes. How much Mulberry Tree Village could keep of the harvest, how much would be portioned out to the villagers—all would be determined by the success of this reception.

The assessment team finally made its entry into the village. The head of the team was vice-chairman of the county revolutionary committee; before the Cultural Revolution, he was but a petty clerk.

On Jindo's orders, I led the assessors to the office quarters of the production team. There the banquet was already set: broiled lamb, scrambled eggs, goblets of wine. The children of the village were all glued to the windows, their mouths watering. Jindo did not keep the guests company. (He said he could not bear the sight. "Every mouthful they eat, I feel they are chewing my own flesh.")

Jindo instructed me to put plenty of water in the wine, reminding me to keep the assessors from drinking too much. Once dead drunk, those immortals would blubber any kind of nonsense and then stick to their words no matter what.

After the assessors finished their meal, Jindo led them to the fields. The villagers working in the fields held their breath.

It was apparent to every eye that the wheat was good. The vice-chairman glanced at the wheat rippling in the sun and, while picking his teeth, casually assessed the harvest at two hundred and ten *jin* per *mu*!

At mention of this figure, Jindo paled. If you take

two hundred and ten as a starting point, you will
never beat it down to an acceptable figure. He tried to
put it off by a joke.

"Two hundred and ten! Why, you won't reach this
figure even if you add last year's crop to it."

"Then what would you say?" another assessor asked.

"Well, you have all done farming yourself," Jindo
said. "You should know, what with spilling and spoil-
ing on the threshing grounds and this uncertain weather,
we would be lucky to collect a hundred and thirty
or forty per *mu*!"

The vice-chairman spat. "Do you intend to haggle
with me?" He walked toward Jindo menacingly.

Jindo backed away. "Chairman, please look again,"
he begged. "Our fields have *never* yielded over two
hundred. You know very well the kind of life we live.
We are, after all, from the same region; don't you
care to keep up good relations with your people?"

Somehow, Jindo's words offended the mighty official. He turned and cried angrily, "Why are you holding me up? You are trying to hit me!" Saying which,
he hit Jindo on the chest. Jindo tried to parry the
blow. The vice-chairman then seized Jindo by the col-
lar and started hitting him in earnest. Jindo plopped
to the ground and, holding his face to his hands, burst
into tears. He was a man, a head of household, with
wife and children, and now, to be treated like this . . .

All the villagers working in the fields turned their
faces away, not daring to look. They could not bear
to witness Jindo's mortification.

Jindo controlled himself and stood up with tears still
running down his face.

Before Jindo could speak my anger shot up straight
to my head. I stomped over to the vice-chairman.
"By what right do you hit us?" I spat. "You just try
it again!"

The group bristled up in alarm. "What! You want to start a fight?" one of them cried.

"You just keep your hands off Jindo!" I screamed. They stopped their bluff immediately. Just a bunch of bullies, that's what they were.

Just as I was about to use my fists on them, two villagers tried to drag me back. As they got hold of me, the vice-chairman gained new courage and ordered his men, "Take him to the commune and I'll make him pay for this!"

The assessors rushed upon me. My arms were still pinned by the villagers trying to save me from myself. Without thinking, I kicked out and one of the assessors cried out in pain as my foot connected with his kneecap. The others scrambled back again. The villagers, seeing how desperate I was, held on to me all the more tightly as I cried out, "You son-of-a-dog vice-chairman, I'll beat the shit out of you!"

The villagers overpowered me finally and dragged me back. As I was struggling in their hands, I called out father's name without thinking. My father had been a leading government official in this region before the Cultural Revolution, and recently during the setup of the new revolutionary committee his name was listed as honorary member.

I don't know whether it was on account of my desperation, or because my father's name worked the magic, but anyway the assessing team left hastily without even eating their indispensable dinner. They departed for another village.

Jindo wanted to recall them and apologize. He even moved a few steps in their direction, then sighed and stopped, realizing the futility of it all.

In the afternoon word was sent round from the brigade. To our shock, the assessment for Mulberry Tree

Village was a hundred and seventy *jin* per *mu*! Jindo
and the whole village let out a sigh of relief.

"Good boy," Old Li commended me.

"Good boy!" the whole village echoed.

That night it seemed that every man, woman, and
child in the village gathered in Jindo's house, to offer condolences for the blows he got.

When Jindo saw me, he said, "My boy, cutting
wheat is tiring work. You needn't do it. You just
keep boiling water, to keep the cutters in drinking
water."

Then he turned to the work-point recordkeeper.
"Fuquan, double the boy's work-points for today.
And from now on, give him nine and a half points ev-
ery day."

All the villagers smiled. Then Jindo added: "Go ahead
and cancel all my work-points for today. I did a bad
job, nearly brought disaster to the village." He patted
me on the shoulder.

Jindo's wife sat by, quietly wiping her tears.

Jindo turned to her fiercely. "Why the hell are you
crying? I'm alive and kicking. Why don't you make
some eggs for the boy?" Boiling eggs is the mountain
villagers' highest form of courtesy to distinguished
guests.

As we talked out of Jindo's home, Old Li muttered
to himself, "What a wily fox that Jindo is! Pushing
the student boy to the front to bear the brunt of the
abuse. And it actually worked!"

Old Li's words struck me like lightning. So I was
taken in again! Jindo shrewdly foresaw that the assessment affair was a risky business, and he knew that
students would not stand by and see officials abusing peasants, that they would stand up and pick a fight.
Jindo's ruse worked. But supposing I hadn't had a
father whose name meant something. I would at that

moment be quivering under the lash of the vice-
chairman!

Reflecting on all this, I couldn't suppress a deep sigh.
So long as I can serve the poor underprivileged peasants of Mulberry Tree Village, I thought, I don't mind
being deceived by Jindo anymore.

All those events happened more than ten years ago.
And here I was, at nightfall, on the outskirts of the
little village I left so long ago.

The soft tints of dusk had receded from the western
slopes; in the gloaming, wisps of smoke rose gently
from households behind stacks of wheat. Specks of light
twinkled, like the deep and unfathomable eyes of
Mulberry Tree Village. On the edge of the terrace
fields, the poplars stood tall and straight, their leaves
rustling to a sweet music.

That night I slept at the headquarters of the produc-
tion team. The whole village turned out to greet me.
There was such a lot of talk about. But I did not see
Jindo, the person I missed most.

People told me he was not the production leader anymore, that Fuchun had taken over. When I was in
the village, Fuchun was just a youngster. "And where
is Jindo?" I asked. Someone said he was visiting with
relatives.

I didn't believe it. The lunar month of July is the
busiest season. How could the astute Jindo possibly
be idle?

"Jindo is full of resentment," Fuchun told me.

I wondered: *what about*?

Jindo was never one to stay idle. As far back as the
days when I was in the village, I remember seeing
him digging holes to plant trees whenever he had a moment's free time. He would dig anywhere, on the side
of roads, on terrace fields, on slopes, anywhere he
could.

The year before last, Mulberry Tree Village adopted the responsibility system, part of the current reform. By that time the slopes were dotted with holes that Jindo dug to plant trees. He was no longer team leader, so he turned to tree planting seriously.

But even with the new policy, the backward village could not expect to turn rich in the twinkling. There was no money to buy saplings. So Jindo again resorted to his wiles.

Last year the land was parceled out and rented as private plots. Jindo offered to rent five *mu* only.

Five *mu* could only produce enough grain for basic food. Getting rich was totally out of the question. The villagers could not believe how such an astute farmer like Jindo could be so dense.

But Jindo had his own plans. "I'm renting twenty *mu*," he explained, "but will only farm five. I'd like to exchange the fifteen *mus* of land for saplings." At the time, all the peasants wanted to lay claim to as much land as possible. Jindo took advantage of the peasant mentality to get hold of tree saplings.

All the villagers laughed uproariously. So that's why Jindo only plans to farm five *mu*. He has made his calculations after all.

Jindo even resorted to blackmail. "If you won't give me saplings, I'd rather let those fifteen *mu* lie fallow." In the mountainous area, where arable land is so scarce, this was a great waste; but nobody knew where to get the required amount of tree saplings.

Jindo didn't achieve his goal after all, and left the village in a huff.

Fuquan said to me: "Who'd believe that he'd go visiting relatives at such a busy time! I bet he's gone to look for tree saplings. This old fellow always knew where his interests lay. I think he's right. It's much more lucrative to raise trees. We're so poor because we've always stuck to farming. Jindo's ideas never go wrong."

Of that I have no doubt.

People said that before he set out, he had sold all the wood and stones and bricks that he had stored up to build a new house. Jindo, who had been dogged by poverty all his life, had certainly set out on a new track. He had plotted for petty advantages all his life. Now he had seen a new road to prosperity.

That night, thinking of Jindo, I didn't sleep a wink. I recollected the affair of the seven *jiao*, and all the things that followed. I feel that as Jindo looks back on his life so far, he must regret having wasted so much energy for so little. It's not worthwhile. But at the time, what could he do? He was a peasant. He tills and sows and harvests big stretches of land, but in his everyday life, he has to measure his spending grain by grain.

Could Jindo be reckoned as wise, diligent, honest, and lovable—as peasants are typically described? I really don't know. This Jindo! Even now I really don't know what to think of him.

THE STORY OF AN
OLD MAN AND A DOG

by Zhang Xianliang

ZHANG XIANLIANG *(1936–   ) was born in Nanking. In 1957 he was labeled "rightist" for his poem "The Big Wind." For twenty years he was exiled to the Wild West (Ningxia province), where he also spent several years in prison. After his release in 1979, he became the chairman of the Federation of Arts and Literature for Ningxia province. He is now the president of that organization and the vice-president of the All-China Writers' Union. He has published many short stories and novellas, including "The Herdsman," which has been adapted for the cinema.*

I.

During an exhibition of animal paintings by Wei Meilin, I was mesmerized by a watercolor rendering of a dog. And, while I admired the artist's lifelike depiction of the dog's soft, clear eyes with their hint of mischievousness and alert friskiness, I was even more deeply moved by the title of the painting. The artist called this picture "A Little Friend Through All Adversity." I later heard that during the time of troubles the artist had this little friend at his side, but that his friend ended up by being clubbed to death by underlings of the Gang of Four.

A little friend through all adversity! I think that when

a person is no longer able to seek friendship and affection from among his own kind, but instead channels his love to a four-legged animal, he has certainly
experienced painful suffering and has reached the point
of unbearable loneliness. Literary giants like Turgenev
and Maupassant have written masterpieces using the
theme of friendship between a lonely person and a dog.
But the profundity of such a relationship was driven
home to me most vividly through personal observa-
tion. Whenever someone asks, "What animal do you
like best?" I always reply, "The dog!" This is because I saw with my own eyes the growth of a close
relationship between a dog and a lonely old man.

This dog was exactly like thousands of other village
dogs. He had no obvious special characteristics and
was hardly a precious purebred. He was a yellow, lo-
cally bred male dog. Perhaps his coat was a little more
lustrous and his body a little stronger than other dogs,
but he never once performed any stirring deeds that
would result in literary or cinematic fame.

His owner was also like hundreds of millions of other
farmers. If I had not worked in the production brigade that he was in, and if the special relationship between him and his dog had not attracted my interest,
I wouldn't have noticed this extremely ordinary old village farmer either. He was a bachelor of about sixty
who was neither tall nor short. He had slightly stooped
shoulders and always had an unhurried and grave look
about him. When he wasn't busy, he would squat on
his heels under the base of a wall or sit cross-legged
on his brick bed, lost in thought and holding a long
pipe between his lips. There was line after line of
wrinkles carved into his dark reddish-brown face. His
eyes, though not large, would sometimes flash with
the knowledge of a man rich in experience. Of course,

his hair and his beard had both turned white, but he
was not by any means bald. In short, you only had to
see him to know that, although he carried with him
the joyless withdrawal common to those alone, he was
still an alert and healthy old man. As far as work in
the production brigade went, he was a jack of all trades
who had done a little of everything. Sometimes he
worked in the fields; sometimes he drove a horse cart;
and sometimes he tended to the animals. Whatever
the brigade assigned him to do, he did, and he never
fussed about the work-points he was given.

He lived by himself in a cramped adobe shack on
the west side of the village. In the front yard rose a
large solitary white poplar tree. Inside the shack there
were only a brick bed and two old wooden boxes.
However, the old man kept his room very clean.

Village dogs generally don't have names. No matter
how much an owner likes him, a dog is still called
"dog." Similarly villagers are rarely addressed by their
given names. So it was that everyone in the village
called this old man Old Xing. As time passed, the given
name of the old man was gradually erased from people's memories.

Old Xing and his dog were inseparable companions. When the old man drove his cart out on long-
distance business, he also took along the dog. If he
worked near the village, he would be greeted at the
end of the day by his faithful dog. The dog would hurl
himself forward as soon as he saw Old Xing and lick
his face and hands.

Old Xing only received two or three hundred pounds
of unhusked grain a year. Adding a few vegetables
to this, he was barely able to sustain himself and had
no extra food to give the dog. However, when Old
Xing started the fire to cook, the dog always remained
at his side. He would wait until Old Xing had eaten,

locked the front door, and started off to work before he raced out to hunt for wild game. He seemed to know that his master was unable to feed him anything and he never yipped at the old man's side begging for handouts.

During the lunar New Year holidays, the production brigade would butcher one or two sheep and divide the meat among the brigade members. Old Xing was likely to tell the dog, "Tomorrow they will butcher the sheep at the sheep pens. Go down there and lick up a little of the blood. There will be some intestines left behind too." The brigade members rarely had a chance to eat meat, and when Old Xing received his allotment, he did not rip all the flesh from the bone. He always used the back of his cleaver to smash the bones that still had some meat on them and then gave them piece by piece to his dog. "Gnaw them carefully. There's a lot of meat there. Your teeth are in good shape; mine won't do." Old Xing said very little to other people, but with his dog he was talkative.

To the man, this was not a dog, but his close friend. During the summer nights when the brigade assigned him to watch the vegetable gardens, the dog stayed by his side. In the winter, when he fed the animals at night, the dog endured the bitter cold with him. On many nights the old man would hold the dog in his arms so they could provide one another with warmth. On the long, quiet, and lonely nights, it seemed as if only the two of them were left in the world.

In fact, though, Old Xing once had a family, once had a wife.

II.

Before liberation, Old Xing had worked as a farm laborer for over ten yeas and had never been able to afford to marry. After liberation, he was allotted several acres of sandy river-bottom land. That year he was just a little over thirty years old. Through his hard work and skill in agricultural production, those several acres of sandy river bottom, to everyone's surprise, produced good crops. At that time, he believed strongly in the future, and life actually improved year by year.

The year he reached forty, other people spoke to him about a wife. Of course, no suitable girl was willing to marry a forty-year-old man. So he married a woman almost as old as he. But she was a sickly female, and eight months after the marriage, she died. During most of those eight months, he was continually at home taking care of his bedridden wife. In no time at all, he completely depleted the savings he had accumulated over the years. However, the wife's death coincided with the year in which the cooperative movement was being implemented in a big way.

The tragedy that Old Xing had endured made him realize that one could not withstand unpredictable natural and man-made disasters by going it alone. Therefore, he put his few acres of sandy river-bottom land, his one donkey, and himself into the production brigade. For one or two years, life really improved. In the presence of a strong collective, his hopes again began to grow.

However, the world is changeable, and life is filled with twists and turns. In 1972, the neighboring province experienced a drought. In the spring of the next year, vast numbers of people affected by the drought poured into the open plains land. They came in groups of three to five, in whole families, or sometimes several families at once to beg for help. Everyone carried a dirty cloth sack over his back hoping to plead for some dry grain to give to relatives who had remained at home. In the restaurants in the cities, on the streets,

and in the waiting rooms of the train stations, these
victims of disaster swarmed like locusts. After the militia drove them out of the cities, they began to make
their way into the out-of-the-way poor villages.

One day at noon, Old Xing was just preparing lunch
when he heard outside the door a voice calling out
in the accent of another province, "Uncle, be merci-
ful. Give me a little." He was moved by the sound
of the plea and opened the unlatched door. He saw
standing outside a thirty-year-old woman with disheveled hair and a dirty face. He let her come inside
and told her to sit on the brick bed. Then he busied
himself preparing enough food for two. After a little
while, the woman saw that the old man was quite
inept at cooking. She said in a small voice, "Uncle, if
you won't be offended, I'll fix the meal." Old Xing
agreed instantly, and after filling his pipe with tobacco, he sat hunched over on the brick bed. The
woman washed her hands and began to prepare the
meal. Her work was deft and clean. Even though they
were the same noodles and the same ingredients that
Old Xing always used, he felt this was the best meal
he had eaten in years. The two of them ate two dishes
heaped with noodles. Old Xing insisted that the poor
woman eat a second helping.

Just as she was about to serve them both a second
dishful of noodles, Old Wei from the east side of the
village pushed open the door and came in.

"Heh, I wondered why you still hadn't gone to hook
up the plow. I see you have a guest."

"Umm . . ." Old Xing, not knowing why his face
turned red, slowly said, "Someone who wants food.
I'll go as soon as we've finished eating."

Old Wei was the uncle of Tiangui, the production
brigade's leader. He was also the head of the committee
of the poor and lower middle peasants.

"Ah, it's a terrible thing to see—a woman having to go to someone's house to beg for food." He squatted on the threshold of the door and rolled a cigarette. "We always hear tales about returning to the old suffering, but it seems to me that we have already returned. Our villagers are suffering again right now. Are you from northern Shaanxi? How many are in your family?"

"Yes, I'm from northern Shaanxi," the woman replied brashly with her head lowered, "and there are two children, a father-in-law, and a mother-in-law in the family."

"Don't be embarrassed. No one's blaming you. In 1929, I had to go out to beg for food too. My wife has also begged for food. How can one be blamed after last year's famine? How is your family managing?"

"Our commune is giving everyone half a pound of grain a day. Since I left it means one mouth less to feed."

Old Wei suddenly moved as if he had an inspiration. "It seems to me that in times of storm, a person begging for food can only encounter trouble. Right now begging for food is not like what it was. Why don't you stay here and cook for Old Xing and do a little housework? Old Xing won't let anything happen to you. He's an honest man. I know."

The woman turned her face away and did not reply. Old Wei turned to Old Xing and said, "Go out and hitch up the plow. Tiangui is hunting for you. After you've hitched up the plow, come back and finish your noodles."

Old Xing stuck his pipe in his belt and went out to the horse corral. After several puffs on his cigarette, Old Wei also went to the corral. Smiling happily, he slapped Old Xing on the shoulders and said, "You dog, you. Your ancestors had all better thank me!

Someone's willing to stay and live with you. She still hasn't said definitely, but if you treat her right and have some kids, her heart will be fixed here. Do you have any money? If you don't, go sign a chit. I'll talk to Tiangui about it. Borrow a little money from the brigade first, and let her buy a set of clothes."

As Old Xing's face broadened into a smile, all the wrinkles on his face came together. As soon as he came in from work that night, his new friend served him a bowl of steaming hot noodles in hot spicy oil soup. She said not a word. After she had combed her hair and washed up a little, you couldn't even tell that she had been a beggar wanting food. After supper Old Xing put his pipe in his mouth and tried to think of something to say. While the woman was washing up, he discovered that the stove and chopping board were all shiny and polished. The oil bottle and salt jar had also been arranged neatly.

"Old Xing? Congratulations, congratulations!" With these words, large-framed Brigade Leader Wei pushed open the door and entered the shack. His eyes swept the room and, allowing himself a smile, he said, "Good. This looks as it should if two people are going to live together. It's true that everybody should have a mate. Here's ten *yuan*. Tomorrow you can have the day off to take your wife to the marketing and supply cooperative to buy a little something."

Old Xing quickly got down from the brick bed. He took a filled pipe and handed it toward the brigade leader. With his face gleaming in welcome, he said, "Sit, sit!"

The brigade leader didn't sit, but he brought out his own cigarettes and gave one to Old Xing. He smiled and said to the woman, "You're from northern Shaanxi? That region is really suffering from drought, I know. Were you farmers at home? Are you able

to manage the sieve? To operate the sieve is considered skilled work and only girls with nimble hands
are able to do it."

"I can," the woman replied softly.

"Good. Day after tomorrow you start to work. Our
brigade is just now selecting the seeds. There still
aren't very many who can handle the sieve. You will
get the same number of work-points as the others;
we don't discriminate against people from other dis-
tricts here. And besides, Old Xing is a good man.
He has contributed a lot of manpower to our brigade.
Settle down and live with him. Overcome whatever
difficulties occur! Then you won't lack porridge to eat."

Old Xing never imagined that in half a day he would
tie the knot again. This certainly wasn't any fairy tale.
It was exactly as the brigade leader had said. There were
many marriages of this type in the neighboring villages. In the villages during the years of the Cultural
Revolution, legal concepts were extremely weak. A
woman without a man and a man without a woman
could live together simply because they were willing
to and people would recognize them as a family. Legal approval wasn't required.

III.

Within a few days, the young wife had skillfully
changed Old Xing's house inside and out. Originally
the white alkali at the base of the adobe wall had
spread all the way up to the top of the brick founda-
tion; one layer of adobe had even eroded away. Now
the house was clean, warm, and dry. Even the four
bleak walls were a great deal brighter. Every day at
noon or evening when the two of them returned from
work, Old Xing would chop the firewood and light

the fire while his wife kneaded the flour and cut up the vegetables.

At this time Old Xing truly felt every second was precious. He was deeply in love with his new wife.

Although the woman never breathed a word of it, she understood Old Xing's feelings. She never rejected his warmth; she even repaid him with even greater solicitude. And a poor solitary old villager having acquired a spiritual comfort and satisfaction, needed nothing more. A dish of noodles fixed by his wife with some chilies added, a patch made by his wife with fine stitches, and at night a warm breath by his side—these were quite sufficient. Therefore, during this time, Old Xing suddenly seemed to be ten years younger, and when he walked, he shot along with vigorous steps.

However, as time went on, there was a dark shadow that gradually stole into Old Xing's life. His wonderful dream, he feared, would turn into a nightmare.

If you have ever lived in a village, you know that anyone from another district, especially a woman from another district, cannot avoid being discussed by the women of the village. After a short time, rumors began to spread in the village about this aloof, solitary beggar woman. The women used their meticulous logic to reach a conclusion—namely, this woman must still have a husband in her home province.

One day, when Old Xing was pulling a cart of manure, Brigade Leader Wei came up to him. "Old Xing, you don't want to be too careless. Tell your wife to get her registration card sent over. If she doesn't, you can't guarantee anything."

In fact, this was, of course, the sore spot in Old Xing's heart. He had also gotten wind of some of the rumors in the village, but he certainly didn't believe them. However, he knew that if her registration was not transferred and if she didn't have any more children, his wife would have to return home sooner or later. People with village registrations had difficulties leaving their old areas. He had already talked to his wife, asking her to write a detailed address and to move her registration and her children. But his wife always lowered her head and replied simply, "It won't work." And since he didn't have the heart to press her, he didn't inquire further.

"You don't want to be muddleheaded," Brigade Leader Wei went on to say. "When I have the address, I'll go to the commune to get an approval of transfer permit. But if she already has a husband . . . it will be difficult to arrange."

At dusk that day, Old Xing drove his cart home to eat. He saw his wife, sitting as usual on the threshold, using the last glimmer of light to sew and patch. When several youngsters ran under the white poplar to play, she stopped her work to watch them. Then with her head leaning against the door frame, she fixed her eyes on that hazy, distant place. Old Xing knew that she was thinking of her babies, but he couldn't find any words to comfort her. He could only take a jacket and cover her shoulders. "Don't get cold." He sat with her, pondering on how to bring up the question of the registration again.

This woman who had wanted food was a sensitive person. She saw from Old Xing's expression that he had something to say. Therefore, after the evening light had completely disappeared behind the western mountains, she gathered up the needle and thread in her hands and went into the house. She climbed on the bed and lay quietly, waiting just like a prisoner in an interrogation room.

Old Xing was already sitting on the bed, hunched

over his pipe. Drifting dark smoke and an uneasy silence enveloped the small room.

Old Xing smoked until his lips felt acrid. Only then did he work up the nerve to speak. "Mother, you really ought to let Brigade Leader Wei go to the commune to write up an authorization for you. When we have transfer approval, we'll go collect your babies and bring them here."

His wife still kept her head lowered and said nothing.

"Um," Old Xing slowly intoned. "If . . . you still have a husband at home, uh . . . we can talk about it fairly." When he reached here, Old Xing ran out of breath. In fact, he had no idea how to proceed.

"No," his wife said softly but determinedly, "I don't have one."

"Then . . ." Old Xing's eyes lighted up. "Then, what's wrong?"

After a moment, his wife began to cry. Tears fell one after another onto the old rung on the bed. Old Xing quickly stood in a panic and moved near the front of the bed. "Then is it because I don't treat you right?"

"No." His wife used the back of her hands to rub her eyes. "I have wanted to tell you all along, but I was afraid you wouldn't want to have anything to do with me."

"What are you saying? Who wouldn't want anything to do with you? If you're willing to put up with me, then everything's all right."

"My . . . our family belongs to the rich peasant class."

"Huh." The rock in Old Xing's heart dropped to the ground. He tapped his pipe against his shoe soles. "I thought it was a major problem. Now everyone works to eat. What difference does it make if you're rich peasant class or not!"

"You still don't understand. Where I live, they won't let the so-called rich go out to beg and I can't allow my children to suffer. I ran away secretly. They won't even write a certification that I fled, let alone one to transfer my registration. I still don't know what sort of criticism my husband's parents have undergone because of this. I know you are really a good person. Next spring, if you'll give me a little grain, I must go back. As soon as spring begins, the days are even harder for my family." And with that, she kneeled and with great respect bowed to Old Xing.

"Hey, hey! What are you doing that for?" Old Xing sprang up and helped her sit up. "You have gone too far when you speak like this. Isn't everything in this house yours? We'll think of some way to get your registration taken care of. What will you do if you go back? That place is impossible because of the drought. As long as the blind sparrow hasn't starved to death, there is always a way."

IV.

On the next day, Old Xing hauled manure again. Brigade Leader Wei joined him once again. Old Xing explained what he and his wife had talked about the night before. The brigade leader didn't say anything for a long time.

Finally he said, "This is more difficult to arrange than if she had another husband."

"What's so difficult about it?" Old Xing shouted. "When they are so poor they have to beg, how come they are still considered rich farmers?"

Brigade Leader Wei glanced at him for a second, but he knew there was no way to explain so that the old man would understand. Old Xing had never partici-

pated in any study meetings. As soon as a movement came along, this old farm laborer would be
assigned to the most important post that required solitary work. All the other workers would come down
to participate in the movements. Therefore, Old Xing
had become the commune member most "politically
unaware."

"It's difficult to arrange; difficult to arrange!" Brigade Leader Wei pulled off his hat and scratched his
scalp. "The problem is that if we send an approval slip
for transfer, they won't release her there and it will
cause trouble. Damn! It looks to me like you just go
ahead and live with her whether she has a registration certificate or not. Our brigade for the time being
can still squeeze out rations for one person. If there
is grain to eat, that will do. But don't tell anyone else
about this; act as if it never happened. You still need
to keep her feeling secure. Wait until the next spring
festival and then we'll see. Right now we'll go one
step at a time. Who knows by next year what changes
there will be."

That year, on the basis of their work-points, the two
of them were given over five hundred pounds of grain
and one hundred and twenty *yuan* in cash. After they
brought their grain and money home, the brigade
asked Old Xing to take his cart into the city to do some
sideline work, hauling sand for three days to a building site. Old Xing put the bread his wife had baked
into his bag and drove the cart to the city.

It was on this trip that he met the yellow dog. The
dog was still small then. He had been born wild and
grew up that way. No one had ever fed him. When
Old Xing halted his cart at the work site to eat his
food, the dog was suddenly there staring at him. Old
Xing tore off two small pieces of bread to give the
dog. After this, he spent the whole day following be-

hind Old Xing's cart. On the fourth day, the morning Old Xing headed home, the dog ran behind the cart all the way out of the city. Old Xing couldn't stand to watch the pathetic creature any longer and, in a moment of compassion, he lifted him up into the cart.

At noon man and dog arrived in the village. While on the outskirts of the settlement, Old Xing noticed that there was no smoke emerging from his chimney. An ominous apprehension suddenly shook him. Just as he reached his shack, Old Wei's wife came to find him.

"Old Xing, your wife said yesterday afternoon that she was going to the supply and marketing cooperative. She gave me the key to your door. But last night she didn't come back. What's happened?"

Old Xing took the key and opened the door with shaking hands. The room was even cleaner than usual. The covers, the mattress, and Old Xing's padded clothes were all folded in clean piles on top of the bed. Atop the pillow were four new pairs of shoes placed in a row, but there was no person to be seen.

In a little while, lots of villagers were standing around inside and outside the house. Some people urged Old Xing to go look for his wife at the cooperative, but this was really a stupid suggestion. Everybody understood what had happened. Old Xing, in a stupor, sat on the edge of the bed hunched over. He didn't hear anything. He just repeated over and over again in his heart: She's gone, she's gone! She didn't even wait till spring!

Old Wei cut his way in through the crowd and said, "Old Xing, don't sit there like a dummy. Check and see what she took with her."

Soon Old Xing's neighbors discovered that besides the old battered clothes she wore, she only took with her one hundred and twenty pounds of grain and fifty *yuan*. She hadn't even taken the half of the grain and money that was her share.

"This really is a good woman!" everybody said, heaping praises on her. But this just made Old Xing feel even more heartbroken.

When it was almost time for work, Brigade Leader Wei quickly entered the room and said to Old Xing, "As luck would have it, the commune is sending a tractor into the city just now to haul some chemical fertilizers. Go to town quickly and go to the bus station and the train station to hunt for her. A woman carrying over a hundred pounds of grain won't find it easy to travel. I found out that yesterday afternoon she caught a ride on the third brigade's cart, which was taking cabbage into the city. It was almost dark before they reached the city." The brigade leader, fearing that something might happen to Old Xing, also sent along a young man.

Old Xing went into the city in a daze. All the faces in the vast crowds were the faces of strangers. He and his young companion tried the bus and train stations, but without success. No one remembered seeing the missing woman. The young man said, "She must have gone like she came. She must have jumped on a freight car." They then explored the empty freight trains. She wasn't there either.

On the afternoon of the next day, they caught a ride home. On the road, Old Xing still clung to one thread of hope. "She's a good woman. She may still come back." The young man also tried to comfort him. "She must have been thinking of her children and went back to see how they were. She'll probably come back to me, this time with her kids."

Old Xing returned to the village, feeling discouraged yet hopeful. Just as he took the key to open the door, a fuzzy-haired thing stumbled at his feet and woofed up at him. It turned out that for a day and a half, the little yellow dog had never left the door of the house he recognized as his master's. Old Xing picked him up in his arms and they entered the cold, empty house together.

From this time onward, Old Xing resumed the life he had led ten months earlier, except that he added one pleasant recollection, one poignant memory, one fierce hope—and one yellow dog.

For a year Old Xing kept hoping for her return. He always kept the room neat and clean, kept everything as it had been when she was home. Every day he expected her to throw open the door and charge in.

Gradually the patches she mended were worn through; the clothes she had sewn for him had holes in them; the shoes she had made for him were almost all worn out. Slowly Old Xing's hope and longing became a secret pain buried at the bottom of his heart, while the top of his heart was again blanketed by hopelessness.

In the days that followed, there was only the yellow dog to comfort him. Whenever Old Xing seemed lost in thought during the rest period or at night, the dog snuggled close beside him and made him feel that he still had at his side a living thing that held the deepest affection for him. The yellow dog, which by now had grown large and strong, became a living link between Old Xing and his wife.

However, even this link was wrested from him in the end.

V.

After the movement began to study the theory of the dictatorship of the proletariat, Old Xing's production brigade was like all the other production brigades. As soon as the movement began, a work committee was sent out by the county. In the daytime farmers worked the land; at night they had meetings. They had practically no time for themselves. One night during a big meeting, there came a proclamation that caused all the farmers complete bafflement. The proclamation specified that the villagers should "eliminate" all dogs within three days. So that there would be more food for the farmers themselves, all dogs were to be killed. Lack of compliance with this order would be equivalent to harboring a class enemy.

For the first few days, Old Xing really didn't take this notice very seriously. He had his own simple farmer's reasoning. He thought to himself: *I've never heard of any country's poverty being caused by raising dogs. In the old society even beggars had a dog with them.* However, to his surprise, in a few days one farmer after another who owned dogs took those dogs and killed them. Even Old Wei, who had kept his big black dog for five years, hung it from a tree and used water to drown him. It turned out after all that the dogs were even a road to profit. Some people in the city heard that the village was going to kill its dogs, so they came one after another riding their bicycles to the countryside to buy dog meat. The meat of the dog alone brought three or four *yuan*, and if the farmer took it into the city to sell, he was able to get forty or fifty *fen* for each pound.

After ten days, Old Xing's big yellow dog was the only one left alive. The militia, wearing their red armbands, had noticed this dog and had already gone through Old Xing's village twice carrying guns.

On this day four old men were winnowing grain on the threshing ground. When the wind stopped, they all got together to chat. When the talk got around to Old Xing's dog, Old Xing said in some temper, "However poor we are, we can't lay the blame for our poverty on the dogs. In fact, who in our village has ever fed a dog? Don't they hunt everywhere for wild things to eat? My dog is already raised to be like this."

One old man said, "It doesn't depend on whether you feed them or not. If you use your own grain to feed your dog, who is going to bother with you? I heard it was because some people had their dogs take state-controlled corncobs home to chew on."

This was so funny everybody laughed. Old Wei said, "If the village dogs were able to do this, we wouldn't have to farm. We could just take our dogs out to perform everywhere."

One old man who in the past loved to listen to the ancient books said, "That night when I went home from the meeting, I thought about it a little while too. In fact, it has nothing to do with the feeding of grain. It's just like Old Xing says, who among us has ever honestly fed his dog? I've figured out that it's related to the movement to criticize Confucius and Lao Tzu."

Except for Old Xing, who was still frowning, everyone laughed.

"Now look. Loyalty, filial piety, moral integrity, and faithfulness are what Confucius and Lao Tzu talked about. What are these four virtues? Loyalty refers to the horse. Everybody knows the horse is most loyal to man. When Guan Gong died, his horse, Red Rabbit, wouldn't eat anything. Filial piety refers to the sheep. Lambs are able to kowtow to their mothers

as soon as they are born. Moral integrity refers to the
tiger. When the mother tiger gives birth to a cub,
she knows extreme pain, and afterward she won't let
the male tiger trouble her again. Faithfulness refers
to the dog, of course. In the current campaign to criticize loyalty, filial piety, moral integrity, and faithfulness, it seems to me that my interpretation is valid
and they are starting out the campaign with the dogs.
Otherwise why would they say that raising a dog is
equal to harboring a class enemy?"

The old men, who were filled with the wisdom of
experience, all understood Old Xing's implications,
and they all chuckled in mutual understanding. Finally
Old Wei sighed and said, "Of course, there are other
explanations, but it seems to me that the leaders really
think that dogs eat grain." He faced Old Xing. "Talk
is talk, fun is fun, but you had still better put down
that yellow dog of yours quickly. If you don't, that
gang of militia will be forced to kill him. They're all
brutal young men. And they don't listen to reason."

After supper, Old Xing squatted at the edge of his
bed, puffing on his pipe. The dog was lying on the
floor with his head raised, wrinkling his nose to sniff
the familiar smoke. Old Xing pondered during the
time it took him to smoke several bowlfuls of tobacco, and he thought through to a plan, namely to
seek official protection for his dog. Therefore, he put
on his shoes, locked the dog in the house, and went
to the home of the brigade leader.

Brigade Leader Wei's house happened not to have
any other visitors. The brigade leader was lying on
the brick bed and his daughter was sitting under the
lamp sewing up shoe bottoms.

"I thought it was something important," Brigade
Leader Wei said when he heard Old Xing's plan. "It's

only a dog and the leaders above have this directive.
Why don't you just kill him and let it go at that?"

"Let it go at that?" Old Xing said angrily. "He's been
my companion for years. I can't bear to kill him. I'll
guarantee that I'll never ask the brigade for relief grain,
then it will be okay. My dog will eat *my* grain."

"Actually it's not just a matter of eating grain; it's a
fact that dogs harm the crops."

"Tiangui, you're a villager. When have you ever seen
a dog harm the crops? A dog isn't a farm animal and
he isn't a chicken or a duck. How can they say that a
family can raise a chicken, but I can't raise a dog?"

The brigade leader's daughter understood Old Xing's
feelings. She said softly from one side, "Right. Uncle Xing doesn't have anyone at his side. Having a
dog keeps one from feeling bored and in low spirits."

These words aroused even further the compassion
Old Xing felt for his dog. "Tiangui, I'll tell you for
certain. If anyone wants to kill my dog, they will have
to kill me, Old Xing, first."

The hearts of all three of them sank. Brigade Leader
Wei's smile disappeared and he scratched his short
hair vigorously.

"Old Xing, you have your difficulties, I know. But
I also have my difficulties, and who can I find to talk
about them? If you don't have anything to do tonight,
why don't the two of us talk?

"You saw me grow up in this village. The year I
grazed mules everywhere, you were a farm laborer
for Wang Hai's family. After liberation, when we
formed mutual aid teams, and when we formed the
cooperative, we were both together. Then I was filled
with the spirit of youth and wanted with my whole
heart to lead all of us along a path of mutual prosperity. You know this. One, I have never prostituted
myself, and two, I have never been corrupt. Why is

this? Isn't it so I can do some straight talking for all
of us? You are just one person, but if you get enough
to eat, then so must everyone else. Through good
and bad we can all pool together. From my position,
the whole brigade of over three hundred hold out
their tongues to be fed and hold out their hands to be
clothed. If people don't get to see a little ready cash,
no one will have the drive to work next year. You're
worried about one dog; I'm worried about a lot of
people—over three hundred."

With considerable agitation he sat up on his heels on
the bed. "Look," he continued, "we get through this
year, the spring festival next year will bring this and
it will bring that. If no one has the drive to work,
can I make them? We're all poor and middle peasants;
we're all of the same village. But I've been thinking
too that a movement is always like a gust of wind.
Once this storm blows over, we'll engage in sideline
work again. If we don't engage in sideline work, we'll
all keep on being poor and never accomplish mecha-
nization. But you don't want to meet with the head
of the windstorm. We must all toe the line on the
big points. It's not worthwhile for a little place to hold
out against the intentions of the top. As for killing
the dog, it's really like not picking up a watermelon
in order to fight over a sesame seed. I feel that it's
meaningless too. However, the upper echelon has already elevated this business to a key program and has
said that not to kill the dogs is tantamount to harboring counterrevolutionaries. The head of the work
committee that has come to our brigade is also a member of the county party committee. The day it's figured out that the brigade had ten dogs, but has only
killed nine of them, the work committee will say that
our vanguard brigade didn't even carry out the policy
of killing the dogs. To tell you the truth, Old Xing,

if everything goes wrong and they find out that I, Wei
Tiangui, supported you in the matter of the woman,
the worst that can happen is that I won't be the brigade leader any longer. As for this dog, get rid of
him and let it be. Let the leaders be satisfied. Afterward, it will be easier to arrange things for the brigade. As soon as the head of the work committee goes,
you can raise another dog. How about it?"

At first Old Xing hadn't really taken what he said
to heart, but as he kept listening it became clearer.
When Tiangui mentioned his wife at the very last, Old
Xing was filled with all random emotions. He knew
that Tiangui had helped him wholeheartedly. Could he
allow Tiangui to get into trouble over a dog? He lowered his head and struck it furiously. With great sorrow, but with determination, he said "Tiangui, I can't
allow you to get into trouble. Everything you said is
true. Tomorrow have someone come to kill him. I
can't do it myself."

That whole night he didn't sleep. He sat on the
earthen bricks protruding beneath the bed and smoked
in a daze. The dog didn't have any idea that these were
his final hours and still affectionately laid his head on
Old Xing's thigh. Old Xing petted the lustrous, silklike
fur.

He stroked his dog lightly, just as if it were his child.
Chinese farmers, he recalled, are calm and restrained
in the face of unavoidable disasters. Now that he discovered his life no longer had any meaning, what was
the use of keeping a dog? He thought aloud: "You go
first; I'll come a little later."

He lifted his head and looked around his little room,
trying to find the marks left behind by the woman
who wanted food. Almost every square inch of this
small adobe house had been swept from top to bottom by her and everything in the room had been dusted

or washed by her. But she was gone, and all that remained was the deep mark engraved on his bleeding
heart. And yet, he didn't blame her for leaving him.
Moreover, her leaving without saying anything still allowed him to keep a little hope.

The next morning he let the dog, who had been fed
until he was very full, go outside. It still hadn't
reached noon when he heard in the fields the sudden,
clear, cold sound of a rifle from the corral. He knew
without doubt that someone had shot his dog and his
heart was violently flooded with a surge of guilt and
remorse. When he raced to the corral, the person who
had executed the dog had already sauntered off and
there was only a bunch of children around his dog. The
dog was lying stretched out on its side and from the
bottom of his stomach came a wisp of rich, red blood.
One eye, whose pupil was already enlarged, was looking sideways at the dark blue sky with an expression
of fright and unease—just like the expression in the
eyes of that woman who wanted food.

Old Xing bent his head over the dog's body and he
sobbed piteously.

VI.

Not long afterward, when the work committee dispersed after completing their assignment, village sideline work and rural household sidelines were, sure
enough, resumed secretly. Moreover, from the neighboring villages the sound of barking dogs could be
heard faintly. However, Old Xing's dog could not be
resurrected. Old Xing himself became weaker and
older every day. After several months he even lost the
ability to take care of himself and had to depend entirely on the neighbors to bring him sustenance.

On the coldest day of the winter this year, his neighbors thought it strange that by noon he still had not opened the door, and after they had pried open the door of that solitary adobe shack, they discovered that he had died sometime during the night. He lay straight and stiff on the bed.

Some people said he had had a heart attack; some said he died from old age; and some said it was cancer. Only Old Wei grumbled in his grief and said, "In politics, all they can do is criticize Confucius. In production, all they can do is kill dogs. It's not enough to target people for attack, they still have to attack animals. If Old Xing's dog were still here, he would have barked and we would have known sooner. . . ."

EPILOGUE

Three and a half years later, young Yang, a county postal worker in the commune, received a letter from Northern Shaanxi that was addressed to Old Xing of the Fifth Production Brigade. Yang didn't give it much thought and sent the letter back after noting on the envelope: "Person deceased, return to sender." Later when there was a break during a commune meeting, a group of people were standing together chatting and young Yang mentioned the letter as a piece of news. On hearing this, Wei Tiangui, who had already become the party secretary of the brigade, ferociously hit the young postal clerk on the back and reprimanded him. "You rascal, you, why didn't you open the letter and look at it? It must have been mailed by that woman who wanted food. We don't even know how she is getting along now. Besides, Old Xing left behind two boxes that are still stored in the Fifth Brigade's storeroom."

(Translated by Beatrice Spade)

FAMILY CHRONICLE OF
A WOODEN BOWL MAKER

by Jia Pingwua

This second short story by Jia Pingwua was first published in The Chinese Writer, *a Beijing literary journal.*

Way back during the Forties, in the county of Shan in Shaanxi province, there was a great landlord by the name Zhou, his given name being Shouwa. Within a circuit of over a hundred square *li*, all the land belonged to him. Beyond the walls of the county seat, within an area of sixty *li* as far as Niantze Village, was a stretch of lowlands surrounded on four sides by rocky hills. The soil was of that dark, rich quality especially fitted to growing opium. All Zhou's opium-growing tenants were settled in that area.

Every year during the lunar months of July and August, when the carrots were all pulled up, the poppy would also be ready for harvesting. In those months the stems were waist-high, thick enough for a young cow to be lost under the growth—and the flowers were white and beautiful to the eye.

In the early mornings the farmers would wind a blue, hand-woven belt around their waists and attach a gourd to the belt, this being the opium gourd. They would then go into the fields, split open the bulb with their knives, and the milk-white fluid would appear.

It would turn black and congeal the moment it was released. The farmers would carefully scrape the sticky little lump.

All this unprocessed opium was sold to landlord Zhou; circumventing him was out of the question. Of course, the price was very low, but to the peasants it was still more profitable than growing corn or potatoes or peppers.

At that time opium dealing was ostensibly declared illegal by the government. But in reality most of the military and most of the local officials as far down as the village elder were addicts. Moreover, Niantze district was remote and secluded, so the opium traffic was carried on without interference.

Later, landlord Zhou, who monopolized the sale of opium, was killed in a feud with local bandits. His business fell apart, but the local growers had become addicted and some of the smugglers had made fortunes, so the poppy trade still continued. The locality seemed to possess an evil influence; some of the population made fortunes while others went bankrupt; under this influence, the good people turned to evil ways, while the bad went from bad to worse. Gradually the place became notorious as a haunt of bullies, hooligans, and roving bandits.

But always, as the saying goes, there are exceptions. The Huang family was one such exception. Years ago Huang had also grown poppy on Zhou's land like all his ancestors. His grandfather was an addict who, when overpowered by craving, became a shivering, tearful bundle, a disgusting sight; in desperation he would crawl into the poppy fields and roll some unprocessed opium, and he finally died in misery. After his death, Huang's grandmother vowed that no member of the Huang family would ever touch opium. Only when one of them was ill, suffering from a toothache or diarrhea, would they be allowed to drink some water soaked with the poppy husk, or boiled with poppy leaves.

Soon after the downfall of landlord Zhou, Huang's grandmother and both his parents died, and Huang was left on his own. He gave up poppy growing entirely. Thus, he was very poor. In spite of his healthy way of living and the hard work he put into farming his parcel of land, he still could not feed himself, and so he acquired a trade: making wooden bowls. At age thirty, then, he became an itinerant craftsman, going the rounds in the countryside, making wooden bowls on order.

The fact is, Shan County never boasted of a pottery; all through the generations, the population bought their pots from the tradesmen of Yao County. So in those times, a piece of pottery was worth a lot of money. Very few families could afford a set of bowls. As for the children's eating bowls, which were often dropped and broken, they were invariably wooden ones. So wooden bowls were greatly in demand, and Huang was able to maintain a living. At the age of thirty-six, he became pretty well known. He managed to take for his wife a one-eyed woman, and he fathered a son. That is to say, he finally managed to set up a family. But as a bowl maker he could not earn enough to keep his wife and son. The villagers advised him to try a hand at poppy growing, but he would resist.

"That is not a reliable business!" he would say. The villagers would shake their heads over his stubbornness.

But Huang had stumbled on the right path after all. In 1949 the People's Liberation Army descended into the hills and opium became illegal. Those who made fortunes by the opium trade lost their lives, or as the saying goes, "Their heads made a change of habitation." The addicts deprived of sustenance lay shivering in bed.

Huang congratulated himself secretly. He held steadfast to the belief that keeping on the right track reaps its own reward. After the land reform he was allotted land. He did not give up making bowls, but worked harder than ever on the land.

Thirty years elapsed in the twinkling of an eye. Huang became an old man, his back stooped in the shape of a lobster; his son was as tall as the garden wall and he was married and had children of his own.

For the last three decades after the liberation, because of the numerous political turmoils that racked the nation, Huang stopped his little business of making wooden bowls; he had given up all hope of handing down this craft. But now in his old age, the policy of the government changed. Formerly, peasants had no land; then the Communist party gave them land. Now that the land was in their own hands, the Communist party reminded the peasants that their vision of the future should not be limited to tilling the soil. Understandably, the old man was full of hope and fear at the turn of things.

He summoned his son and said, "My son, I have been living in this world for more than sixty years. The land is still the same land, but the population has doubled and trebled; now the government encourages us peasants to undertake trade and industry. That is sensible advice for ensuring peace and prosperity to the country and to the people. Now I've been thinking, why don't we restore our family tradition of making wooden bowls instead of staying home and staring at the land all day long!"

"That is true," the son replied. "I have also been thinking of turning my hand to something."

So father and son shouldered their axes and went into

the mountains and gathered clumps of willow and walnut and pine suitable for carving out.

Old Huang's art was ripe. It had mellowed with the years. His son cut the clumps roughly into the shape of a bowl and the old man would hollow out a bottom for the bowl and then apply it to the shaver. In the old days the shaver was fixed onto a mill set on a wooden stump. When the mill was set revolving, a bowl would be carved into shape in half a day. But now with electricity (and Huang's son's facility with electrical gadgets) a bowl could be carved in an hour. The whole family rejoiced.

But after practicing their art for two weeks, the son gave up. Sales of the bowls were very bad. Most families, it seemed, were only interested in porcelain bowls. So the son lost interest.

His father said to him, "My son, you are envious of those in the village who are doing business in transportation and brick making. Yes, they can get rich overnight, but our art is longstanding. Thirty years ago—"

The son knew that Old Huang was going to repeat his homilies about shunning opium and interrupted him: "Yes, yes, I know you were right about that. But now times are changed. Clinging to your old art won't get you anywhere." The father was going to remonstrate, but the son cut him short. "You are too old to understand, I refuse to talk to you."

Old Huang was furious, of course, and abused his son soundly. The son was equally furious.

The old father was full of sorrow and anger, but age was against him; he puttered about helpless. Certainly the world belonged to the young nowadays. But when he saw his son running about without direction, he said to himself: "All right, let's wait and see what you're worth—a dragon or a worm. Try being

on your own and then you'll know what having a father means. . . ."

The son was a very clever fellow, but a whole month
passed and still he had not decided on any kind of
work. He had no capital to start with, so could not
buy a tractor or truck; also he did not want to smug-
gle wood and herbal medicine and evade government
inspection. What could he do, stranded in this valley, so far away from town and city? He would return home empty-handed every evening, sit at the
table, and consume bowl after bowl of food.

"There's no more salt in the house," Old Huang
would say. "You better go and buy some. I cannot
feed you and your wife and son on nothing."

The boy knew his father was making fun of him.
He would shrug as if he didn't care, but then he
would lie awake all night.

On the second day of the second lunar month, there
was no rain, only rumbling thunder. According to
local tradition, on this day thunder without rain is the
herald of spring, when all the earth wakes up to a
new life.

But young Huang was still oppressed. He didn't remain home to eat the traditional stir-fried corn beans
but went glumly to a former classmate's house to drink.
He came back at midnight. Stumbling drunkenly in
the wheat fields behind the village, he came across a
piglet lying on the ground, wailing piteously.

"Whose pig is this?" he cried out three times, but
there was no answer. He cursed the careless housewife that let a piglet run loose at night and, scooping
up the piglet in his arms, walked home, thinking to
return it to its owner the next day.

Back home he dumped the little animal on the floor
in the middle room. After explaining the situation
to his wife, he fell asleep.

Strangely, nobody came to claim the piglet. Old Huang looked it over, saw that it was perfect on every point as far as piglets go. "Perhaps this is not a lost pig!" he exclaimed. "Maybe it was purposely thrown away."

The son then looked at the piglet's tail and saw that it was flat and turned up twice. In this area there is a superstition that piglets whose tails are flat-shaped and turn up in two circles are the embodiments of lamb and will be devoured by wolves. There were a lot of wolves in the vicinity and nobody would risk raising such unlucky piglets.

Old man Huang picked up the piglet by its hind legs and was on the point of throwing it out again, but his son stopped him. "This is just a local superstition—not grounded in truth. I want to raise this piglet, and let the wolf come if it dares!"

The old man could not dissuade his son. From that moment on, young Huang had his hands full. He couldn't service this piglet more devotedly if it were his wife. He would personally prepare all its meals. Then he would watch it eat and eat until the silly thing straddled with legs apart, unable to move. And the piglet filled out like a balloon. In the eighth lunar month, it was killed and produced one hundred and twenty *jin* of meat. When sold, along with the head, the trotters, the heart, the liver, and other innards, the meat fetched eighty-five *yuan* and three *jiao*.

Old Huang was clearly impressed. He thought to himself, My son must be born for great things. Except for young Huang, the inauspicious piglet would not have been preserved; it would have turned up for a wolf's breakfast long ago. He told his son: "Since this has turned out so well and you are not good at other things anyway, why don't you keep on raising pigs? Winter has come. There's plenty of carrots. I suggest you buy and raise another piglet."

Young Huang went to market several times but never brought back any piglet. Just when his father thought he had somehow changed his mind, one day young Huang brought back two half-grown pigs of eighty *jin* each. The old man was disgusted and ordered his wife not to raise a finger to help with feeding. "This is pure nonsense!" he exclaimed. "Such big eaters they are. They each cost thirty to forty *yuan* for a start. How much will they ever make?"

The son did not mind what his father said. He kept feeding his pigs steamed carrots and sweet potatoes. The two pigs were big-boned, but would not put on flesh. Their reddish hair hung on them forlornly. But two months later, the pair shed their layer of hair and began to puff out, milky white and sheeny, like a pair of young cows. Huang the younger sold them to the state collector and made a net profit of one hundred *yuan* for each.

With this two hundred *yuan*, young Huang did not rush out on a buying spree. Instead he laid out his profit on four eighty-*jin* half-grown pigs and a load of corn, which he ground and mixed with sweet potatoes and carrots and fed to the pigs. At the end of the year, he made another five hundred *yuan*.

Huang the younger's raising of half-grown pigs was a success story in the whole of Niantze Village. He was the object of universal envy and emulation. Everybody in the village gave up raising piglets and threw themselves into raising half-grown pigs and force-feeding them with high-quality grain, in the hope of making quick money.

Young Huang contemplated them with amusement while he strolled along the market studying different trends. He decided to stop buying half-grown pigs. In-

stead he brought back a big bulky sow. His entire
family protested.

"You have just now found the key to success," cried
his father, "and now you're up to some new nonsense. Nowadays sows are not worth a cent."

"But, Father, don't you realize, precisely because nobody is raising piglets anymore, there'll be a scarcity
of half-grown ones. As sows are cheap, this is the best
time to buy. You just sit and watch."

True to the son's predictions, the sow gave birth to
twelve little piglets, all warm and pudgy and cute. Just
when they started running about to look for food, there
was a scarcity of pigs in the market, especially of piglets, and their price soared. Huang the younger brought
his month-old pigs to the market; he would not sell
them piecemeal. No! He sold them by weight, three
yuan, five *jiao* for every *jin*, and his brood sold out
in a matter of minutes.

In the mountainous areas, there was not much out-
let for side industries. Pig raising was considered a
real bonus. Nearly every family undertook pig raising; some invested all their savings, looking on pigs
as vital as their own heart, liver, and life pulse—their
only god of good fortune. Raising pigs was something like planting a seed of gold and growing forth
a tree that sheds gold coins without end.

By then, though, young Huang had stopped raising
pigs.

He had made eight hundred *yuan* by several deals.
With two hundred, he repaired the middle room,
which had been leaking; he spent another hundred on
a cupboard and a square table and another on clothes
for the family so that everybody turned out respect-
ably clad.

"You are old," he said to his father. "You should
give up making wooden bowls."

"You have just made a few *yuan* and you better not put on airs before me!" Old Huang retorted. "Do you think your little deals will last you forever? As for my wooden bowls, indeed there is only a small market, but all my old customers are loyal. I don't make much, of course, but I don't stand to lose. A man's life stretches out in front of him. How long do you think your few hundred *yuan* will last?"

The father kept to his old craft, professing to have no envy of his son's rise in fortune. The son shrugged and let him be.

Pig raising turned the tide in Huang the younger's fortunes, and now that he suddenly stopped raising pigs, the village was intrigued.

One day the old man journeyed into the northern mountains to sell his wooden bowls and his son accompanied him. There were a lot of sheep in the mountains. Every family raised one or two, primarily for meat, and also for the milk to feed their cows. The mountain people refused to drink sheep milk themselves, though, considering the taste repulsive.

Huang bought five head of sheep at fifteen *yuan* each and milked them every night. When the milk was plenteous, he got as much as five *jin* from each sheep, altogether making twenty-five *jin* a night. He would store the milk carefully and, hitching it to his bicycle, pedal himself to the workers' residence area ten *li* away. The factory workers had plenty of money and were mostly southerners who were concerned over nutrition. Huang's twenty-five *jin* of milk would, therefore, be sold instantly. He would start out at dawn and come back before the morning was over—an easy way to make money. Thus, after six months, he bought another three head of sheep and had heaps of money in his pockets. He was the envy of the village.

The other villagers had great difficulty selling their

pigs to the state collector because of the surplus. The peasants in need of ready money to buy supplies for the New Year Festival killed their pigs themselves and sold the pork cheap. Most of them couldn't even make a profit.

In their apish ways they next started to follow Huang the younger in raising sheep for milk. In a very short time, the whole village was roaming with sheep, but some sheep owners turned to cheating for profit and would distill the milk with a lot of water, and the reputation of the local milk was damaged. Huang the younger could not get rid of his eight sheep on the spur of the moment, so he started to drive them to the workers' residence area. He took his time, playing on his mouth organ, while the sheep, also in no hurry, would nibble at fresh grass and a drink of the pure mountain water. When they reached the residence area, Huang would milk his sheep just as the customer ordered it, ensuring the quality of his goods and thus taking away the business of his dishonest competitors.

This notion of selling fresh milk was a novelty. Everybody in the village was impressed by his originality and astuteness. Even his bowl-carving father thought his son's head might not be so empty after all.

Just when his business was at its best, Huang the younger, to everybody's surprise, sold his eight head of sheep. He went to Linbao County of the province of Henan and for the price of two *yuan*, five *jiao* brought back thirteen Holland-breed chickens. During the long journey back, by bus and train, by water route and land route, by day and night, five of the thirteen chickens died. Those chicks were not particularly big, but very solid. Their color was a bright yellow, with a reddish haze. The villagers proclaimed that success had gone to his head and that Huang the younger would make a mess of his business yet.

They would ask him: "Is this the phoenix that you have transported from afar?"

"Yes," he would answer.

"And will this phoenix lay you eggs of silver and gold?"

Of course he could understand the implications, but he would answer all the same, "Wait and see."

Ten days passed and then twenty. Still nothing happened. The newly bought chickens had nothing to show.

All the villagers who raised chickens gathered eggs every day; when they took their eggs to the state collectors, they would pass by Huang's gate on purpose. Holding an egg against the sun, they would exclaim how big their eggs were.

Huang the younger ignored them.

Old man Huang's sixty-fifth birthday came around, and he went to buy several *yuan* of eggs from his chicken-raising neighbor.

"Isn't your own son raising chickens?" asked the neighbor.

"I don't call that raising chickens. That's playing with pigeons."

"But pigeons lay eggs too! Everybody says that your son is capable of wonders, even able to pick a star from the skies."

At that, Old Huang blushed, ashamed of his son. The old man walked back home and scolded his son for letting his success get to his head. He ordered Huang the younger to kill all the good-for-nothing chickens who were wasting feed. Needless to say, the son kept his chickens.

And on the twenty-ninth day, the chickens began to lay. Each and every one of their eggs was heavier by one *liang* than ordinary eggs. He stored up a basketful very soon, but kept the news to himself. Of

these eggs, he would neither eat nor sell so much as a
single one. He hatched them all, getting eighty-three
chicks. Ten died and twelve were male. The remaining matured and started laying. Huang would collect dozens of eggs every day. He sold all his eggs to
the local Agricultural Technical Center, at five *jiao*
each.

The news spread and the whole county was stunned.
Everybody was talking about the superior quality of
the Holland-breed chickens and buying the new breed
from the technical center. Huang was the only sup-
plier. For a whole year he had not made money, but
now the money came pouring in.

When the Holland-breed chickens were popularized
in the whole district, young Huang turned to planting sugar-leaf chrysanthemums, and the next year he
planted saplings on part of his land. When the saplings were grown, the campaign to plant trees was in
full force. Each sapling sold for three *jiao*, five *fen*—
nine times more profitable than planting grain.

Since starting his business with raising pigs, young
Huang had put aside something after every deal to
expand his business. When he finally sold off his saplings, he had six thousand in the bank. He bought
himself a four-wheeled tractor and took to long-distance
transportation. In the last few years the mountain people had become rich and all had their eyes fixed on a
tractor. But the mountain area was too far removed
from the city to get enough business orders, while the
price of gas went up. Clearly there was not money
to be made by tractor transportation.

Huang the younger made twenty thousand and decided to stop. He went to the county capital and then
to the provincial capital. He came back one day in great
haste to borrow money, saying he planned to buy a

bus and start a bus line from Niantze Village to the provincial capital.

"Nowadays everybody is doing business. The buses are overcrowded. Running round-trip every other day, I'll have all the business I can handle. I'll get back my capital in the matter of a twelvemonth. That will mean having a bus of my own for nothing."

Old Huang had lighted a match when his son was speaking. He was so astounded by this news that he held the match in midair and only remembered it when the fire burned his fingers.

"Oh, my son," he cried, "I am no match for you. The young have taken over the world. But there's a limit to everything. The best policy is to leave well enough alone. There is no end to the money one can make. Remember the adage: the highest tree collects the strongest wind to itself. You must not raise yourself too high over others. Now our whole family is prosperous. It is time to stop. One step too far will lead us straight into trouble. Remember in that time when everybody was raising poppy—"

"Yes, yes, I know all that. But these are the 1980s. The world is far beyond your imagination. Why don't you go out and see it for yourself? And anyway, I'm not stealing or robbing anybody. How can I bring trouble on you or the family?"

Old Huang saw that the son was flush with recent success. The young, he thought to himself, never look backward. They just plunge on, not caring to leave a stepping-stone for retreat. That night he murmured his fears to his wife.

Even during the day he had no peace of mind. His heart was full of evil forebodings. Under these circumstances he set greater store than ever by his bowl making.

He told his wife, "I keep carving out wooden bowls

not for the money but so that our son, and then his son, will have something to fall back on. Just you wait and see. What are we anyway, that our son should be so rich? It is not right, and will bring evil in its wake."

Huang the younger went ahead and bought his bus and hired a driver at a monthly salary of eighty *yuan* and started his round-trip bus line from the township where the commune was seated to the provincial capital. He himself could not drive, but he went along with the bus, selling tickets while learning to drive. The peasants flocked to use the bus and business was excellent.

This spectacular success astounded all seven counties of the region. Some jealous souls, however, banded together and wrote letters accusing the young Huang of stealing business away from the state-controlled transportation service. Before the month was over, the transportation authorities of the region ordered Huang to close down his operation.

The bus line stopped operating. In the village some were indignant, some sympathetic, and some were gleeful. "Socialism prevails after all," one villager said. "Huang the younger is rightly punished for turning capitalist."

"Just give up and forget it," Old Huang advised his son. "Let them confiscate the car. You should offer incense to the gods that you are not sitting in jail! How could you believe that your good fortune will last forever! Don't you see, when you first made money, people envied you, but conceded that you are quite a character; then when your good fortune grew out of bounds, you lost your neighbors' good opinion."

Huang the younger was very downcast. He wrapped his bedroll around himself and stayed in bed for three days.

On the fourth day he hired a lawyer to represent him in court.

It worked. He won his case. His bus started running again.

The day his business resumed, young Huang decorated the bus with bands of red silk tied to the front, then stood up on the top of the bus and let off a string of firecrackers. The scene was one mass of lively sound and color. The entire village joined young Huang in his victory celebration.

Within six months all the buses in the region had been rented out as private enterprise. But the young Huang had already made thirty thousand *yuan,* far in excess of his investment. The villagers speculated that this young Huang was not an ordinary mortal, that he was probably going to start a chain of bus lines.

But he didn't. He didn't touch the thirty thousand, but added another twenty borrowed from the bank and hired a building contractor to build him a four-story building at the foot of the hill in front of the mountain.

The building was quite imposing; it could be seen eight or ten *li* away.

On the day it was finished, the young Huang, dressed as if for a special occasion, went to the county township and invited over to the site the head of the county, the head of the local bureau of education, the head of the commune, the head of the local primary school. He called these officials together and publicly announced that he was offering the new building to the local school.

EPILOGUE

A framed certificate of honor now hangs in the middle room of the Huang household. The story of a peasant donating a school building made headlines in all the provincial papers. Meanwhile, young Huang's bus operation continues to thrive.

One reporter asked Huang the younger for the secret of his constant success. "Were you born lucky?"

Young Huang smiled and pointed to his wife. "It's all due to her."

Everybody was nonplussed and looked to the wife. Huang's wife then revealed that she had three brothers, one working in the provincial research institute of policy, one in the agricultural bureau, and one as the head of a factory in a neighboring province. Whenever young Huang wanted to start something new, he would always consult his brothers-in-law.

When the young man was being interviewed, Old Huang was not at home. He was out selling his wooden bowls. Actually he avoided the reporters on purpose. At the moment he was sitting on the doorstep of one of his faithful customers, enjoying his pipe.

"This wooden bowl is a real treasure," he was saying. "Porcelain looks better, of course, but porcelain bowls break easily and, once broken, they cause heartache. Whereas this wooden bowl will not break if dropped. If it does break, your heart need not ache over it. Now, don't look down on handicrafts; handicrafts endure. You'll not burst with profit, but on the other hand, you won't starve. The old saying holds: a trickle of water flows long. Mark my word: keeping to your place always ensures good relations with your neighbors."

SHORBLAC: A DRIVER'S STORY

by Zhang Xinliang

This second story by Zhang Xinliang was published in Shanghai in Encounter Monthly.

Oh, please don't doze off. On long-distance rides, I get scared when the fellow sitting next to me falls asleep. It's catching, you know.

Have a cigarette? . . . What, you don't smoke! . . . You work with your pen, and yet you don't smoke! Well, *I* do. Drivers are not allowed to smoke in the big cities, but here we're free to do what we like. Otherwise we'd be bored stiff. Here, things aren't the same as in the interior. Here, you can drive thousands of *li,* with nothing in sight. Your eyelids keep getting heavy.

Look at this endless plain of oval rocks. . . . Yes, this is the Gobi. Perhaps you'd always thought of the Gobi as a vast desert. Well, it's not all desert. Over here it's rocks, bigger than a fist or a human head. After we cross the Gobi, we'll be in the mountain regions. A section of the Tianshan Mountains. Even they aren't what you imagine from watching films. This section of the mountain is just bare rocks, looking like they'd been beaten out on an anvil.

We'll cross the mountain by way of the Dry Ridge. Isn't that some name? But accurate. It's stone dry.

117

Even a teardrop will evaporate before it leaves your
eye. No grass, no trees, not even birds or ants—it's
like being on the moon. You'll see it directly. Out here
it's tough to keep driving for hours and hours, without nodding off. Lucky for me, you're here today. And
a reporter too. We can chat a little.

I'm sure you've seen a lot of China. But if you don't
come west to Xinjiang, you never realize how big
your country really is. There's an adage that in Xinjiang
even a beggar must ride on a donkey. Otherwise,
having eaten his fill in one village, he will starve to
death before he reaches the next. That saying refers
to the old society, of course, but it gives you an idea
of the vastness of the place.

I like picking up passengers. Whenever I see somebody walking along the road, I always slow down
in case the guy needs a lift. Just look! All this space
and not a sign of life. The mountains in front so
forbidding, the skies so clouded. And a single human
being trudging on alone. You sort of take pity on
him. And also respect him. Perhaps you don't feel it
so much riding up here. But try making this journey on foot, step by step. Then you'll know how it
feels.

With a passenger sitting next to me, we keep each
other company. Driving a long-distance delivery truck
like this one, I'm always faced with the machine, rarely
with people. On the road, even when I do come across
someone I know, we barely have time to acknowledge each other before the car whizzes past. The machine is less than an animal. When I was a kid, I used
to drive a donkey in my home village. The donkey
is a stubborn thing, but at least it's alive. You can talk
to it when you're bored and it will flap its ears, as if
it understands. Driving a car or truck—well, the soli-
tude really overcomes you. That's why whenever we

get to a stop, we drivers always get together to shoot
the breeze. We just want to wag our tongues. People should be with people.

A few years ago a new boss was assigned to our fleet.
He expressly forbade giving lifts and he established
a lot of nonsense rules and regulations. It turned out
just as I suspected. The fellow was himself accepting
gifts of wine and cigarettes in return for transporting
of private goods. So he was fired.

And don't imagine that giving people a lift is such a
small thing. He hails; you stop; he climbs up. All
done in the twinkling of an eye. But maybe your passenger will think: *good men are not so hard to find after
all*. And once you see his contented smile, you also feel
a warmth spreading over you, and you resume driving with renewed energy, having forgotten about your
drowsiness. I don't speak a lot as a rule. It is enough
to have somebody sitting near me. Today I just can't
stop talking. I love to be with educated people. . . .

How did I come to Xinjiang? That's a long story.
Maybe by my accent, you can tell I'm from Henan
province. I finished junior middle school in my county.
At that time what dreams I had! When I saw the PLA
men on film, I decided to become an army officer. I
read a novel, and I wanted to become a writer. Then
I met a doctor, and I considered being a doctor.
It seems I've dreamed of everything except becoming
a truck driver. During my last year at middle school,
I wrote a poem that was printed in the school paper:

> "My dreams are many, like the stars in the sky,
>   Sparkling and bright, they shine over my
>   head. . . ."

Not bad? Oh, don't make fun of me. I was just seventeen. The teacher said that I showed promise. After
all, I was just a country boy.

But 1960 came round, and with it the hard times. My parents had nothing to eat. I couldn't go on studying, so I returned to my village to support my parents. But back home all I could do was to starve with them. I was the only child, and my parents could not bear to see me starving.

"Go, child," they said, "go and look out for yourself in the big world outside. After all, you've had nine years of book learning. Won't that earn you a bowl of rice?"

Well, you know, from the earliest days, we Henan people have been known for roving, roving through the provinces, by lakes and mountains, finding ways to survive. Whenever there is a flood or disaster at home, we get on our feet and off we go. At that time it happened that someone in our village had settled in Xinjiang; he sent a letter saying that in Xinjiang you could get a job and fill your belly. Xinjiang had been living in my imagination through a song we sang in school: "Xinjiang, O Land So Wonderful." So to Xinjiang I decided to go.

At that time residence checks were very strict. Leaving your home village was just as bad as robbery. We waited for a moonless night and stole out of the village. My father saw me to the crossroads as far as the boundary of the commune. He couldn't move a step further and crouched down by the roadside, panting. I took out the two cornbread cakes that my mother had smuggled into my pack and stuffed them into his shirt. "Father," I said, "please go back, I know my way, I have brought a map. When I get a job, I will send you money."

Young people have no regrets when leaving home. I didn't shed a solitary tear. Although my stomach was empty, my spirits soared, and I couldn't wait to fly far and wide. All I could see was a glorious fu-

ture in front of me; I never stopped to think about my
parents. I only began to understand their feelings as
I grew older. But even so, if you'd asked me what my
parents' parting words were, what they looked like,
I really couldn't say. Only that my father made a big
shadow crouched down on the roadside. In the past,
whenever I drove alone at night, I would always see
that shadow ahead of me. Crouching on the roadside.
It was like the permit stuck to my front window.
It was part of my vision. I couldn't get rid of it.

   Sometimes I would forgive myself. I would think
back and feel that if my mother had seen me off that
night, we might have said words closer to the heart.
My father was a taciturn old peasant and I was a
young man of few words. Well, so it happened that
after living on my parents for eighteen years, I left
them without offering a few words of comfort.

   All right, on with the story.

   That is how I left for Xinjiang. At the time the train
went as far as Weiya. Of course, Weiya was then
nothing compared to the flourishing place it now is. It
was just a cluster of a dozen clay cottages, set on a
sandy plain. And around this cluster of cottages, tents
were set up, one after another, in an endless chain.
The fact is, Weiya was the railway terminal. Everybody going to Xinjiang stopped there.

   In the train I had feared that it would be hard to get
employment without a certificate. But at Weiya an
old-timer told me, "If you do not have the commune's written permission to move, your voter's card
will do; if you don't have a voter's card, any letter from
a relative here will suffice. But those loudmouthed
recruiters for the hardest work and the greatest dis-
tances do not require any certificate at all. They just
look you over, and so long as you have all your limbs
intact—well, to hell with the certificate!"

The old man who gave me all this information was probably only forty or forty-five. He had a ragged jacket slung across his back; the covering was all soiled and greasy. He said he was versed in medicine and wanted to practice here, so he avoided the screaming recruiters. He did seem more or less educated. I showed him my middle school diploma. His eyes glistened at the sight. "Good for you!" he cried. "This could get you a job as an office worker. Don't you mind those hawkers. Go over there." He pointed in the direction of one of the recruitment tents. And off I went.

This particular tent was unlike the rest. A paper sign stuck to the outside had the words XINJIANG CULTURE BUREAU, WEIYA RECRUITING CENTER written in brush and ink. The person in charge seemed refined and he was certainly quieter than the recruiters outside, who were shouting themselves hoarse.

In the middle of the tent was a stove converted from a gas tank, and by the stove a bench of unvarnished wood, where applicants sat to be interviewed. The interviewer sat behind a desk, also of unvarnished wood. He was quite fat. I remember this because at that time, people who carried any flesh on their bones were a rare sight. It turned out that even here a diploma was not absolutely indispensable. If you didn't have one, Fatty would give you an oral examination on the spot. The questions were along the lines of "name the continents and the oceans"; "what type of state is the People's Republic of China?"; "who invented the table of the elements?"; and identifying quotations of Confucius and other philosophers. Fatty was from Shaanxi, a learned man, he seemed, and quite friendly. When my turn came, I displayed my diploma, and he seemed satisfied. He inquired about my family, how and when I arrived, in whose company, and so on. He registered my name as a school-teacher and told me to return the next morning to board the bus for Umruchi.

My elation was beyond description. I was soaring over the mass of tents, higher and higher over Weiya. Life had opened up a new path for me. I realized I had always wanted to be a teacher. I imagined myself, after a long career of teaching, white-haired, specta-cled, surrounded by scientists, writers, officers—all former students of mine. All well educated and deeply appreciative of me.

Just as my imagination was soaring in this manner, two girls came up to me. They were about my age, dressed more or less like students, with four braids be-tween the two of them. They were also from Henan, actually about one hundred *li* from my home village. The girls asked me whether I had found employ-ment. I said yes, a nice job too. I told them the whole procedure and bragged that Fatty trusted me and gave me a teaching job right away without an examination. They were very downhearted, because they had no hope of finding a decent job. And if they did heavy manual labor, they would collapse in a few days. Which was true. They were so thin and sallow, not at all like teenage girls today. So I said offhand: "Why don't you also try your luck at that tent and be a pri-mary schoolteacher?"

That night, I slept in one of the mud cottages which doubled as an inn. I don't know whether it was gov-ernment run or privately owned. It consisted of a heated wall and two long *kangs* on either side, but now the wall was damp and cold, and on the *kang* were neither pillow nor blanket. Even so, it cost three *yuan* a night. When I finally squeezed myself onto the *kang,* my hands came across a piece of woolen matting. The inn-keeper had a sort of conscience after all.

At the inn I learned that people changed jobs many times, always on the lookout for better pay. You people back east, heading from home to school and then from school to office, you are used to the orderly life. But it's thanks to this liberal employment policy that Xinjiang has changed from the most backward part of China to its present state in the last thirty years. If employers had acted as they do in the interior, treating job-seekers as criminals, judging only by a piece of paper and not the person himself, why, Xinjiang would still be desert wilds today!

Anyway, the next morning I got up. Realizing that first impressions are very important—especially for teachers—I paid thirty *fen* for a mugful of water and cleaned my face. When I arrived at the gathering place, the other recruits were already boarding the bus. Fatty stood aside checking names off a list. The moment he saw me, he flew into a rage.

"Go away," he cried. "I thought you had an honest look. But you're a crook after all. We don't want you. Go away."

"What have I done?" I asked, appalled.

"What have I done?" he mimicked my country accent. "What do you mean, a young man like you, running around with two young girls? What exactly are your relations with them? Why did you say you arrived alone when I questioned you yesterday?"

"I have nothing to do with the two girls," I cried. "If you have no faith in me, please give me an examination."

"Examination! You all say you are out of junior middle school. But you can't do simple addition and subtraction, and you take Gorky for a Chinese writer! Preposterous!"

Educated people are stubborn by nature, I suppose, but Fatty was more stubborn than most. It was evi-

dent that the two girls had lied to him about their qual-
ifications and dragged me down with them. Anyway,
he was absolutely set in his prejudices; wild horses
couldn't sway him to my side again.

The bus started off. I was left standing there forlornly. Fatty stuck his head out of a side window and
shouted, "Young fellow, the basic requirements of a
teacher are honesty and propriety. Without these, all
your book learning counts for nothing."

So much for my dream of being a schoolteacher!
Those scientists, writers, and officers whom I was
to have taught disappeared as if by magic. Fatty also
disappeared, leaving me splattered by the mud of the
bus. I turned back dejectedly and saw the two girls
standing together and looking at me very timidly.

"What have you done, you two? You have ruined
my chance!" I was ready to pour out my anger.

The girls held down their heads. "We didn't know
what to do," one of them said. "We never finished
primary school."

"Fatty wanted to give us an examination," added the
other. "So we said no need for examination, that we
were your classmates and that you brought us over with
you. But later it turned out . . ."

I saw their tearstained faces and relented. Drowning
people would clutch at straws. They did not intend
to harm me. I turned away and strode toward the
hawking recruiters, as boisterous that morning as they
had been the day before. The two girls followed me.
"Please take us with you," they cried. "You are a
good man. We'll go wherever you go."

"No," I said. "Goodhearted or not, my going around
in the company of two girls is enough to damn me.
Didn't you hear what Fatty said?"

"But what shall we do?" one of them asked. "We
have no money left, and there's no one we know.

We've decided to apply for manual labor. There's no other way out."

"Well, you can try. Don't go for the heavy work, though. Take some lighter job, and go slowly at first. It's better than the village back home. At least you will not starve."

They applied and left in a big truck that very afternoon. Just before the truck started off, I sold one of my shirts, then ran up to them and gave them each two *yuan*. Around us, recruiters were still hollering, "Come and join. The milk flows as freely as water!" But the two girls were in tears. I felt something stick in my throat, as if we were indeed classmates who had made it to this strange place together and were now to part.

The fact is, there is not a corner in Xinjiang that is inaccessible to us drivers. Many years after that, I was passing Kurle. A truck was parked in front of me, and people were unloading baskets of pears. One woman moving baskets of pears looked very familiar. It suddenly dawned on me that it was one of the two from my province. She worked very deftly. It was evident she was married and had born children; she had put on quite a lot of weight, and every gesture denoted self-assurance. I looked at her for a little while, but I didn't stop and speak to her. What could we have said to one another?

Meanwhile, back to my story. I was still stranded in Weiya. I still hoped to find work with educational requirements. I vowed not to sink to manual labor like the two girls who never finished primary school.

In the evening I joined other rovers in small talk. The truth is, people drifting at large in alien places watch out for each other. No matter how bad their own prospects might be, they are still interested in offering information and advice. They heard my story, passed my diploma around, and finally came to the unanimous conclusion that Hami was the place for me. They said there are openings for accountants in Hami.

I agreed that being an accountant was a fine profession. I was quite good at the abacus in middle school. If Hami was the place for me, so be it.

At the time the bus starting from Weiya was always crowded. For a ticket on a southbound bus, you sometimes had to wait an entire week. I could not afford to wait. I had only a few *yuan* left and no more clothes to sell. So I decided to hitch a ride with one of the delivery trucks.

The parking lot for these trucks was in the west part of town. It was a sandy space crisscrossed with tire marks and spilled gasoline. The trucks, around one hundred of them, were parked anyway and anywhere, according to the whims of the drivers. I milled around the place, afraid to open my mouth. The sun had risen, and the trucks began leaving one after another, and I was still hesitating. Just then, I heard a driver speak in my native dialect. So I stood next to him, watching him fill his gasoline tank.

Comrade reporter, the Chinese people's sense of local attachment is strong indeed. Those two girls came up to me because they heard my accent, and now I stuck to this driver because I recognized his dialect. After a little while the official who had been talking to him left. He turned, saw me, and said, "Hand me that bucket of water, my boy."

I handed him the bucket, and asked him timidly, "Where are you driving to?"

The driver was kind looking, with a ruddy face. He noticed my accent at once. "So," he remarked, "we are natives of the same province. Where are *you* headed?"

I said I was going to Hami. He was going to
Umruchi, he said, and could take me part of the way.
He told me that he was transporting a gasoline con-
tainer, so smoking was absolutely forbidden.

He added water to the truck and told me to be quick
with my luggage. I waved my little bundle at him,
saying it contained all I had in the world. He laughed,
opened the door, patted me on the back, and started
the engine.

On the truck that day, I told him about the political
situation in our native province. He shook his head
sympathetically. He then asked who I was looking up
in Hami, asked what relatives I had out there. I took
out my diploma and told him all my hopes for the
future.

"Don't look down on manual labor," he said. "The
world is created by working hands. Being a worker
is the most honorable thing in the world." He confessed he had been a driver ever since joining the army
in 1947; he entered Xinjiang in 1949 and could have
been promoted to officer rank, but he refused. After
he was demobilized, he continued working as a driver.
All the way we talked—and the more we talked, the
more we liked each other. Before we reached Hami,
he had decided to take me on as apprentice.

So I passed Hami without getting out and applying
to be an accountant. Instead I followed my new friend
to Umruchi. He became my mentor.

By now my mentor has long retired. He is seventy
years old and spends all his time tending his plants.
I often visit him. He always says, "Don't bring me anything except flowers." Do you see that orchid over
there? I bought it yesterday for fifty *yuan*. I'm taking
it to him tomorrow. I know he'll be pleased.

Do I bore you? You reporter fellows like to write
about the bigwigs, heroes, model workers, and what

not. I haven't done anything remarkable my whole life. I'm just an ordinary man. An ordinary trucking company employee.

Hang on to your seat. After the next turn, we'll be up the mountains.

Anyway, after my apprenticeship, I was committed to driving. The days passed like the wheels of a car. Happy days rushed by at full speed, while the bad days were like dragging through mud and slush. But anyway, good or bad, long or short, the days have gone by. I've been a trucker for twenty years now. During this interval, I've gone through several changes of trucks: the Soviet brand Gas, our homemade Liberation, the Czechoslovakian Skoda, and also Rumanian cars. This Nissan is my latest.

A car's age is reckoned according to mileage, rather than the year in which it's made. I feel it's the same with men. Some cars and trucks live to fifty or sixty, all smooth and easy, without having gone through any trials. They should be considered young. Some are born to hardships and might be considered old before they're thirty.

I really have nothing to complain of. What am I after all, just a peasant boy, and now driving this big truck with tens of thousands of *yuan* worth of goods under my care. This in itself is proof that I am somebody. During those years when family background counted for a lot, I was the only one around here who had a spotless background. That's why I was always assigned the outside job, driving along the international highways. And I always worked hard. The bosses trusted me and I didn't want to let them down. But deep down inside me, there was a wound that would not heal, like a lump of ice that would not melt.

My parents died the year after I left. They died on

the construction site of the local irrigation plant. My uncle wrote that my mother called out to me repeatedly before she died. After she was dead, they found two postal money orders I had sent to her. She never went to the post office to cash them—there was no grain, either at the grain store or in the market. It wouldn't have helped even if I had sent her sackfuls of bank notes. My uncle used the money to make a coffin of thin boards for my mother and to repair my father's grave, my father having died a few months earlier.

In 1964 I used my savings for a visit to my home village. My parents' graves were overgrown with grass. The trees that had been planted when they were first buried were as thick as my arm by then.

I went to have a look at the little back lane down which I had left my village that night, and the place where my father and I had our last parting. Everything was changed. The little back lane had become part of a paved highway. The place where my father had once squatted down was now right in the middle of the highway and tractors ground their way over it in an endless stream.

My mentor was right. Life is like driving: you must always look forward. A glance or two at the rear mirror is okay, but if you keep looking backward all the time, the truck is sure to overturn. So I came back and resumed my job as driver.

It is easy to talk about looking forward, but one fact faced me: I was absolutely alone in the world. No words can express that feeling of desolation. Drivers do not really see each other. When I leave off work, my partner in the next shift drives off, and when his turn is over, I take off.

Soon after my return, the Cultural Revolution broke out. During that period you couldn't trust anybody, not even old acquaintances. People never said what they really thought. As for strangers, the first thing people tried to determine is whether they were class enemies or not. The way I am speaking to you right now, on first acquaintance, was unthinkable at that time.

Comrade reporter, what do you think is the most painful thing in life? As I see it, there is nothing more painful than being cut off from your fellowmen. Just try to imagine: you get up in the morning, put on your underclothes, then your woolen sweater, then your padded jacket, and over that padded jacket you put on an invisible armor. Only then do you venture abroad. Everybody walks about concealed behind his own plate of armor. So, although there are lots of people working together in one unit, they don't really know each other.

In those days I would always go about my business silent and glum. One day my mentor said to me, "You should think of marrying. You're nearly thirty and still single. If you have a wife to look after you, you will shake off this mood." Right, I thought, why didn't I think of it before? Yes, I should get married.

But in Xinjiang, it was hard to find a girl. This is a world of men. You hardly ever see an unmarried girl. Luckily for me, I go everywhere in my line of work. Not long afterward, I was driving through Dabang city. A couple of us drivers from the same company happened to be stopping there together. At lunch the subject of my marriage was brought up, and one driver exclaimed, "I've got exactly the right girl for you! Look over the world and she's right there under your nose, as they say. There is a girl here, as a matter of fact, who has just arrived from Shaanxi. Let's go and see her."

The girl came from Mizi County of Shaanxi province. That year there was a drought in Mizi, and she had to leave home to escape starvation, just as I had done in 1960. This girl was just past her twentieth year, and had actually gone through primary school. She was pretty, with big eloquent eyes, although her braids were not long. Her aunt had a little tea stall at the crossroads, and when she learned of my interest in her niece, she did not insist on any bridal gift, only that I get her niece urban registration and grain coupons.

The aunt's terms were not hard to meet. The administrators of our company had always thought well of me. Whichever faction was in power at the moment, they all needed a driver. Getting urban residence and grain coupons for my prospective wife was no problem at all. I talked the matter over briefly with several of my driver acquaintances and made up my mind that very day to go ahead with the marriage.

When I went back and told my mentor of my intentions, he disapproved. "You don't know anything about her. How can you rush into marriage like that? Don't be in such a hurry. Let me look for somebody suitable."

I said, "Oh, I've been running around for so many years, and met so many different kinds of people. I believe I'm a good judge of character. This girl looks straight and steady, not the flighty sort. I've decided to have her." The truth is, after all those years, I had never thought of marrying, but just dragged on from day to day, bored and lonely; but once I did consider marriage, I couldn't wait. Unfortunately I didn't heed my mentor's advice.

You look young. Are you single? . . . Yes? Well, I can tell you something about the philosophy of marriage. I'm an expert. I've been married twice.

Living together as man and wife—there is nothing

momentous in the daily routine. You must rely on
your spouse's every gesture, every glance, to judge the
success of your partnership. Book learning does not
help you. You must rely on intuition. If she loves you,
you feel the warmth in her hand even if she gives
you a slap; if she is false, her very embrace will chill
you to the bone. You can get away with pretense in
public, but at home you go through three hundred and
sixty-five days together and share the same bed at
night. The heart cannot be cheated.

This girl from Shaanxi was a good wife. Nimble
with her fingers, a fine cook and seamstress. Never
gossiped or stirred up trouble with our neighbors. She
even kept a record of every cent she spent. Whenever I came back from work, there was always a hot
meal waiting for me, and all my clothes were washed
and mended without my having to remind her. A perfect housewife. But as to affection, there was not a
drop.

I tried hard to make her love me. Those years of
the Cultural Revolution, you know how it was. Everything so mad and chaotic, you couldn't do anything for your country even if you wanted to, so we
all turned our energies to building up our little homes.
I had a lot of furniture made. What people called
Czechoslovakian style and Polish style. Varnished all
bright and shiny. And also a pair of sofas and a stan-
dard lamp. I had saved when I was assigned to drive
in Pakistan, and my monthly pay was enough to keep
the two of us in comfort.

But she persisted in treating me as if I were her lord
and master, or even worse. She never so much as
smiled in my direction. She never touched the furniture, would never sit on the sofa. She just did not
consider them hers, and she never touched the clothes
I bought her. It was not a matter of saving; it was

quite clear she wanted to keep a distance between us.
After work, or when my day of rest came round,
she would always find an excuse to keep as far away
from me as possible. If I suggested that we go out
to a film, she would mumble, "What is there to see?
The old *Sha Jia Ban* and *Weihu Mountain* over and
over again!" Which was true, of course. So we would
stay home—in silence. Even in bed at night, she
would lie as still as a corpse, with no response whatever, leaving me discouraged and humiliated.

As I said, people can walk around behind invisible
sheets of armor, but my wife wore that armor right
into the home. And why? I ask you. After all, am I
blind, or pockmarked, or disfigured? True, I'm no
movie star like Da Shichang. But at twenty-seven or
-eight, my looks were tolerable. Besides I was good-
tempered and had not a blot on my character. Then
why? The problem nagged me day and night. It was
at that time that I took to smoking, and drinking too.
Although I never drank excessively. Still don't. I have
to drive, after all.

Thus we dragged on for six months.

Once, I was part of a convoy of truckers sent to Yili.
We unloaded our cargo and checked into the Oasis
Hotel. That evening for dinner all the drivers got together over kebab and wine. With the wine flowing,
we started talking about women—a safe topic. When
we were well into our fourth or fifth bottle, the subject turned to the women of Mizi County—so desir-
able for lovemaking. The others began to tease me,
because they knew my wife came from Mizi. When
the noise was at its height, a young fellow who was
already drunk blurted out, "Be careful, your little wifey
has someone else for her dearly beloved and not you!"

The minute he said it, there was a dead silence. The
others looked at the young fellow, trying to signal

to him with their eyes. He realized that he had over-
stepped the bounds of propriety. He kept his head
bent over his kebab, without saying a word.

The others tried to distract me by cracking jokes,
but I had no heart to mind them. When the young
fellow got up to go to the bathroom, I followed him.

In the corridor I pulled him by the sleeve. "What
did you mean, just now? Don't be afraid, you'll not
be held responsible."

The fellow blushed and stammered, "I was joking,
I didn't mean anything."

By this time an old driver had followed us out. He
said, "Since you've blurted it out, let's not keep him
in the dark any longer. Come on, let's go in and spell
out the details."

And so, over drinks, my fellow drivers told me what
had long been public knowledge. It turned out that
three months ago, while I was on the road, a young
peasant from Shaanxi made his way to my house,
asking for my wife. Before long, the neighborhood
gossips—better than a team of detectives—found out
that the young man came from the same village as my
wife. He had just been demobilized and had come
over a thousand *li* to seek her. The young fellow soon
got a temporary job as a stoker in the meat product
company right across from our residence compound.
When I was away, he would often steal over, then
the two would close the door and speak low.

"Don't be hurt, and don't be rash," my fellow drivers advised me. "To tell you the truth, we decided
to keep it from you because we saw you were a happy
couple, and we didn't want to stir up trouble. Besides, suppose the information was wrong. You always keep your thoughts to yourself. We were afraid
of the consequences."

My throat was constricted and I made an effort to

keep back tears. "Thank you for your good intentions," I said. "You should have told me sooner. We are not the happy couple you imagine. Actually, for the last six months, I have been quite miserable."

When they heard this, they were indignant. Some suggested that we beat up the fellow and send him packing. Some said he shouldn't be let off so easy; he should be taken to the police. The older ones advised caution.

My mind was in a turmoil, like a kaleidoscope. All kinds of possibilities churned round and round, some deadly, some kindly, some base, some upright. I could not decide on anything.

I returned home and observed her sharply. She was the same as before. The household account was in order, and the house was spick and span. There was nothing to complain of. Even if I had wanted to have it out with her, I wouldn't have known where to start a quarrel.

I stayed home for a few days, because my truck was due for an overhaul. After this general checkup, I started off for work one morning and discovered that there was still something wrong with the gearbox; whenever I changed gears, it would emit a queer sound. In those days, the repairmen were completely irresponsible. So I spent the whole morning working on the truck myself. At noon, I went home, a wrench dangling in my hand. I opened the door and there they were, the two of them.

She was sitting on the bed. The fellow sat on a little stool by her. They held their heads down, the picture of misery. Both were shocked at my sudden return and stood up immediately. My wife stepped forward and stood between us—to protect him from me, perhaps, but more to defy me, as if saying, "Hit me if you want to have it out!"

While I stood there dazed, the fellow slipped out in a flash.

"Who—who is he?" I yelled at my wife.

She sat down again without a word. By and by, two big tears coursed down her cheeks, then dropped to her breasts.

I cannot bear to see women cry. All my rage dissolved at the sight of her tears. I put the stool out of the way and sat down on the sofa. I wanted her to say that he was a cousin, an old acquaintance from her home village, and I would be satisfied.

But she would not speak to me, not even to tell me a lie. She just sat there crying silently.

I decided to confront the stranger, so I dashed out of the house. The fellow had built himself a hovel against the big chimney of the meat product company. He used the chimney as a support and erected two walls of clay against that, making a nondescript crescent-shaped lean-to.

The fellow was not a coward. When I pushed open his cardboard door, he seemed to be expecting me. He politely asked me to be seated and poured out tea. You know the saying: one does not slap a smiling face. What was I to do? I couldn't just walk in and hit him. I sat down and listened.

The fellow told me that he and my wife grew up together in the same village; as children they went to the mountains to collect firewood and in school they were classmates. At seventeen or eighteen, with their parents' consent, they became engaged. But he was recruited by the army, so they planned to marry after he was demobilized. Meanwhile there was a drought and her father died. Her mother was helpless, so the girl joined her aunt in Xinjiang. Her aunt knew of her previous engagement, but when I came into the picture, she was tempted by my salary and city residence

and forced the girl to marry me. As for the girl, she
saw that her aunt wanted to be rid of her. And with
her fiancé thousands of *li* away, she lost her nerve
and married me. But later she told him she had never
ceased to think of him.

Finally the fellow said, "We are all young people.
Let me be frank with you. I have come to ask her to
divorce you and to go back with me, or settle here in
Xinjiang with me. She doesn't love you, but she says
you are a good man and she could not bear to hurt
you. I must tell you that we did nothing shameful
behind your back. We have known each other from
childhood; you have known her but six months. You
married each other without love. Even now, how much
affection do you have for each other? But we were
in love when we became engaged. The three years I
was in the army, I thought of her every single day.
I cannot stop loving her. You must understand and forgive. Strike me if you must, but please realize I didn't
do any wrong. I'm the injured."

But my anger had not subsided. "If you didn't do
anything shameful, why did you run away at the sight
of me?"

He blushed. "You had a massive wrench in your
hand. I was afraid you'd do something rash."

"So you ran away without a thought of what I might
do to her. Is that how you love her?"

He hung his head and muttered, "I was at the door
all the time."

Suddenly she rushed in. Perhaps she thought the two
males were going to settle it by a fight.

After a long silence I finally said to her, "Let's make
an end of this. Things have come to this pass. You
must make a decision. You must choose one of us, and
right away."

She began sobbing again. It seemed that she was

pouring out all the tears she would ever weep in her whole life. After a little while the young man said in brokenhearted tones, "You had better stay with your husband. Now that I see all is well with you, I am at ease; we are not destined to be man and wife. Let's just forget the past." The minute the fellow finished, she burst out afresh, in an uncontrollable fit of crying. That was clear enough indication of her choice. Why go on torturing her? I took pity on her. I was not destined to enjoy her affections and that's that.

"Her preference is as clear as day," I said. "If she stays with me, she suffers, I suffer, and you suffer. We are all rovers from the interior. The poverty of the countryside is the root of all these problems. But China is big. If you are willing to work hard, you will be able to make a living. You can build a new life here, the two of you together."

When I said this, she slowly calmed down. I felt I had alleviated her suffering. But at the same time, her lack of affection for me brought home all the loneliness and desolation of my situation. Tears welled in my eyes. In fact, all three of us stood there in tears.

We completed divorce proceedings very quickly. You can imagine all the gossip going on around me. But I did not heed a word. One must be firm in handling one's own affairs. One afternoon when it was all over, she came to the house to collect her own things. She cooked a last meal for me, and then still hovered about the place, not ready to go. At last she said softly, "Would you like me to stay for the night?"

This was the first time she had spoken to me with some feeling. Of course I understood what she meant. Poor country girl, it was the only way she knew to show her gratitude. But it was gratitude and nothing else. I said, "No, you had better go. Go and start your life with him. Don't worry about anything else.

We're no longer husband and wife, but perhaps we can still be friends. If you have difficulties, let me know."

How that couple worked! In the first few years they just lived in that hovel built against the chimney. They made adobe bricks for sale. The last three years, private enterprise was restored, and now they have a little food stall, specializing in Shaanxi food—lamb dumplings, oatmeal pasta, fried lamb, ravioli, cakes with date meat stuffing, fried pancakes. And their business is very successful. Right now they have several thousand in the bank.

After a time the memory of my marriage wore off, and I became used to the solitary life. Comrade reporter, there is one advantage in being a driver—we go everywhere and see the world. And Xinjiang really is a marvelous place. In spring I drive along the banks of the Selimu Lake, looking at the deep blue water, the white swans, the mountain overgrown with flowers, and the pines reaching out from the gullies. In summer I open the window of my truck and let in the first winds from the mountain. On such days I'm immediately filled with hope and the joy of living.

Now, we are at the top; and now, downward. As the saying goes, the way up the mountain is easy; it's the downward path that's hard. But don't worry. I have driven over this route so many times, I know the way perfectly.

You want to hear some more? . . . About my second marriage? . . . All right, so long as you don't fall asleep. It is quite interesting. It happened when I least expected to marry.

Two years after my divorce, I was driving along this road one day. The wind was very high, sand whirling against the windows of my truck. One could not see beyond five meters. I had just passed Kumish and driven into the Poplar Ridge. By then the sun was set-

ting, the ridge was flanked by high cliffs, and streams
ran down a fissure in the middle of the cliffs. In the
ridge the wind was milder and visibility was very
good.

I drove slowly in the direction of the wind. Suddenly, way ahead, sitting on the side of the road, I
saw a woman in a gray scarf with a child in her lap.
She wore a cotton padded coat and she wrapped the
child under her coat close to her breast, presenting a
very bulky appearance. It was hard to judge her age.
She had two bags by her side. I thought she wanted a
lift, so I slowed down. But when I stopped in front
of her, she did not raise her hand, but only peered into
my face.

"Where are you going?" I shouted to her.

She said she was going to Shorblac.

"Then what are you waiting for?" I cried, "Hop in."

She looked at me timidly. Now I noticed that her
cotton padded coat was silver gray, and her scarf was
rabbit wool. These were stylish clothes, from Shanghai. The child was around four years old. His delicate little face was blue with cold. Wrapped in his
mother's coat, he stared out at me with frightened
eyes.

Just then, another gust of wind swept over us, passed
through the ridge, and shook the poplar trees till it
made them howl. I did not have my coat on and was
trembling with cold. I asked her to hurry. She still
hesitated, pressing the child against her breast as if I
was going to take it away.

I knew why she hesitated. To be frank with you,
there are indeed some rascals among us drivers, who
would take advantage of women. It was clear that this
woman was waiting for the bus, or an older driver,
or another woman in the car, for safety's sake. She did
not trust herself with a youngish driver like me.

The wind was blowing harder. The sun had disappeared behind the mountains and the trees were by then a dark mass swaying in the wind. If she missed my truck, she'd never get another chance. I took out my driver's license and waved it in her face. "If you don't trust me, keep my license. The last bus has gone by. How can you get another lift? There's no car driving along this route tonight. I know. Consider the child. Please."

She did not move to take my license. She looked at the child in concern and scrutinized me. Then she got up, as if she realized that there was no choice. I picked up her bags and pushed them into the front seat.

I have picked up many passengers, including kids of four or five. Children that age can never sit still. They try to move the gears, or the knobs or the dials, or else they look out the window, hollering at this and that. Strange, I thought, this little fellow, unmoving in his mother's lap, not making a sound.

Thus we drove on in the pitch dark. Xinjiang is like that. Night descends without warning. The child began to cough. The woman kept patting the baby and trying to wrap him more closely. I slowed down, and listened. He was breathing heavily. I put out my hand. His forehead was burning! "The child is ill!"

The woman did not know what to say. She cried softly.

I stepped on the gas and rushed on. The child continued coughing while the woman sobbed. In front of me the lights of Ushtala twinkled in the mountains. Ushtala was a tiny community of half-a-dozen households. Passing trucks would stop here for the night. But I did not stop. The truck rushed past the one-storied guest house.

"Stop, stop!" the woman cried, banging on the door.

"Don't be afraid," I told her. "We must rush to get

a doctor. I know this place better than you do. In Ushtala you can't even find a barefoot doctor."

"I don't care. I want you to stop! Stop!" She freed one hand to grasp me by the sleeve.

One of my arms was in her grasp. I used the other hand to steer. In front of us was a curve. I was tense. "Don't be afraid. Let me assure you, I have no intention of harming you." I'm sorry I didn't have my commendations or certificates of honor with me. That way she might more easily have been convinced.

"Where are you taking me? Please set me down!" The woman had become hysterical.

The turn was coming into view. At the curve there was mountain on one side and a deep ravine on the other. No joking matter. I freed my arm. She still tried to hold on, as if clasping my arm would stop the truck.

"Now look here," I shouted in anger, "don't I need to stop at Ushtala? I need a break myself! But I'm taking you to a hospital. I beg you, let my arm go. Let me show you something."

I think she saw the dangerous curve. At any rate she freed my arm. I made the curve smoothly and then took out a white drinking mug from underneath my driver's seat. "See, this is a prize I got. I told you, I mean you no harm. Hold your child; I beg you, don't give me any more trouble."

Looking back, I realize how preposterous it had been. What does a white drinking mug signify? But it worked as a kind of peace offering. I don't know whether it was the mug or whether she had become resigned to fate. But she became silent, only holding her son closer. I drove them into Yenjie.

You know what hospitals were like in those days. Finding a doctor on night duty was harder than looking for a pin in a haystack. I drove through the empty streets of Yenjie, calling at one hospital and two clinics. The lights were on, but nobody was on duty. I shouted myself hoarse and lost an hour for nothing.

"Damn it!" I climbed back into the driver's seat. "Let's go to Kurle. I know a doctor there."

It was in the small hours of the morning when we reached Kurle. I didn't bother to go to the hospital but headed straight for the home of a doctor I know. Within minutes the doctor had assembled a nurse and a pharmacist, and mother and son were soon installed in a ward of the nearby hospital.

There was nothing for me to do. I drove my truck to a guest house, emptied the water tank, and dozed for a little while. With dawn I was on the road to Aksu.

A week later I came back by way of Kursh. I thought I should thank the doctor, so I brought him fifty *jin* of Aksu rice.

As soon as he saw me, the doctor told me that the little boy had recovered and would be released from the hospital the next day.

After unloading, I checked into the local guest house. I had nothing to do that night, so I made up my mind to have a look at the child.

I arrived at the hospital ward, a tin of canned fruit in each hand. First I saw the mother. She was sitting by the child, who was lying in his cot.

Only now did I see her clearly. She was at most twenty-seven or twenty-eight, with a pair of big eyes. She was pale and pinched around the cheeks, with a sad look. When she bent down over the child, I saw that she had a gentle look, not like the hysterical woman to whom I'd given a lift.

She looked and saw me. Her eyes lighted up suddenly. "I am sorry about the other night. I have been frightened. From past experience."

"It's nothing. How's the child?"

"Doctor said it was a case of acute pneumonia. A minute later and there would have been no hope. I owe my son's life to you."

She looked very grateful and her eyes welled with tears.

I felt uncomfortable and bent closer to play with the child.

Evidently the little fellow was brought up in Shanghai, for he spoke with the local dialect; his skin was clear and delicate and his features resembled his mother's. I played with him and asked him, "What do you want to be when you grow up?"

The child lisped out the words one by one: "My—mummy—says—when—I—grow—up—I—must—be—a—driver—like—you!"

I turned my head away and laughed in embarrassment. The child's words touched me more than any honorary citations. A little soft hand seemed to be rubbing itself against my heart and all the words that had been locked away were crying to be set free, but I could not utter a word.

The child held me by its little hand and babbled on. As I answered his baby talk, the feeling overcame me that this was my son, that I was responsible for him. How will he survive, I wondered, coming from a city like Shanghai to this desert land where water is more precious than oil?

"Didn't you say you were going to Shorblac?" I asked the mother. "I'll take you there tomorrow."

She blushed and hid her face. "Is that on your way? I don't want to bother you any further."

"Don't you worry about that. Just get your things ready by tomorrow."

The next morning I changed assignments with another driver. He would take my truckful of matting to Umruchi while I carried a load of chemical fertilizers southward.

Then I went to fetch them at the hospital. They were ready. The mother was smiling behind her woolly scarf, eyes shining. The child held out his arms to me to be lifted up and turned to say goodbye to the nurse. What a marvelous day it was, how sunny and bright. I had never been so happy. It was as if I were fetching my wife and newborn baby from the hospital.

On the road the boy was playful. He kept touching the gear, fiddling with the digital board. He had never ridden in a truck before. Everything was new and interesting and his questions were endless. For the first time I felt that my cab was full of life. The motor sang happily and the seat was soft and springy.

Around ten we arrived at Cunke. After the fertilizers were unloaded, I bought some bread and shut the door.

"And now for Shorblac!"

We were gradually approaching the Tarim Basin, skirting the Takelamagan Desert. Much of it was buried in sand. You can only pick out the route by the marks left by tires. The places all have names ending in -blac. Blac means springs. That doesn't mean that there's a lot of water around. On the contrary, the towns are so named precisely because water is so scarce. Consequently, the farther we drove, the more desolate the terrain became. At first there were some straggling poplars, but soon the wind rose and there was nothing but whirling sand in sight. We drove on blindly, as if in fog.

As the truck lost speed, the boy lost interest and slept in his mother's lap. The smile disappeared from her face. "Come," I said, "let's make him comfortable."

I stopped the car and made a little nest for the boy behind my seat. He was as comfortable as in a rocking cradle. The child snored softly, the breath from his little nostrils blowing softly against the back of my neck. How I loved it.

Our truck was the only thing that crept, like an insect, over that vast expanse of sand. The loneliness brought the two of us together. She sighed and said softly, "This is the kind of place I'm going to."

The prospect was certainly bleak.

"Will the boy's father come and meet you at Tieganlike?"

She fell silent for a moment. "He has no father," she finally replied.

"Oh!" I was surprised. And then, somewhat elated, though I couldn't say why.

She smiled bleakly. "Nobody knows. Not even my own family. But I feel I must tell somebody. I can't bear it alone."

She came of a capitalist family. In 1964 she graduated from senior middle school. She came to Xinjiang sincerely intending to remold herself and help build the border. When she first arrived, she was a teacher, but after 1967 a group of "makers of revolution" took over the leadership of the farm, and she was sent to work in the fields. With the advance of the Cultural Revolution, she was more and more discriminated against.

But one day the commander of their group suddenly decided to give her the use of a gun and asked her to go with him to hunt for wild goat. She was thrilled—not everyone was allowed the privilege of going off on a hunt. So off she went with the commander—who took her to a patch of woody hollow overgrown with willow and raped her. Soon after, she found herself pregnant. She dared not accuse the man, had no means of abortion, and was too ashamed to ask advice from anyone. She went back to Shanghai to give birth. To protect her parents from shame and sorrow, she told them she had married in Xinjiang. She left the child to be reared with her parents. But because of recent unrest in Shanghai, she had gone back to reclaim her child.

She said, "I will bring him up. The child is innocent. My classmates advise me to leave him, but I am determined to have him with me. I have gone through everything. Nothing can daunt me anymore."

"And what about the scoundrel?" I asked, full of anger. Now I understood why she was so frightened of me at first.

She smiled bitterly. "Transferred to some other division to be chief of security."

It often happens in this way. You can tell your life-long secret to a complete stranger, as I am telling you mine. She told me her story very calmly, with no show of emotion, as if relating somebody else's story.

Without knowing it, I began to admire her. I asked in concern, "Why don't you marry again?"

She said there were no more suitable men among the Shanghai youth, and she did not want to marry the local men. Some Shanghai girls did, she said, but for her that would mean giving up the last hope of moving back to Shanghai.

I picked up my courage and remarked, "I am also from the interior. My experience is, the quality of your life is determined not by where you are, but with whom you share it."

She smiled wanly. "This is just a platitude."

I retorted, "There's a proverb in Pakistan: the mouse should keep away when the cat's around. A platitude, if you like, but a matter of life and death to the mouse. It is the same for human beings: what one regards as a platitude is also truth."

She looked up and sighed. "Perhaps you are right. But the truth is so far removed from reality."

Luckily for us, the truck was empty, so by the time the sun was setting, we made it to Shorblac. This was an oasis in the desert. The place was beautiful and the land fertile. But life was completely wrecked for the young settlers by scoundrels like the one she had come across.

A ragged group of men and women came forward to meet the car. They were full of complaints. One particularly ragged young fellow, nicknamed "American G.I.," patted me on the back and said, "Thank you so much, master driver. If we were in Shanghai, we would treat you at Lao Zheng Xin, or if you prefer Western food, we could go to the Red House. But here . . ." He shrugged and spread out his hands in a gesture to show his helplessness.

I knew that it would be very hard for them to put me up for the night, with nowhere to sleep and not much to eat either. And anyway, she was just back and needed to unpack. "I must return to Tieganlike," I said. "Please don't trouble yourselves."

But the child ran up and held my hand. "You must also stay here," he said. "I won't let you go."

I stooped and patted him on the head. "I must go and pick up goods in my truck. You must stay with your mother."

He held his head to one side, as if thinking it over. "Are you coming back?"

"Yes, I'll come back," I said.

"In the big truck?"

"Yes, in the truck."

"Promise?"

"Yes!"

She was standing by. I stood up and said, half to her, half to the child, "I will surely come back."

Back in Umruchi I could not drive away the memory of the two of them. I went about like a man distracted, as if I had left my heart in Shorblac. When my mentor was home, I went and told him the whole

story and my feelings. He struck the table with his fist.
"Good! What are you waiting for? Go to her quick!
Shorblac in Mandarin means spring of bitter water. A
wellborn daughter of a capitalist family, who has been
soaked in bitterness. She is invaluable. She is worth
her weight in gold."

I bought a lot of New Year supplies and several toy
cars and got a lift from a fellow driver. I arrived at
Tieganlike on the eve of the lunar New Year, and
walked all the way to Shorblac, braving wind and
snow. When I pushed open the door to their house, it
was just the time for the midnight feast according to
Shanghai custom. . . .

Later she asked me, "Why did you love me?"

"There's no why about love," I replied.

I told her the whole story of my marriage to the
Shaanxi girl. "Looking at it from the outside, I am
better off in many ways than her peasant lover. But
she prefers him, would rather lead a hard life with
him, living in a hovel. In the past I could never understand. Now I understand: it is love. I love you as
that girl loves her peasant lover. There's no why about
it."

She listened, on the verge of tears.

Well, comrade reporter, here you are. Where shall I
stop the truck? Oh, no problem, I'll take you right
up to the gate.

Now? Oh, now everything is just fine. My wife is
deputy principal at the Shorblac Middle School. She
and my son come and stay in Umruchi for summer
and winter holidays. As for me, my boss did me a
favor and assigned me to this route, so I am home once
every week. Our son is already in middle school. But
now he doesn't want to be a driver anymore. His idea
is to be a writer. He wants to write about me and
his mother. I say, "Oh, come on, your mother and I

are not worthy of writing about, and anyway there are details of our lives that cannot be published—or you'd be criticized for wallowing in the seamy side of our society."

"Oh, Father, you don't understand," he says. "Truth is the soul of literature." Well, who knows whether the little fellow is right.

The year before last my wife's father was rehabilitated, and his salary and the interest on his investments were returned to him. If she had not married me, she would have had a perfect right to return to Shanghai. Once, when I was in high spirits and had drunk too much, I told her, "Of course you're sorry you married me. Otherwise you would be now in Shanghai, your father's heiress."

She was silent. But at night, as she lay beside me, she cried bitterly. "Do you know what you are saying? Didn't you say yourself that it's not important where you are, but with whom? Why should I want to be in Shanghai or be an heiress? What do you take me for anyway!" I knew that my joke had gone too far. Finally, though, she forgave me. Ever since then I've been careful not to overdo the booze.

Shorblac, Shorblac, spring of bitter waters. My wife, who drank of those bitter waters, is a treasure. But I believe that all of us born of hardships, all who have drunk of bitterness, are precious. We all have hearts of gold. What do you say, comrade reporter? Do you agree?

ANECDOTES OF CHAIRMAN MAIMAITI

by Wang Meng

WANG MENG *(1934–   )* *is another Chinese writer who was la-beled "rightist" in 1957 and exiled to the West—in his case, to Xinjiang. He was rehabilitated in 1979 and has been the Minister of Cultural Affairs in Beijing since 1986. "Anecdotes of Chairman Maimaiti" first appeared in China in* Selections of Short Stories and Reportage *(Beijing Publishing House, 1981). Wang Meng's stories have also been translated into French, German, Russian, and Japanese.*

The six life-sustaining elements are: air, sun, water, food, friendship, and humor.

When tears are exhausted, laughter takes over.

A sense of humor is a sense of superiority.

from Gleanings from Ancient Philosophy

I.

How does Chairman Maimaiti manage to retain his youthfulness?

On the sixth day of May in 1979, the wind was calm and the sun mild. The willows were just beginning to sprout. I was in the Great Cross Restaurant in the city of Umruchi, and whom should I see but Maimaiti and his twin brother Saimaiti, whom I hadn't laid eyes on in ten years! And what a sight they were!

On Maimaiti's face were furrows carved by the passing years, but he still retained a head of thick black hair, a vital-looking, ruddy face, and a hearty laugh resounding with good humor. His brother Saimaiti, by contrast, had a stooped back, a pair of dim eyes, clouded by closing shadows of death, and he spoke every word with a gasp, as if he had a pain in the side; his hands clutched feverishly at a bottle of heart-reliever.

We were overwhelmed at this unexpected meeting. After the courtesies were over, I asked, "Where have you both been all these years?"

"I was under a calamity," cried Saimaiti.

"And so was I," rejoined Maimaiti.

"The minute the Cultural Revolution occurred, I was labeled Black Gang and thrown into the cowshed."

"I was denounced too, and put away in 1966."

"I was beaten," wailed Saimaiti.

"I got blows," echoed his brother.

"I was made to bear rocks down from the mountains."

"I was sent to carry coal up from the mines."

"I was officially labeled counterrevolutionary and my wife divorced me," cried Saimaiti.

And so it went, on and on, with each man relating his tragic experiences.

"If you suffered the same calamities," I asked in amazement, "how is it that you, Maimaiti, have retained your youthfulness while you, Saimaiti, have . . . well . . ."

At this, Saimaiti beat his hands upon his sides in despair and let out broken sighs while tears sprang to his eyes.

But Maimaiti answered with a smile, "No secret about that. My brother is always pulling a long face, while I, as the chairman of the department of art and literature, never pass the day without fun and jokes."

II.

The first offense of Chairman Maimaiti: he gave away a secret.

In 1966, the whole country was swept by a revolutionary tide. Yet the citizens of an Uighur village in faraway Xinjiang had not the faintest notion of who and what were to be overthrown, and *how*. As a saying in Uighur has it, "they were not given the news." Even so, from force of habit acquired after many years of following the Party in one campaign after another, the townspeople took immediate action and started to make revolution in a muddleheaded way. We might say they drew a tiger using a cat as the model.

In the twinkling of an eye, things got going. What with denouncing Dengtuo, memorizing quotations, exterminating pigeons, burning the Koran and what not, a pretty good show was soon in the works. Young people, Party members, and Youth League members were excited and thought it all great fun, as if tasting forbidden fruit; conservative old folks were tense and alarmed, afraid to make the slightest wrong move. An excellent situation arose wherein class struggle was the key issue.

Maimaiti's uncle, Muming by name, was party secretary of the fourth brigade (now renamed the Struggle Brigade) of the New Road Commune. Muming took the lead in shaving off his handsome beard and throwing off his embroidered cap, gown, striped trousers, and high-kneed boots. This Uighur gentleman of fifty years of age went and sold his kid-skin jacket and used the money to buy a suit of army green with cap and shoes to match. Over his right arm was a red band printed with the words *Red Guard,* while across his shoulder hung a bright red plastic satchel, such as

children carry to kindergarten. And in the satchel were
the precious red book and the precious portrait. Thus
did Maimaiti's uncle Muming make his brand-new
appearance across the horizon.

Precisely at this critical moment in history, Muming's
daughter Tilacs decided to marry the handsomest
young fellow in the village—the brigade's newly ap-
pointed political director, Mulajiting by name. As
soon as this fact was made known, the commune Party
secretary and leader of a model work team from the
village summoned Muming, his daughter, and his future son-in-law. (I have to add that this occurred during the interval in history when overthrowing "the four
obsoletes" was in force.) The officials requested that
the young couple make a clean break with "the four
obsoletes"—that is, they must renounce old tradi-
tions, and old customs. The celebration was to contain no killing of lambs, no feasting, no wine, no
dancing, no presents, and, of course, no reading from
the Koran. In short, they were instructed to hold a
new-style proletarian wedding.

"What do you mean by new-style wedding?" asked
Mulajiting in full Red Guard attire.

"It means reciting Mao's quotations; it means listening to speeches by leading Party officials from the
commune, the county, and the district; it means that
the bride and bridegroom make three bows to the
portrait of Chairman Mao, one bow to all officials present, and one last bow to each other. It means no
dowry and no bridal gifts; and newlyweds give each
other gifts of the precious red book, the precious
portrait, a hoe, a sickle, and a dung raker. It means
no fun and games; the bridegroom must go water
the fields on his wedding night, opening up and seal-
ing off irrigation channels, and the bride must make

forty wooden sign boards in red and yellow carrying
inscriptions of the quotations.

Muming was aghast. He thought that shaving his
beard and changing his clothes had been quite enough
of a revolution, and now it seemed that he was miles
away from carrying out a full revolution. As for
Mulajiting, his brows were black as thunder, and only
the whites of his eyes were showing. He had assumed that as political director, he would earn work-
points with his verbal facility rather than his physical
strength. He had never bargained for this, acting out
wedding-night shenanigans! Meanwhile, the bride-
to-be was drowning in her own tears; she was a maiden
who knew exactly what she wanted. And what she
wanted was an *old*-style wedding.

The commune secretary and the work-team leader
were scandalized at this response. They criticized the
three very severely and ordered Muming to take the
young couple back and give them a sound political
lecture. They then sent for the Youth League secretary, the head of the Women's Association, the chairman of the Committee of Poor and Lower-Middle
Peasants, and asked them to talk to the three, con-
centrating on one at a time in order to break down their
resistance.

Finally, though no one was particularly convinced,
the date was set for the new-style wedding. On the
great day speeches were given, photographs were taken,
"East Is Red" and "Great Helmsman" were sung, and
quotations were dourly recited. After it was over, the
whole affair was reported in the local papers, broad-
cast by the county broadcasting station, and finally
found its way into the national news.

Ten days later the *real* wedding took place quietly.
Lambs were slaughtered, rice was cooked, presents
of silks were exchanged, and all ceremonies observed.

In a word, nothing was missing. What was more remarkable, there was actually not much risk over this
underground wedding—because all the reporting and
spreading of the good example had been dispensed with.
Moreover, Uighur hair grows faster than other Chinese
hair, and one advantage of the ten days' delay was that
Muming was again sporting a sprightly little beard.
Although this took off some of his revolutionary pres-
tige, it restored him his native style.

And now back to Maimaiti. He, of course, knew the
background details of his cousin's wedding. While
chatting one day, he summed it up thus: "The advantage of the new-style wedding was that it delayed the
real ceremony so that my uncle's beard had time to
grow. The disadvantage was that my uncle was out
of pocket for an extra fifty *yuan*. Apart from the ex-
penses for the real wedding—the lamb, wine, cakes,
and cooking—he had to pay for the melon seed,
candy, and cigarettes of the new-style wedding."

At the time Maimaiti was being investigated for his
liberal tastes in art and literature. His conversation
was reported and he was attacked as a foe of the Cultural Revolution. To protect his uncle and cousin,
Maimaiti stuck to his confession: he had fabricated everything and no underground marriage had ever taken
place. For his loose tongue, Maimaiti was summarily
locked up.

III.

Chairman Maimaiti finally becomes a writer of universal recognition.

Since childhood, Maimaiti had had great respect for
the printed word. Promoted to the head of his department in 1958, he had often been thrown together

with poets, essayists, and fiction writers. Which made
him all the more eager to become a man of letters.
He threw himself into writing with a will, plodding
at it day and night. Finally he did manage to get some
pieces published, a few lines of verse here, a few para-
graphs of prose there. But these efforts were issued
without *éclat*. Readers and critics were not aware of
him. Old established writers and newly discovered
young talent never claimed him as one of themselves. He had applied to join the Writers' Union, but
he was rebuffed. It was very discouraging.

Luckily for him, since he had been branded Black
Gang, he had been herded together with writers he
envied. He was sentenced to work together with them
on a collective farm. One day in spring of 1967, they
were digging up stumps of grapevine, and they suddenly heard a clamor of gongs, cymbals, and horn-
blowing. The group of men of letters at work knew
at once that a detachment of revolutionary Red Guards
would be passing their way. Calling out a warning to
each other, they hastily made themselves scarce, hiding out in the overgrown grass or under the canals,
hoping to escape disaster. Unluckily for Maimaiti,
he was suffering from an infection of the ear and did
not hear his comrades' warnings. He did not notice
anything out of the ordinary until the young revolutionaries sprang upon him.

"Who and what are you?" one of them demanded
of Maimaiti.

"I am a member of the Black Gang, a threefold
antirevolutionary element." Maimaiti lowered his head
and held his hands at his side, swiftly taking a peni-
tent position as he answered in a broken voice.

"What was your former position?"

"Head of the department of art and literature."

"Oh, a capitalist roader! What's your main crime?"

"Attacked the campaign to overthrow the four obsoletes. Also wrote antirevolutionary articles."

"What articles?"

Maimaiti offered a long list, not even omitting re-
ports of a few hundred words.

"And what else?"

Maimaiti proceeded to recite a long list of all his articles rejected by publishers.

"You know Zhou Yang?"

"Yes, I know him." How could Maimaiti have ever
known Zhou Yang? The fact is, in Uighur, the words
know and *know of* are the same. Thus Maimaiti's answer provoked a hailstorm of denouncements. "So!
This is a big catch! A real bad one!"

With that, the little revolutionaries knocked Maimaiti
to the ground and kicked him in the back and stomach. One of them dipped a paintbrush in ink and
painted something on the back of Maimaiti's jacket.
Their violent deeds accomplished, they marched off
with vigor, shouting slogans all the way.

A full twenty minutes passed before the men of letters ventured out of their hiding places. Some spoke
words of comfort to Maimaiti, some tried to help him
up, some blamed him for not heeding their warning
cries.

Maimaiti pushed away their helping hands and stood
up shakily. He spat blood from his mouth and, ig-
noring the blood and dirt on his face, he pointed to
his back and asked his mates what was painted there.

"Evil liberal writer Maimaiti," they said in unison.

"Well and good," he cried elatedly, in spite of his
bashed lips and gums, which hindered speech. "Who
cares if you folks don't give me recognition! The *people*
consider me a writer!"

His mates laughed and laughed until the tears ran
down their cheeks.

IV.

Romance in the cowshed.

On the farm the so-called Black Gang had to fetch
water for their daily use from a mechanical well two
li away. This was a piece of hard labor in which everybody had to take turns. But once in the month of
April 1968, Maimaiti took upon himself the task of
fetching water for ten days running; he practically monopolized the water bucket and the shoulder pole.

"Hey, what are you up to," one of his pals asked
him. "What is behind this zeal to fetch water?"

Actually Maimaiti had nothing to hide. He answered
gleefully. "At the mechanical well I got acquainted
with a beautiful girl!"

"A beautiful girl!"

"Exactly," Maimaiti answered smugly. "Her beauty
outshines the sun and the moon, her long black braids
send out innumerable hints of love. In her presence I
faint, I burn, I swim in my own tears. She is my
happiness, my torch, my delight."

His friends did not believe Maimaiti. They decided
to tail him and find out the truth. Maimaiti, of course,
saw through their intentions, but didn't seem to mind.
And so his "beautiful girl" was revealed as a hag in
her fifties, with a big tumor on her neck, a filmy
growth over one eye, and a hunchback to boot!

How they made fun of Maimaiti, calling him a fool
and a liar. Maimaiti took it all very good-humoredly,
smiling quietly to himself. After his friends teased him
to their hearts' content, he said with a wry smile:
"How can you answer to the name of writers and be
so dense? How did you ever manage to write anything? Just think, we have been shut away for a full
twenty months. What a long and dreary twenty

months! In this kind of existence, anybody in skirts with a scarf over her head is a beautiful girl to us!"

Strange to say, this time nobody laughed. A dead silence. Only Maimaiti chuckled to himself for a long, long time.

V.

The current situation with Chairman Maimaiti.

When Maimaiti was released from labor camp, he was named to his former position as department chairman. Filled with his own recent experiences—and in reaction against tear-jerking "literature of the wounded"—he took up his pen and wrote a long novel about the Cultural Revolution. A good friend teaching Chinese at the Central Institute of National Minorities translated it from Uighur into Chinese.

Maimaiti then asked leave and, at his own expense, traveled to Beijing and personally handed the manuscript over to the editor-in-chief of the Chinese Literature Publishing House. The editor-in-chief, out of special consideration for national minorities, not to mention a department chairman too, personally read the manuscript and pointed out its defects: loose structure, nonexistent form, lack of seriousness.

"But I insist you publish this novel," Maimaiti said. "Just think. If people read this, they will not commit suicide in future political campaigns!"

His words struck the editor-in-chief. Probably he himself had contemplated suicide in the past. He agreed to reread the manuscript in this new light. "Suicide prevention," he mused. "Could that be a good reason for publication?"

★　　★　　★

In the Great Cross Muslim Restaurant, Maimaiti
told me about his unsuccessful venture into publishing
and asked me to approach the editor-in-chief and
say something in his favor. "If gifts would help,"
he added, "I have plenty of dried grapes and oil to
offer."

"The main thing is that your work must be high
quality," I told him severely. "If it's good, all the
publishers would be willing to take it. This talk about
gift giving is pure nonsense."

"Quality? It's really hard to tell. It seems I am only
recognized as a writer when getting kicks and cuffs."

Just then, a waiter in white uniform placed our dinner before us. Chairman Maimaiti opened a bottle
of wine and noisily poured us both a glassful. He raised
his glass and toasted me.

> "O life, you are not all sugar and honey,
>   But certainly not just a bitter fruit.
>   Sometimes you are stifling,
>   But in time you will open up and spread out.
>   Sometimes you are dull and dreary,
>   But in time you will wake up, colorful and
>   lively.
>   Sometimes you are as cold as ice, but a fire is
>   burning beneath.
>   Sometimes you are sad, but joy is deep down,
>   ever-present.
>   Jail, whips, swords—can they hinder life from
>   going on?
>   Threats, rumor, and libel, did they ever stamp
>   out the joy of living?
>   Do not weep; tears do not become a man.
>   Talk not of tragedy; tragedy is putting on airs.
>   Let us have a good laugh together.
>   The power of laughter is the power of life!

Laughter is knowing how to get on with the
business of living!
Laughter is the courage to go on with life!
Laughter is the love of life."

His song at an end, Chairman Maimaiti finished off
his drink in one deep gulp.

THE PROGRESS OF THE MILITARY PATROL CAR

by Tang Dong

TANG DONG *(1951–   ) is a native of Shaanxi province. He joined the army in 1970 and was posted to Xinjiang, an event that serves as the background for "The Progress of the Military Patrol Car." This selection won the 1983 National Short Story Prize. Since 1976, Tang Dong has worked as a scriptwriter for the Drama Troupe of the Political Department of the Umruchi Military Zone. He is presently a member of the All-China Writers' Union and the Dramatists' Union, and he is an executive member of the editorial board for* The Chinese Writer *magazine.*

I.

The nights of June in the Karakunlun Mountains are cold, piercingly cold. The wind sweeping down from the snowy peaks scoops up armfuls of dust and pebbles and thrashes them against the body of our car. The road is quite smooth and not steep, but the car creeps slowly, just as slowly as when we first started out from the hospital at the base of the mountain.

"Comrade, please go faster," I repeated to the driver.

The driver, a raw-looking little soldier, doesn't appear to hear me at all. His hands are secure on the wheel, his eyes fixed on the road. He swerves for any little puddle, any stone the size of a fist.

I can't bear it any longer and shout into his ear: "Hey, go faster, faster! Can you hear me?"

164

He slowly turns his head and gives me a withering look. "This car cannot go fast."

"This isn't the city. You won't be fined for speeding!"

"This car must not go fast," he mutters to himself.

"Damn you!" I can't help crying. "Is there breakable glass? Are we carrying munitions that will explode?"

"What what what . . ." The driver turns to me angrily, stares at me icily. Then he quickly resumes an impassive expression and says quietly, "You don't know. This car can't go fast. It has a problem. . . ."

"But what about my patient?"

"Don't worry. So long as we keep going, we'll be on time."

The driver looks firm and determined. Evidently there is nothing I can do to rush him. I lie back on the seat and think about my patient—Shanguan Xin. I feel my heart being clawed and torn by a vicious cat.

Yesterday morning, at the hospital at the foot of the mountain, the short dumpy director waddled to the washroom and sought me out, asking me to go treat a patient at the No. 5700 outpost. This kind of assignment occurs when the doctor at the outpost is not readily available and the clinic headquarters (which is halfway between the hospital at the base and the outpost at the top of the mountain) has no staff to spare.

When they send an army nurse like me, it usually means a slight illness. Our task is to treat the patient on the spot, if possible, or to bring him back in the car. It is a hard job, going up the mountain, but it means glory. We girls say "I've been to the outpost!" just as Napoleon's old guards would say "I've been to Austerlitz!"

But yesterday I had not expected to be sent on a mission up there. The fact was, a month ago, I was sent to No. 5700 outpost and was taken ill on the Daban road; we call that section of the mountain road the Fearful God of Heaven. Since then, I have had a sinking feeling in my heart whenever No. 5700 is mentioned. But this time I was more than willing to go. Shanguan Xing was there. Xing named for a star, as he is to me.

I don't know what made the leadership so generous. They actually sent me in an emergency car. When we reached the clinic at headquarters, it was already night. And we were only halfway to our destination.

The emergency car was not equal to the high and dangerous Daban road ahead, so we had to change vehicles. As if everything had been ordered ahead, a military patrol car waited in the yard of the clinic, its front lights on. The carriage was tightly wrapped in canvas; seen from a distance, it looked like a huge slab of marble.

The head of the clinic handed me a tin of canned oranges. I ate a few mouthfuls and walked up to the car, my whole body already aching from the first half of the ride. I knew I had the whole night before me.

Suddenly I noticed the number on the car: G2-00112. Wasn't this Shanguan Xing's patrol car? "Xing, Xing," I called out.

A young soldier in a soiled army suit walked from behind the car. He stared at me.

"Did you call Shanguan Xing?"

"Yes, where is he?"

"At the outpost."

"Oh, so he's the patient after all! Is he very ill?"

"I don't know. I've been on an assignment for three days. I'm just back."

"You are . . . ?"

"Just the probationary driver of this car." He tried to smile, but only made a grimace. "Don't worry. Shanguan Xing is so healthy, I'm sure you can deal with his little problem. Please get into the car."

So saying, he took my oxygen tank and first-aid kit and put them into the front seat.

Just look at this car! I couldn't help fuming inwardly at the administrators of the clinic. Why didn't they provide us with a decent car?

II.

"Are you Comrade Moon?"

"What do you mean—*moon*?" I asked. "My name is Qin Yue!"

"Exactly. Yue, isn't that *moon*? Everybody says you are kind to patients, as tender as the moon!"

The new arrival was a large-headed soldier, dusty and disheveled. He held his fur hat with one hand, while over his other hand lay his greatcoat. His hair was a ragged mass of wild straw, and an untidy stubble of beard covered his face. He reeked of petrol and sweat, as if he had just come from an expedition.

"Are you ill?" I asked him, puzzled, as I pushed over a bench.

"No. In the Karakunlun Mountains, you're only ill when you're on a stretcher. I'd like to borrow something."

He put his hat and coat on the bench and extracted a pair of scissors from a holder on the table, the pair we keep for cutting bandages. He started to cut at his beard and hair in front of the mirror in the corner of the room.

I got over my surprise and cried: "Hey, you can't

barber yourself here. This is the outpatient clinic!"

"Sure. A man's face faces outward, doesn't it? Isn't it the outpatient clinic's job to fix up the outward part?" he drawled, while his broad, greasy back shook under his jacket as he chuckled.

So, I thought, another of those mischief-making scamps! Our little hospital at the military base is often invaded by their kind. They would come slouching in, humming a tune, some with a cold or a headache, but most perfectly healthy. They just want to have a look at us young nurses—to nurse their eyes, so to speak. They are utterly shameless, planting themselves in the clinic and trying to engage us in conversation. When we get angry and shout at them, they say our service is poor. Sometimes we complain to our superiors, but they always make light of the matter, saying, "They mean no harm, those young men; just imagine, they're up in the mountains year in, year out; they hardly ever see a bird, not to mention a pretty girl. Next time they appear, try to be more flexible." What sensible advice! Just what does it mean to be more flexible?

"Comrade, please leave." I tried to be patient. "This clinic is for treating the ill, not for haircutting. It won't do to mess things up around here. Please go."

"Don't be angry. I just need another three seconds—one, two, three."

The scissors were replaced with a clatter; but immediately, as if by magic, the soldier produced an electric comb from his pocket, plugged it into a socket, and stood again in front of the mirror. He swished the comb through his hair, trying to produce a wavy effect.

I had never expected to meet such a dandy on the Karakunlun front. I was both angry and amused.

"Will you never finish?" I shouted.

"Sorry. Just one last bit of tidying-up."

The electric comb was getting overheated, and let out wisps of bluish smoke as it worked through his hair.

"You folks at the base are real lucky, with electricity all the time. The generator at our outpost has stopped functioning for six months."

"Too bad! Serves you right for playing the dandy! Just look at your hair. Is it worth the electric comb?"

"I have as much right as the next man to . . . Look, I'd rather not talk if you don't mind."

"Who wants to hear your nonsense! Will you leave or not? I'm going to report you."

But he was immovable. With precision he stood at attention and reported himself: "Karakunlun border troop No. 5700 outpost, driver of patrol car and captain of service groups S-h-a-n-g-u-a-n X-i-n-g! Isn't that a wonderful coincidence? You are Yue, the moon, while I am Xing, the stars."

At first I was speechless with anger, then I stuttered, "You, you, you just wait!" And I rushed out to the doctor on duty.

When I brought back the big, burly duty doctor, the scamp had disappeared. The clinic was spotlessly clean.

III.

Was there a jolt? I suppose so. I did feel a slight jolt. But the driver treats it like a major accident. He jumps out of the car, goes back to inspect something in the trunk, fusses about for a while, then walks around the car until he is sure everything is all right. Finally he climbs back in and we resume our slow journey.

"So that's the way you care for your captain, is it?"

I ask. "Let him lie waiting while you squander time. If it were the other way around, I can easily imagine how Shanguan Xing would rush on his errand."

I remember that time, during my first assignment to the No. 5700 outpost. It's shocking that a military hospital like ours, with the border troops under our care, doesn't have an emergency car fit for mountain roads. Whenever we are on an emergency mission up the mountains, we nurses often hitch a ride in a passing car.

On that occasion I was lucky. A military patrol car drove by, I raised my hand . . .

"Where are you going?"

"No. 5700 outpost. There's a patient. Is it on your way?"

"Get in—quick."

The door flew open. I put in one foot when I got a shock, as if bit by a scorpion. What do you think? The driver was the troublemaker at the base hospital the other day. When he saw me, he was also stunned.

"Just my bad luck," I cried, and prepared to get out. He pulled me into the car and slammed the door.

"What are you doing? I'm not riding with you!" I cried.

He let go of me. "You're looking for an excuse to get out of this job," he said disdainfully. "Little coward."

"Watch your mouth!"

"You are a coward if you daren't go to the outpost. It's five thousand seven hundred meters above sea level. Birds can't fly over it; wild goats can't climb it; you're not much better."

"If you think that, you're in for a disappointment." I sat down firmly on the seat.

"That's the right spirit. You're lucky I came along. You won't meet another express car like mine. There's a special bond between us, don't you think? The star and the moon."

"Behave yourself."

"Behave myself? Now what constitutes good behavior? Do you judge by words alone?" He winked at me and stepped on the gas. The car shot off like an arrow, and the speedometer needle leapt to eighty kilometers.

"What are you doing, driving so fast?" I was frightened and cried out in spite of myself.

"Aren't you in a hurry to reach your patient? Do you want me to crawl?

"Oh, you're afraid we'll have an accident? Don't worry. I'm not married yet, so suicide can wait."

He stepped up speed again. The car whizzed past telegraph poles and the road flashed by. I held tightly on the side, my heart in my throat. As for him, he kept one hand on the wheel while with the other he reached out and put on a pair of snow glasses. He lifted back his head and whistled a marching song.

I really didn't know what to make of him. *I must get him under control,* I thought, *or he'll get the upper hand with his pranks. There's a long way ahead.*

IV.

A gust of wind sends a column of dust wafting in the valley gorge. I feel a headache coming on. As I look around, I see that now we are at Dead Men's Valley. . . .

On that trip with Xing, I was also jolted out of my doze by an acute headache. I had meant to get Xing under control, but somehow had fallen asleep on his shoulder. "What a bother." I moved away from him hastily.

"How do you feel?"

"Perfect!"

"Aw, come off it," he protested, "this is Dead Men's Valley. Four thousand meters about sea level. Even I am feeling short of oxygen."

Dead Men's Valley! What a name! A mass of lights twinkled in front of us.

"Dead Men's Valley indeed! Don't I see a military base ahead?"

"Military base?" He laughed outright. "We passed that hours ago while you were sound asleep. Those lights in front of us aren't lamps but burning sulfur, what we call ghost fire. . . ."

He drove in a zigzag to let me have a clearer view of the road on both sides. Indeed, the road banks were cluttered with bones and skulls. You could even see the eyesockets on some of them. My hair stood on end.

"Do you know where these skeletons come from?" He cleared his throat as if for a lecture. "Here is the silk road of ancient history. In the daytime, you can see a big white pillar. According to legend, Xuan Zhuan used to tie his horse to that pillar. And there's a deep cave, where the traders and pilgrims used to take shelter. All these skeletons are those of traders and pilgrims throughout the ages; there are skeletons of horses, oxen, camels, and of course, human beings. I think it's thrilling, that we are actually guarding this ancient silk road."

He stopped the car and rushed out. I heard the sound of bones cracking. The sulfur fires swam around me. I was alone and frozen with fright.

"Come back," I ordered, not wanting him to perceive my fright.

"Coming, coming," he answered. And suddenly he was beside me with a parcel. "Just put that under your feet, will you?"

I touched it. It was icy cold. I looked. My God, it was a bag of bones! I cried out in fright and pushed it away. "Why do you meddle with them?" I was so angry and frightened I could hardly speak.

"They are very useful, let me tell you. But if you object, I'll store them in the back."

He patiently picked up the pieces of bone that I had scattered and stored them away. Then he picked up a skull and asked, "Who do you think he was?"

"Go away!" I cried, and slammed the door.

He stood aside and smiled as he looked over the skull. "Perhaps he was a hero who conducted cultural exchanges between China and the West. Perhaps he used to lead processions of camels over these high mountains, and one day he ran out of provisions and was caught in a storm and he and his procession collapsed here. Or perhaps he was a smuggler of ancient relics and died here, punished for avarice. Whoever he was, let's treat him humanely."

He scooped out a hole by the road, buried the skull, and placed a boulder over it. That done, he resumed driving.

He drove at great speed. The world was silent around us except for the sound of his motor and the rushing wind. I felt suffocated, hoping to get out of Dead Men's Valley as soon as possible.

"It's so boring like this. Won't you talk to me? Please, please."

I turned my head away and didn't answer. I'd had enough of his tricks.

He feigned dejection. "When beauty is so grand she won't open her mouth and so smug she won't look at people, she's no beauty after all."

I turned to him fiercely. "I don't want any of your comments. To tell you the truth, that affair at the base hospital is not over yet. When we get up to the outpost, I have plenty to say to your superiors."

I thought that would silence him effectively. I was wrong.

"Oh that! I've already reported it myself and made whatever explanation was necessary." He turned and saluted me.

I still wore a grave face. "You needn't feel compelled to keep me entertained."

"Then what do you want me to do?" He sighed. "To tell you the truth—only you mustn't laugh at me—that day, I wanted to get my picture taken. You see, somebody in my hometown was going to introduce me to a girl. I needed a photo of myself. We don't often come down the mountains, so I planned to get the job done on that trip. But I looked a fright. I had to tidy up for the picture, and the barber next door said I was too dirty; they wouldn't touch my hair. So I went and bought that electric comb. I thought others at the outpost could use it too. If I had the money, I would have bought scissors and mirror as well and wouldn't have gone to your clinic to do the job. But anyway, all my trouble came to nothing. The girl didn't like my looks. I blame myself for being so foolish. Since then, I've taken drastic measures. See!"

He took off his hat. His clean-shaven head looked perfectly like a gourd.

"This, I say, is the style of a soldier. Take me as I am. If not, off you go. That's my attitude."

I couldn't help laughing. The car bumped suddenly and our heads collided. It hurt so much the tears welled up in my eyes.

"Oh, my dome is smashed!" he protested.

V.

We are now out of Dead Men's Valley, in front of a
river with no bridge. Luckily the flooding season is
over. The river is dry, and we can cross safely.

Even so, the driver stops.

He gets out of the car, and one by one carries out
of his way several boulders of moderate size. Only
then does he steer the car slowly and carefully across
the riverbed. I am so impatient I could scream. At
this rate, when will we ever get to the outpost?

Shanguan Xing is ill, waiting for aid. I think of the
time he drove me across this same river.

That night the swollen river was frightful to see.
Under the car lights, the icy waters swirled in all directions, shooting up one moment, tumbling down
in a whirlpool the next.

I looked at him, then back at the flood. "What's to
be done?"

He threw a few stones into the river to test the depth,
thought it over a few minutes, and decided to risk
it.

"Are you sure we can pass?" I trembled. "The
water is so deep."

"No problem. This is a patrol car—with very im-
pressive horsepower."

And so we went down the river. The water immediately covered the lower part of the car. He sat as
still as a statue, steering the car. The water in front
formed a sheet of ice moving in a fanlike mass. I was
dead frightened that the car would overturn and be carried away like a leaf on the water. I clutched with
both hands tightly, until I realized I was clutching
Shanguan's arm; I let loose quickly, as if burnt.

Suddenly the car bumped against a big boulder. It

made some sputtering sounds and then stopped. All at once pieces of ice began to crash at the car and water started to seep in from the door. I cried out in fright.

Shanguan was also tense. He cursed under his breath and fiddled with the ignition, but the car wouldn't budge. With the car in the middle of the river, we couldn't even open the door to escape. I thought: *this comes of your bravado, you braggart.* How I hated him at that moment.

I smelled alcohol. I turned and saw him finish a bottle of whiskey and throw it out the window.

"Turn the other way," he said.

I didn't understand but turned around all the same. I heard him fumbling with his clothes. He was going into the river.

The river, so deep, so cold. How could he? As a nurse, I felt it my duty to keep him from hurting himself.

"No, you mustn't! It's too cold!"

He was fumbling under his waist.

"You don't know what you're talking about," he said hotly. "Do you expect us to sit here forever?"

"We'll just have to wait until daylight for help to arrive."

"Wait for daylight! The patient is waiting at the outpost; the generator in my car is needed. Neither of these can wait. Besides, my car will be wrecked, soaked in water for so long."

"But you'll freeze."

"I've done this before, and never came to harm. Don't be uneasy. If you'll just put your feet up on the seat and turn the other way . . ."

I didn't know what to do and obeyed him mechanically. I heard a splash and the banging of the door as it slid open and closed in a trice. A gush of water swept into the car. I looked and saw him waist-deep in the water, tugging fiercely at the generator. The handle beat against the water and the whole car vibrated with the movement.

I glanced into the water and my heart froze. I felt as if it was I and not he standing there. Countless needles of steel seemed to be drilling into my very bones until my heart was ready to burst.

Suddenly the car began to puff. It's working! I opened the door and called, "Come in quick!"

His teeth were chattering as he entered. "Please turn, turn . . . don't mind me. . . ." he said in embarrassment as he struggled into his clothes.

I didn't obey. In fact, I helped him on with his dry clothes.

Suddenly he began to cough. Once, then again and again until he couldn't stop.

VI.

Once back on land, I gave him medicine and rubbed his chest and legs with alcohol. He was in good shape. I knew he'd recover in no time.

The car sometimes disappeared in the morning mist, only to emerge again in the bright glow of dawn. Even with the beauty surrounding us, I was preoccupied with Shanguan. For me he represented a big question mark, as well as a big exclamation point. It was my turn to draw him out.

"By your accent," I said, "you seem to be a native of Xinjiang."

He was surprised at my speaking to him at all. "I grew up in Xinjiang. My native place is Soozhou."

"Soozhou? Such a beautiful city! Why did you come to Xinjiang?"

"Why do you ask?"

"Didn't you say that driving is boring and you wanted to talk?"

He frowned as if at some unpleasant memory, but then quickly brushed it away.

"So you want to hear the story of my adventures? It's the old old story."

His father had been labeled a rightist in 1957. On the eve of the Cultural Revolution, he had been sent to the Tarim Basin area in Xinjiang for labor under surveillance. He brought his two sons with him, as his wife had divorced him on political grounds. (It was called "drawing the line" in those days.) In the deserts of Tarim, Xing had shepherded sheep, driven cattle, and farmed the land. Altogether he spent fourteen years there.

My mood changed. My spirits became heavy and something seemed to gnaw at my heart.

"And now," I asked him, "is your home still in Tarim?"

He coughed gently. "In 1979 my father's verdict was reversed and he went back to Soozhou with my brother."

"Why didn't you go back?"

"There were a few things to dispose of, like the house we lived in and a few sticks of furniture, so I stayed on, planning to join them later. Then the army started recruiting, and I signed up."

"Yes, but you have suffered so much. You should seize the chance to go back."

"Do you think?" He smiled bitterly. "Yes, I did plan to go back to Soozhou. But you can't imagine how I've longed to be a soldier. In the old days that was out of the question. After all, I was the son of a class enemy. But my father was rehabilitated, and the army opened its arms to me. I couldn't resist the chance."

"But what does your father say?"

"He was not in a position to say anything."

"Why?"

"He died right after he arrived in Soozhou."

"Died of illness?"

"No, of happiness." He sighed. "As soon as he reached his native city, his unit allotted him housing and assigned him a new job and presented him his back salary as compensation. He held the bagful of bank notes, laughing and crying. And had a heart attack."

"How ironic."

"I know. Decades of oppression and hard life didn't kill him, but he died of wealth and happiness."

I was silent.

"Stranger things followed that," he added. "My brother abandoned my father's body and started a terrible row with one of my uncles about the bag of money. That's not decent behavior even between ordinary acquaintances, not to mention blood relations. Whereas at our outpost, once we were cut off by snow and had no vegetables for three months. When the cook managed to make some soup from leftover garlic, we all passed it around and finally gave it to two sick comrades. That's what I call compassion."

The car raced on faster than ever.

"I never imagined you had been so unfortunate," I remarked with sympathy.

He smiled forlornly as he took out a pinch of tobacco and tried to roll it as he held on to the wheel.

"It's good for me. When life is too smooth, it's not good for you. Adversity is my teacher and my only wealth. When I'm at the brink, I don't think of the depths down below, but of a ladder."

I pondered his words.

The car bumped and the tobacco dropped from his hands. He took out another pinch.

"You shouldn't smoke," I said.

"I'm not an addict. I need to smoke to keep awake."

I now noticed that he was very very tired, that his eyes were bloodshot.

"Then let me help," I said, and took the tobacco from his hands.

"Do you know how to do it?"

"I can learn, can't I?"

A strange gleam seemed to light up his face.

The weather suddenly changed. A leaden sheet of gray moved over and enveloped all the surroundings in one dull mass.

VII.

We are still grinding on. And the whole world has turned white, it seems—as if all the ice and snow in the world are gathered here. On the winding mountain road, our car veers close to the chasms below. No wonder it's called the Heavenly God's Daban; possibly the gods themselves cannot cross Daban.

The driver is enough to drive me crazy. At every opportunity he stops and checks the canvas covering the back of the car. I lie back in the seat, without even the energy to tell him to hurry. My head is racked with pain. Hold on, hold on, I remind myself. This time you must make it across Daban.

I remember that last ride I took with Shanguan. The weather was awful. As we neared Daban, a snowstorm overtook us. The wind and snow came down on us like an army of wild horses. The mountains seemed to turn upside down. Grains of snow covered the windscreen in a thick coating.

Steering with one hand, Shanguan opened the door

and stretched his neck out to have a better look at
the road. He was soon covered with snow. His face
turned blue while his bloodshot eyes began to water
and coated his cheeks with ice.

I felt the cold stabbing at my own breast and pulled
at his sleeve. "Come in. You'll catch cold."

He shouted at me through the wind. "We mustn't
stop! The snow hasn't cut off the road yet, so we
must hurry. Once we get to Daban, we'll be all right."

The car moved on inch by inch. We were twenty-
five or thirty kilometers from the top of Daban
heights, when the snow thickened and our wheels were
buried in snow.

Suddenly the car slid on a sheet of ice hidden under
the snow. It backed suddenly and started to slide
down. "Jump!" he cried as he opened the door and
pushed me out. I was on the ground before I knew
it. He finally stopped the car—just at the edge of the
road. One wheel was halfway sticking out over the
abyss. The misty depths seem to yawn like the mouth
of a huge wolf.

He removed some boulders from under the snow and
pushed them against the jutting wheel, then started
to dig away the snow clinging to the wheel. So hard
were the ice and snow, it was like beating against
iron. Every few blows of his pickax would make only
a slight mark in the ice. Seeing him so tired, I insisted
on helping, and made him hand over the pickax. My
fingers were so numb that, after two or three strokes,
the pickax flew from my grasp and hurtled down the
abyss. I was so ashamed of myself I could have cried.

"Never mind. I'll find a way."

He helped me to the side of the road where there
was shelter from the wind. Scooping up a wall of
ice, he laid down his fur coat and made me sit down.
He then took out a slab of iron and began hitting at

the ice with that. In the falling snow, he was covered with white. He knelt there and dug on, sparks of ice flying about him.

Every time I started to move, my stomach would turn. So I sat there doing nothing. I had been in such a hurry I did not even bring my fur hat, and soon my cheeks were stinging with cold. I tried to cover up my ears but something cold and slimy fell into my hands.

"Oh my ears! My ears have fallen off!" I cried, not even daring to look into my hands.

"What's happened?"

"My ears, my ears have dropped away." I was on the point of crying. What was a girl to do if she lost her ears?

He rubbed at his eyes and looked at me again. "Ears? What are you talking about?"

I pressed the object in my hand and it cracked to little bits and turned to water. So it was the coating of ice over my ears that had fallen off!

He smiled and said, "Cover your ears with your hands."

I knew what I should do. Only I couldn't lift my hands.

"Let me do it for you."

He stretched out his big hands and, covering both my ears, began to rub gently. His hands were soft and warm, and soon blood was circulating through my cheeks and ears again. Then he took out his coat from the driver's seat and covered my head with it. Then he went back to work on the ice.

The warmth of his hands stayed with me; I felt my cheeks burning. . . .

The snow fell thick and fast. Shanguan came back from digging, his expression grave. I knew the situation was serious.

"The ice and snow are too thick. I can't dig through them." He put down the slab of iron. "It's not too far now. I'm going to walk up to get help."

"Walk?" It seemed impossible to me. "Let's wait. The people at the outpost will surely come to look for us."

"Of course they will, but who knows when, and then they don't exactly know our position. I must go. You wait here; I'll be back before dark."

"No. I'll walk with you."

"This is no joking matter. It's a good thirty kilometers in the snow. And at this altitude too! How can you manage?"

"I can, I can. . . ."

I struggled, but fell at the first step.

"Don't be afraid," he said as he helped me sit down. "There are no wild animals here. You only have to stay wrapped up. Also, you better stay on this side, in case the car slides."

He built up the wall of ice around me higher and thicker and then took out from the back of the car the parcel of bones and placed them beside me. Then he poured petrol over the bones and lighted up a fire. So that's why he had gathered those bones!

"And here is the lighter. Keep it and strike a fire when you feel cold. Take care."

"And you too." I held his big rough hands, ready to cry. My heart felt empty.

He looked at me hard, then saluted comically. Within seconds his broad outline disappeared in the hazy whiteness ahead.

On the snow his tracks were visible, like an unending chain, tugging at my heart.

VIII.

We have finally made it over the Daban of the Heavenly Gods, and I can make out the rows of grayish barracks at the top of the mountain. The nearer we get, the more anxious I become. I would give anything to fly straight to Shanguan.

But, as if to exasperate me further, the driver stops again. He takes out a piece of rag, goes to a puddle nearby, soaks and wrings the rag, then starts to wipe his car.

It is more than I can bear.

"Can't you wait till we get to the outpost?"

"No, we're close to home. It's better to spruce up first."

"Don't you know your captain is ill? What I need is time, time!"

"Still, I think it's better to do this now. Our captain would always wipe his car here, before driving in."

"Okay, you wipe. I'm walking over."

"No, please. In this mountain altitude, you'll be ill if you move about too much."

I jump out of the car, shoulder my first-aid kit and oxygen tank, and rush onward. But I haven't walked a dozen steps before I am overtaken by dizziness. My breast constricts and my legs collapse under me.

The driver rushes over, grabs me, and says sternly, "Control yourself, will you! Supposing . . ." He doesn't finish. "Ready in a moment," he says awkwardly.

He rushes back, wipes the last few strokes, dusts the canvas covering, and drives the car to my side. He is no speedier than before.

The evening sunset casts a mantle of scarlet over earth and sky. Mountain and valley lie quietly under the snow. The wind is still blowing as layers and layers of snow are swept up and down. . . .

I still remember that day after Shanguan left to walk to the outpost. He finally reached safety, and the commander placed him in sickbay, then came down personally to fetch me. He and a company of soldiers found me according to Shanguan's directions. Thanks to the fire, I did not catch cold. They dug out the car. Fearing I would not be up to the journey to the outpost, they had brought my patient along on a stretcher. I had not, therefore, gone onward. My patient was transported back with me. The commander drove the car himself. Thus I never met Shanguan again, although he was always in my thoughts.

The car zigzags its way forward. We have reached the barracks. Dozens of soldiers stand at attention on both sides of the entrance. What are they doing? Is this for me, or for their car? Suddenly I see that each of them has a white flower in front of his breast. What does this mean? I tremble unaccountably and rush to the commander who had driven me down the mountain that last time.

"Shanguan, where is he?"

"Comrade Qin Yue." He holds my hand and hesitates. "Forgive me for not telling you sooner. Comrade Shanguan has died. . . ."

I feel dizzy and see hundreds of white flowers swimming around me. Somebody holds me upright. Then I see something totally unexpected: the canvas covering the G-00112 car is lifted and the soldiers take down a covered stretcher. It is Shanguan.

So we have been traveling together all the way. Now I understand why the driver drove so slowly, so carefully. . . .

I rush up to the stretcher and gaze at Shanguan's face, so firm and composed. I feel the world has frozen. . . .

The commander is talking. "On patrol duty a few days ago, the car was sunk in a snowdrift. Shanguan went forward to test the way and fell into a ravine dozens of feet deep. We took him up and sent him to the military clinic, but they were not able to save his life.

"His last wishes were to return to the snowy mountains, at the outpost, to be among his comrades. He loves the cleanliness of the snow. He is ever a soldier of Karakunlun."

His last request was that Comrade Qin Yue attend him to the grave. He has no mother, no sister, no fiancée. I am the only woman he has ever known. I am to leave the breath of spring over his tomb so that he may feel its warmth. . . .

The commander explains that he decided to keep this news from me until I had reached the outpost—in case I cannot bear the strain under the high altitude, for fear that I might never make it to the outpost. . . .

I do not approve of his decision. If I had known, I would not have allowed Xing to ride alone behind me. I would have sat by him and we would have kept up a silent conversation.

The commander gives me four letters. Shanguan wrote them to me but never posted them. I look at the dates. He has written one every week since our last trip together. I open the last letter. It is a poem.

> I am a star,
> You are the moon.
> We are both
> Up in the eternal skies.
> You give me light,
> I give you light.

In the beautiful night,
Our yearnings give forth light!

I write this poem on my wreath. I know that
however long I live, I will never forget him.

DAUGHTER OF THE YELLOW RIVER

by Wang Jiada

WANG JIADA *(1940–) was born in the city of Lanzhou in Gansu province. He received a degree from Lanzhou University in 1965, and for the last twenty years he has been an editor at various literary magazines. His "Daughter of the Yellow River," originally titled "The Clear Cold Waters of the Yellow River," was first published in 1984 in* Dangdai, *a Beijing literary journal. A feature-length film version of the story has also been completed.*

People called her Granny Duo. Actually she was only twenty-five years old. But among country people, seniority carries weight, and her husband (usually greeted as Grandpa Duo) belonged to an older generation. I was then but a child, yet, by overhearing the conversations of my elders, I knew that Granny Duo was considered an improper woman.

Granny Duo's deep black eyes were very expressive. When she looked at you, her long eyelashes would flutter and a strange light would quiver in her pupils.

She also had inexpressibly beautiful hands. Although she was a country woman, her hands were white and delicate. In spring when the flowers were in bloom, she would pound the petals of a nail blossom to a pulp and apply a smudge upon her fingernails, wrapping them with leaves. After ten days, she would remove the leaves and her nails would be dyed red. When gazing at people, she liked to hold her chin in her palm, shielding her face with her pink hand and scarlet nails. When Granny Duo was amused, she would burst out in raucous laughter. Then, coquettishly, she would cover her mouth with the slender fingers and flaming red nails.

Although Granny Duo was a bit short, her figure was well made; walking in town or working in the fields, her every movement was light and dainty. She was, as you might guess, the most showily dressed woman around. In summer she would always wear pink or light green. To relieve the afternoon heat, she would actually remove her shirt and stretch out under the shade of a tree. Often in winter she would wear a tight-fitting scarlet padded cotton jacket. Granny could be quite seductive.

She was also constantly hungry. The tofu peddlers often came to our village in Gansu province, their tofu and salt and pepper carried on sling poles. Sometimes Granny had no ready cash, so she would scoop up some beans and exchange them for tofu. When she got her tofu, she would immediately cut out a morsel and sprinkle it with pepper and salt. The pepper would run down her pretty lips, dying them a deeper red.

Each spring people would come and sell their newly cut leeks. They would walk about the village, calling: "Leek sprouts for exchange!" Granny Duo would always be the first to make a purchase.

Strange to say, her house was always full of people, including the people who abused her behind her back. Her large courtyard faced the sun. So it was especially popular on winter afternoons. Granny Duo would bring out long benches for her visitors. The old men would sit and pull at their long-handled water pipes,

then doze away. The younger ones would squat on the
steps over a game of chess. At noon Granny Duo's
sweet-roots would be cooked (she boiled a potful every day); she would place the pot on the steps and
her guests would help themselves. It seemed that she
was constantly boiling water and serving tea.

When the snows fell, Granny Duo had fewer visitors. She would sit on her *kang,* with legs folded, a
cotton padded blanket thrown over her knees as she
sewed. A few young fellows would perch on the edge
of the *kang* and put their hands under the blanket for
warmth. Granny Duo would sit unmoving, her eyes
fixed on her work, sewing stitch by stitch, sometimes
passing the needle through her hair as if to wipe it.
At these times her black eyes would be like two unfathomable pools of crystal-clear water. Sometimes a
hand would stray too far under the blanket and ca-
ress her feet. At these times her inch-long needle would
prick at the hand and the young offender would retreat, his eyes hungrily seeking out Granny Duo's all
the while. As for Granny, she went on with her sewing, unaware of anything out of the ordinary.

This was Granny Duo, a most attractive young
woman. Why people spoke evil of her was more than
I could make out. Was it because she was twenty-
five years younger than her husband? As far as I could
see, she was very good to him. His stomach was
weak and she would often cook special meals for him,
or send for a doctor.

My elders say that Grandpa Duo had been a first-
rate raftsman in his youth. He spent all his early years
carrying fruits and vegetables up and down the Yellow River. Poverty-stricken for most of his life, he
only managed to accumulate a little money when over
forty. He paid two hundred silver dollars—the sav-

ings of half a lifetime—for sixteen-year-old Granny Duo. (Her father had contracted lung disease, and used the money to pay a doctor.) At the time she was but a child and had no conception of love and marriage. To her husband she expressed respect, as she would respect an elder who fed and clothed her. However, there seemed a distance between them, as if they were eyeing each other through a mist—familiar, yet strange, close, yet distant. Sometimes indeed, Granny Duo would feel a vague yearning, an undefined blankness, but her cheerful nature would quickly dispel such gloom. On the whole she did not complain; she believed that serving her husband and looking after the house was her plain duty. Later on, severe arthritis kept Grandpa from rafting down the river. By mere chance the two of them took in an apprentice, an outsider. Probably that was where all the rumors about Granny Duo started.

It was the year before liberation, during the springtime. The young man came begging his way into our village. He was dirty and disheveled, with a ragged cotton jacket on his back. Tall, dark-skinned, and spare of words, he was named Ergeze, or Second Brother.

There was a threshing ground at the south end of our village, on the banks of the Yellow River, and nearby a hut for guarding the wheat in summer. The beggar settled there. He would often stand on the bank alone, gazing into the distant mountains. Sometimes he would hum a local *huar* tune in a low voice. His voice was beautiful—and wistful, perhaps with longing for his home. But as soon as he discovered that he had a listener, he would stop.

I once asked him about his home, but he just smiled faintly and turned to face the river. He would often stand like that for hours. Sometimes, without warning he would plunge into the river, disappear, and

emerge way over on the other side; he would then
swim ashore and lie down on the opposite bank,
sometimes for hours. Ergeze was such a strange man.

One morning Granny Duo went to the river to fetch
water. As she filled her buckets, she caught sight of
Ergeze lying on the sandy bank. Evidently he had just
taken a bath and was sunning himself. His muscles
rippled in the sun. Granny Duo stood gazing at him
for quite a while, then she approached him.

"Hey, you!" she called. "Come help Granny Duo
with the buckets of water."

Ergeze didn't move.

"Hey! Wake up!"

No response.

"Lazybones! I'm speaking to you!"

She filled a gourd full of water and splashed it over
Ergeze. She laughed as Ergeze shot up, his eyes blaz-
ing, his hands clenched.

But Granny Duo soon recognized her mistake in teas-
ing the outsider. Shouldering her buckets on her pole,
she hastily backed away. From then on, everybody
knew that the wandering stranger had a deep sense
of self-respect and would not be trifled with.

But a few days later Ergeze helped Granny Duo of
his own accord. It had been raining in torrents. Hay
and lumber had been washed downstream. (The local
people called this the "river firewood.") That day
Grandpa Duo took out his raft—eight inflated sheepskin air bags—and went to the middle of the river
to retrieve a floating log. But the log was too un-
wieldy and it overturned his raft. When Grandpa Duo
emerged from the water, his raft had been carried
downstream. The wind was strong and the waves
high. Grandpa Duo was helpless as he saw the source
of his income borne to the mouth of the river gorge,
circling round and round a whirlpool.

Some of the villagers gathered on the banks above the gorge. Granny Duo stood out right in front of the crowd, lost in despair as she followed the raft with her eyes. Another wave would hurl it into the vortex of the whirlpool. But the water was so rapid, who could go to retrieve it? This was no joking matter.

Just then Ergeze appeared on the bank. He looked down into the water, swiftly took off his clothes, exposing his wide chest and solid muscles. Suddenly a soft pink hand grasped him by the arm. Granny Duo stood before him, her big black eyes dilated with fear.

"No, no!" she exclaimed. "It's too dangerous!"

He gave her a glance, gently pushed aside her hand, and stretching his arms wide, plunged into the raging river. Time seemed to be frozen as he disappeared beneath the waters. Granny Duo paled with fear while the sweat stood out on her nose. Soon Ergeze appeared on the edge of the whirlpool, swimming toward the tossing raft. Nearer, nearer—Ergeze was on the point of reaching the raft when he was suddenly caught in the whirlpool.

"Ah!" Granny Duo cried out in spite of herself.

Just then Ergeze made his appearance on the other side of the river, far beyond the whirlpool.

"Come back!" cried Granny Duo. "I don't want the raft anymore!"

But Ergeze didn't heed the words. He raised his dripping head and plunged back toward the whirlpool. Everybody on shore started shouting: "Come back, Ergeze! Come back!"

But Ergeze swam on.

At last he established firm footing, reached out, and with one bold sweep of his arm, caught the raft. Then he pulled it to shore. Once on shore, he didn't even glance at the admiring crowd, nor accept Granny

Duo's gratitude. Tossing his jacket over his shoulders, he bit his lips, blue with cold, and made off.

That same afternoon, Granny Duo boiled a few eggs, made some pancakes, and took them to Ergeze. At the entrance to the door of the hut she heard voices.

Guotai, the lame village chief, was asking Ergeze, "Where are you from?"

"The other side of the river."

"Why are you here?"

"Begging."

"When are you going back?"

Granny Duo peered inside the hut. The old village chief was lifting his staff and shaking it in front of Ergeze. "Three days. You make yourself scarce in three days, or else!" he threatened.

"He's not going anywhere," interrupted Granny Duo as she walked up to Guotai. "We have hired him."

"What is that? Did you say you are taking him in?"

"Yes, my husband Grandpa Duo has accepted him as an apprentice. He'll be part of our family from now on." Granny Duo signaled to Ergeze with her eyes as she spoke.

The elder was astonished. "Do you know anything about his background?" he asked coldly.

Granny Duo laughed outright. "Why should we care about that? You can go and find out for yourself." She turned to Ergeze and addressed him. "Remember, tomorrow morning come over for breakfast, and then you set out rafting with the master."

She strode out of the hut, oblivious to Ergeze's look of surprise. Guotai shouted at her back, "If something happens, you will be held responsible."

The next morning I saw a lot of people standing in the courtyard of the Duo household. It was apparent that something exciting was going on. I dived into the crowd and saw that Granny Duo was shaving Ergeze's hair.

Granny would often give the local children a haircut, not minding the trouble and the dirt. Once, my mother asked the village butcher to cut my hair. The butcher was accustomed to handling a big carving knife, and there was no delicacy in his method. He seemed to be sawing through my hair. I stamped about in pain. So Mother held my head while the butcher sawed away, sweating profusely. It really was like a pig killing. I finally escaped from Mother's grip and shook out my half-cut hair.

The next day Mother acquiesced. "All right, Little Sheng, let's give Granny Duo a try." I knew that she despised Granny Duo and never liked my lingering around her house, but now she had little choice.

When Granny saw my hair, she laughed until her body shook. "Little Sheng, you look as if you'd been gnawed on by a dog," she said. She hastily made hot water, brought out a towel and scented soap—at the time she was the only one in the village to use scented soap—and washed my hair thoroughly. Then she wiped the shaving knife on her knees and, holding my head in position with one hand, she performed her task deftly and gently. When she finished, I felt a slight itching, as if an ant was crawling over my pate. She patted my shiny top and laughed. "There you go, sonny!"

But she had never been asked to cut an adult's hair. That would have been improper. Yet there she was on that spring morning, in front of the whole world, barbering a young fellow about her own age! The crowd looked on, amused, malicious. But Granny Duo did not mind them at all. She sat composedly on the steps of her house, her hand moving swiftly over Ergeze's head with the shaving knife, a ring flashing on her finger. Ergeze was somewhat embarrassed as he lowered his head.

Granny Duo kept her eyes on the moving knife. When she finished, she put her hand lightly on Ergeze's shining pate. "A handsome young fellow like you, why shouldn't you smarten up a bit?" She then went into the house and brought out some of her husband's clothes and made Ergeze change into them. Ergeze looked another man. I hardly knew him.

From that day on, he was part of the Duo family. Every morning he would go rafting with Grandpa Duo, and he mastered the craft in a short time. Grandpa Duo's health went from bad to worse and Ergeze ended up doing the job alone. Sometimes when business was heavy, Granny Duo would accompany him down the river. In the daytime he shared his meals with the Duos; at night he slept in the hut next to the common threshing ground. Gradually the cloud over his face cleared away.

But still, he rarely spoke. Apart from rafting, he had to tend to the Duos' farm. He was thus busy all day long. Only at dusk could we see him squatting in his doorway eating noodles from a bowl the size of a washbasin. He kept at a distance from Granny Duo, never joking with her, rarely looking at her. He seemed to have a deep respect for his master's wife. Only once was his behavior strange and unaccountable.

It was a hot midafternoon. Granny Duo was washing clothes on the riverbank. As she worked, she decided to take off her upper garments, leaving on only a stomach kerchief that exposed her snow-white arms and neck and shoulders. To cool off, she sprinkled some water on her arms and neck. And then she loosened her hair and, kneeling on a slab of stone by the river, she dipped her hair into the water and washed it. When she finished, she held up her hair in one hand and contemplated herself, bending over the rippling water: a young woman in a pink stomach kerchief, clasping her long jet-black hair, gazing distractedly, full of unsatisfied longings.

Ergeze was walking back from the fields at that moment. As he passed the threshing ground, he saw this spectacle on the riverbank and stood riveted to the ground. His eyes became blank. After a while, with a low moan, he turned and flung himself down on a bundle of hay.

There was another occasion that also seemed like overstepping the bounds, but it was not Ergeze's fault. It happened when we were piling up the hay.

In our part of the province, we do not cut the wheat but pull it up by the roots and knot it into bouquets. Then mules or donkeys carry the bouquets onto the threshing ground, where they are piled up until they form pagodas with a wide base and a pointed top.

Grandpa Duo owned no cattle, so all his wheat was carried to the threshing ground by Ergeze. Granny Duo stood on top of the heap and Ergeze handed the bouquets up to her. In earlier years the wheat of the Duos would usually make up two pagodas, but on that day Granny seemed distracted. She stood on top of the wheat and kept piling and kept piling—until the pagoda was huge and towering. By the time her wheat was all tucked away, it was past noon. Except for Ergeze, everybody else had gone home to eat.

Granny Duo, standing atop a wheat pile ten feet above ground, looked down on Ergeze. Her dark eyes sparkled. Even after the morning's labor, she was so fresh, so lively, so delicate. A mischievous light shone in her eyes, and also something more unfathomable.

"I can't get down!" she cried. "Oh, what's to be done?"

Ergeze scratched his bare head, at a loss. "You must find a way."

"No, I want you to do something," Granny Duo

said helplessly, her legs swaying on the tower of
wheat.

Ergeze thought hard. "Supposing I spread some hay
and you jump down?"

"Jump! You silly! If I hurt myself, who would cook
your dinner?"

"Well, then, I'll stand here and you can step on my
shoulders."

"Me! A woman! How can I step on a man's
shoulders?"

"Then what's to be done?"

"Carry me down!"

"What!" Ergeze's eyes goggled.

"I want you to climb up and carry me down!"
Granny Duo looked down at the shocked Ergeze and
smiled mischievously.

Ergeze stood still, not knowing what to do. Then
he timidly climbed up a few feet and stretched out
his arms to receive Granny. She slipped down from
the pile in a twinkling and fell into his arms. At that
moment both blushed deeply. When Ergeze stepped
to the ground, Granny wriggled free. They separated immediately, as if struck by thunder, and stood
apart, unmoving. Ergeze held down his head, his face
crimson. Granny recovered her poise first and, picking
up her broom, prepared to walk away. She took a few
steps, then turned. "Eh, Ergeze, do you have a wife?"

"No."

"Why don't you get yourself a wife?"

There was no reply.

"Why don't you speak?"

Still no reply.

Granny Duo walked away as Ergeze plopped to the
ground, lost in thought, his eyes fixed on something
far away. After a while he started to sing a mountain
tune in a low voice:

"Oh my father, you left in such a hurry, the
      sweat of labor on your body.
Oh my mother, so hard-hearted, you too left
      for that faraway place.
That place of lasting peace, to be with father.
No brothers, no sisters, all all alone, what
      support, what warmth for me?
Found, found, warmth, here on the banks of
      the Yellow River.
But why is my heart so heavy?"

That was all, all that was supposedly improper between Granny Duo and Ergeze. And what did it
amount to, after all? Why should they be blamed for
such a little thing? Oh, those backbiting busybodies!
In all honesty, it was only later, during that unforget-
table raft ride on the moonlit river, that my firm belief in their innocence was shaken.

It was the second year after liberation. Our harvest
of fruit was very good. We had three huge crab-
apple trees, all dozens of years old, the trunks thicker
than my clasp. In the summer the leafy treetops
would cast their shade over the vegetable garden, and
water from the irrigation canals would glide quietly
by as the frogs kept up their incessant croaking. Father put up a bed under the trees, and I slept there
every night to guard the fruit harvest. The fruit hung
heavy and, in the seventh lunar month, the crab apples turned a brilliant red. As the wind blew through
the branches, the ripe fruit would fall to the ground.
Sometimes I could retrieve as much as a basketful in
an afternoon.

One day Granny Duo strolled along and said, "And so,
Little Sheng, now that your fruit is ripe, you don't know
your Granny anymore! You little rascal, how are you
selling your fruit this year? By sea route or land route?"

"You better ask the elders," I replied. "I know nothing."

"But I'm asking you, Little Sheng," she said as she knocked at my forehead playfully.

That evening I brought the question to my father; he pondered a little and replied, "By the land route. Taking the river route means hiring a raft. That is too expensive."

A rutted road winds its way from our village to the city; when not raining, the road is always covered with dust. Father was referring to this road when he said the "land route." At that time there was no bus on this road, only a horse-drawn cart to carry passengers. The cart had a carriagelike covering and two rows of wooden benches on each side, seating ten passengers altogether. We would convey our fruit to the city either on this transportation cart or, more often, by use of our legs.

The advantage of walking was that we didn't have to spend a cent on transportation. But it was very slow and inefficient. We were able to carry and sell only one hundred *jin* of fruit—or less—every day. Later that season my father reconsidered this routine and said to Mother: "Let's hire the raft after all." Unfortunately, the next day Father hurt his back in a fall and couldn't move about.

The picked fruit lay in heaps waiting to be sold. If we waited, the price would drop.

I came up with the solution. "I'm grown up," I said. "I'll sell the apples on my own."

Father looked at me, as if seeing me for the first time. He nodded. "Very well, go ahead. You're a big fellow."

That same night I ran over to the Duos to tell Ergeze the news.

"You're so young," Granny said. "Let me go along and help."

So while Ergeze went to haul the raft to the river, Granny helped me pack the fruit.

Ergeze hauled the raft to the riverbank. He then un-strung the sheepskin air bags and blew air into them with all his might, until his face was all swollen and red. Then he placed the inflated raft on the water and the three of us lifted the containers of apples aboard. Ergeze was very clever. He placed the containers care-fully one on top of another in the middle of the raft and left empty spaces both in front and behind. His place was at the front, holding the oars, while Granny Duo and I sat at the back. We could only see Ergeze's head and shoulders by lifting our heads where we sat.

We started out at midnight. To be on a raft going down the Yellow River! My heart pounded with ex-citement. I looked around me. The moon was hidden behind clouds. A thin mist floated above the river. The banks on both sides were also hidden behind a screen of thin fog, as light as silk tapestry. On shore, likewise, the orchards, melon patches, and fields of grain stretching into the horizon were all enveloped in a mysterious, phantasmal mist.

In far-off cottages we could hear someone singing an aria from an opera to the accompaniment of the plaintive Hu violin. Suddenly the sound of the instru-ment wavered and stopped and then was swallowed by the all-pervasive night.

We took off our shoes, rolled up our trousers, and dipped our feet into the water. Immense stars re-flected in the water played around our feet. Suddenly a night breeze blew over, ruffling the waters, and all the stars disappeared, leaving a chain of ripples cir-cling out wider and wider. The breeze wafted the sweet scent of melon and wild pear and the soothing smell of the soil under the autumn harvest. The Yellow River, caressed by the breeze, lay quiet and beautiful, like a weary traveler, finding rest at last.

"Take a nap," Granny Duo advised me. "You have plenty of work tomorrow."

I shook my head. "*You* take a nap. I'm not tired."

This was my first raft ride on the Yellow River. Wrapped in all the mysteries and wonders of a moonlit night, I was bursting with excitement. It would be impossible for me to sleep.

"All right then. If you won't, I will."

She curled up on the edge of the raft, with her back to the containers. She fell right to sleep. After a little while she even started to snore softly.

I stretched to get a look up front. Ergeze was paddling softly, his head and shoulders moving up and down as the raft glided forward.

Water carts on either bank backed away from us one after another as we went forward. Their great wooden wheels covered with moss revolved lazily, lifting the water in buckets. The croaking of frogs broke the silence in the fields—first one, then another, and finally a chorus, bringing life into the night.

The moon crept out of the fields and shed its light on Granny Duo's face. She was more beautiful than ever. Her long eyebrows, thin and curved, were slightly puckered. One pink hand hung down from the raft and drifted on the surface of the river, letting the water play over it.

At last I got sleepy too. Granny Duo stirred and sat up, saying, "You lie down, Little Sheng. Don't be afraid. I'll stay next to you and shield you." So I lay down, squeezing against the containers, while Granny sat on the edge of the raft, her bare feet playing in the water.

A cloudy mist rose in front of me; I was lifted onto it and wafted to a strange place. It was one mass of silvery water, which disappeared into a bluish mist. A low-keyed, hearty voice sang out:

"A high cliff overhangs the Yellow River.
Two clouds are hovering over the gorge,
The clouds make up a bridge for you to cross.
Come over, flower of my heart."

A voice familiar to me replied:

"The crystal-clear water keeps flowing.
The water cart aloft keeps turning.
If I'm in your heart, keep thinking,
Keep on hoping against the months, the years."

The first voice was now urgent:

"Thinking, thinking all the time.
Longing, longing all day long,
Until the tears keep running.
My tears could set a mill turning,
The mill turning, spinning; the bird alights."

Again that sweet soft voice:

"The stars in heaven cluster together.
The star keeps close to the moon.
The moon caresses the Suoluo tree.
Little sister Duo nestles against her love."

The sounds were very soft, hardly discernible, wafted from afar as if heard across a sheet of water, then again right next to my ears. It was like the lapping of the Yellow River, fashioned by a heavenly art, most appealing to the senses, flowing naturally into each other.

I opened my eyes. Everything had been a dream. The
moon was again behind the clouds. It had turned very
dark. The river looked like a dark satin ribbon swaying
slightly in the wind. The trees on either bank looked
like huge pieces of rock as we flashed past. The silence was eerie.

Suddenly, in fear I called out, "Granny Duo!"

No answer.

I sat up, but was held down by something. I
stretched out my hand and touched a thick rope that
was wound protectively over my waist so that I
wouldn't slip overboard. One end of the rope was tied
to the containers, the other over the edge of the raft.
I untied the rope and looked about me. Granny Duo
was nowhere to be seen. I put my ears against the
containers to catch some sounds at the front. But everything was dead quiet. I couldn't even hear the
sound of oars slapping the water. I got into the kneeling position and looked over the containers.

The two of them were there. Ergeze had put the oars
beside him and was letting the raft glide forward on
its own. Granny Duo sat close by him, her cheek
against his broad chest, one arm encircled around his
waist. Ergeze lowered his head and touched her forehead with his cheek, smelling the sweet scent of her
hair.

Ahead on an islet in the middle of the river, a pair
of cranes were resting quietly. When they saw the raft,
they opened their wings and swept upward as they
emitted their sad cry: "Gah, gah . . ."

I was so frightened. I lay down immediately, tied
up the two ends of the rope, and closed my eyes.
After a while Ergeze sang again in a soft whisper:

"The stars above are locked in pairs.
    The brightest one is over the mouth of the river.

Little sister Duo's eyes are deep and dark,
Her lips are burning red.
Her looks tug at my heart."

And Granny Duo responded:

"The peony is king among flowers.
Youth comes first among men.
My brother is linked to me shoulder by shoulder.
No separation ever,
Until the waters of the Yellow River run dry."

Ergeze:

"Go up the mountain to look at the plains.
The grapes in the plains grow in clusters.
I cannot disentangle myself from my sister Duo.
Will sister Duo stay with me?"

Granny Duo:

"The east is turning white; dawn is at hand.
The cows and sheep in the plains are stirring.
Sister Duo has cried her eyes dry.
The city of Lanzhou is right before us."

Their songs stopped. There was a long silence, broken only by the sound of the river beating against the edge of the raft. Finally I heard Granny Duo say in a weak voice, "I must go back." She climbed toward me over the wooden containers. "Little Sheng, Little Sheng!" she called softly.

I made a snoring sound.

"Fast asleep," she said to herself as she sat beside me.

★　　★　　★

In the distance a cock crowed. I opened my eyes slowly. A dark red light suffused the eastern skies, and then burst out into all the colors of the rainbow to light up the river. The mist that hovered over the river through the night slowly lifted until it finally separated itself from the folds of the earth. With the mist lifted, the trees, the undulating hills, the high white pagodas, and the green melon fields bathed in dew now stood out vividly.

Then smoke began to rise from hidden chimneys from both sides of the river. Soon after we could discern the faint murmur of the marketplace.

Our raft trip was coming to an end. I looked at Granny Duo. Her eyes were shining with a fierce light; her face glowed with happiness. She held her chin in her hands and looked far away. Her eyelashes fluttered as if she was thinking, or hoping.

The market was on a piece of open ground on the bank of the Yellow River. There was a wooden arched bridge ahead called the Sleeping Bridge. Across that bridge was the gate to the city. And just outside that gate was the marketplace.

Ergeze steered the raft to shore and jumped up on the bank. Granny Duo and I helped him to unload the fruit. Granny and I carried the fruit while Ergeze shouldered the raft. In minutes we arrived at the heart of the market.

The huge market space was bustling. There were stalls with all kinds of fruits and vegetables. At that time things were cheap. Melons were sold in heaps, apples by wooden containers. A whole crowd of retail dealers carried baskets on shoulder poles and hawked their goods through the market, looking for a favorable deal as they strolled around.

On the side of the Sleeping Bridge was a row of stalls selling beef noodles, baked bread soaked in mutton broth, and soups of assorted innards. Some of the peasants who had finished their business would sit under the canopy of woven bamboo, hang up their straw hats on the wall, roll up their sleeves, and get into noisy conversations. They discussed the market, extracting information from each other, nodding and laughing boisterously as they ate from the huge bowls of coarse white pottery until the sweat ran down their faces.

Ergeze stood the raft upright, held it in place by placing the oars against it, and ordered me to keep an eye on it. He and Granny Duo left the center of the market. I watched after them until they disappeared into the gateway of the city.

I unfastened my containers, took off the covering of wild lotus leaves, and exposed my crab apples. A middleman with a little mustache came forward and patted me on the head. "Where are your elders, sonny?" he asked.

"I am the elder here."

"That's talking big!" He laughed. "Well, master, how are you selling your goods? Will you hawk them yourself, or shall I help?"

"Would you sell them for me? I don't know how."

And so he squatted down and started his spiel. "Bright red crab apples—the sweet scent of one will last for half a month!"

A crowd came over. The middleman set a high price; the buyers offered very low figures; and thus a fierce bargaining campaign was sparked. Soon a compromise was reached. The middleman counted out the money, took two *jiao* as commission, and gave the rest to me with the warning, "Be careful, my boy!" Lighting a cigarette, he set off again looking for business.

By this time Granny Duo and Ergeze were back. Granny now wore a green kerchief over her head, while Ergeze had a pair of rubber-soled shoes on his

feet. The pair smiled at me. Granny handed me some
meat packed in rice. They had bought it specially for
me.

"Eat, little fool," she said, and looked at me know-
ingly. I had no trouble obeying her command.

Then Ergeze shouldered the raft. Granny Duo and I
followed and we left the market. The Yellow River
is very rapid. You can only float downstream; you cannot row upward. So the only way back home was
by foot, carrying the raft. This raft was made of eight
big-sized sheepskin air bags, two in the middle and
three on each side. The insides were lined with tar to
prevent leaking cracks. With the rowing pole and the
plants, the whole affair weighed almost thirty *jin*. For
a weaker man, carrying that raft back was out of the
question. But Ergeze was incredibly strong. He actually carried it on his back and walked the first twenty
or so *li* without stopping. He had a knack of changing
shoulders every now and then without slowing down.
The raft swayed with his movements as if to the
rhythm of a lighthearted dance. Granny Duo walked
close behind him, with one hand on the raft, her steps
quick and light. I somehow felt that she was keeping
pace with Ergeze not only in her walk, but also in
her heartbeat. Her eyes looked so fondly on him.

We arrived at the foot of the section of the Great
Wall by sunset. This was quite near home. Ergeze
put up the raft and we all sat by the wall to catch our
breath. Granny extracted a few pieces of candy from
her bosom and shared them with us. She looked at
Ergeze with longing and Ergeze returned her gaze
with significance. Slowly they both averted their eyes.
Ergeze drew something on the ground with his fingers while Granny Duo was lost in thought. Later
Granny Duo raised her head, looked at the brilliant
sunset beyond the river, and sighed deeply. We had to

go. After the break we walked even faster. Nobody said a word and we reached home presently.

After hearing about the trip downstream, the rumor mongers in the village went wild. As far as I could see, Granny Duo and Ergeze resumed normal relations. They seemed quite distant. Even so, the rumors about their scandalous behavior spread.

Guotai, the lame village elder, was a distant cousin to Grandpa Duo. In fact, the latter was Guotai's senior by one year, so he always greeted Grandpa as Elder Brother Duo. Actually Grandpa was a bit intimidated by his cousin's presence. As for Guotai, he both pitied and despised Grandpa. As to that minx Granny Duo, he could not bear the thought of her! He had always held that it was the misfortune of the clan that Grandpa Duo had taken such a wife. Such a shallow flirt, so wild and unruly, giving rise to so much gossip. That woman was an outrage to their ancestors!

When the rumors were at their most feverish, Guotai felt he could keep his silence no longer. One day he flatly asked his cousin, "Elder Brother Duo, let me ask you. Exactly whose wife is Granny Duo?"

"What do you mean?"

"Don't you know what's been going on behind your back?"

"What?"

"Your wife and Ergeze. They have been acting like a married couple!"

Grandpa Duo smiled. "Don't be foolish. Ergeze is a poor orphan. He and Granny enjoy one another's company. That's all."

"Ha!" Guotai was so angry his face turned purple. He stared at Grandpa in speechless fury, then lifted his head and laughed mirthlessly. "Just you wait and see!"

And Guotai didn't give up his efforts to attack Ergeze and Granny Duo. In time his malice precipitated the final disaster.

The beginning of the end was the eve of the New Year Festival. The provincial leadership sent down a young woman to organize the New Year festivities. She brought with her a revised edition of a traditional local opera, a Qin Qiang play called *Roaming the Turtle Mountain*. We were all overjoyed that *Roaming the Turtle Mountain* was to be staged for the lunar New Year. When it came to picking actors, many young people volunteered. The most coveted role was that of the heroine: Hu Fenglien. Several village girls auditioned with prepared verses and songs. The female official was clearly not impressed with what she saw or heard. Her eyes wandered over the little crowd who had come to witness the auditions—and her eyes lighted on Granny Duo.

"Come over, please," she said.

Granny Duo edged over, very embarrassed.

"Would you like to take a part?"

"Me?" Granny Duo was so surprised that for a moment she was speechless.

Grown women never took part in acting in our village.

"Yes," the official replied. "I want you for the heroine. You are the living image of Hu Fenglien."

Granny Duo was elated by this vote of confidence. She blushed and nodded.

Other actors were then chosen. All the minor roles were settled very quickly, but they could not find a suitable actor to play the hero-lover, Tian Yuchuang.

Granny Duo gathered up her courage and said, "Let me choose somebody. Ergeze! He would be perfect. He has a beautiful voice."

When Ergeze learned that he was being solicited to

act in a play, he shook his head repeatedly. "No, no, no!"

Then he felt a pair of burning eyes fixed on him and saw Granny Duo looking at him earnestly. He swallowed his unfinished words of refusal and silently joined the group of actors.

Later events proved that Ergeze was indeed a good singer. For years he had sung the local *huar*, and since the impassioned Qin Qiang tunes had much in common with the *huar*, he gave a masterful performance. And so did Granny Duo. But one person in the audience was not pleased: Guotai. For him, the pretend lovers were not playacting. Rather, they were both sending out covert messages of love.

Directly after the performance, he dashed over to Grandpa Duo's in a fury.

"Did you watch the play?" he demanded.

"Yes," Grandpa Duo replied.

"What do you think of it?"

"Nothing."

"What!" Guotai gave him an angry look.

"Not bad, considering it's just peasants acting."

"Your wife and Ergeze's acting was the personification of lewdness!" Guotai laughed dryly.

"This is the new society," Grandpa Duo said complacently.

"Nonsense!" Guotai couldn't contain himself anymore. "What has the new society to do with a bitch in heat!"

"Cousin!" interrupted Granny Duo, who had just arrived home. "To whom are you referring?"

"You better be careful," Guotai warned, looking at her threateningly. "People are talking about you!"

"Which of those shameless busybodies is slandering their grandmother? Let them bite their own tongues!" said Granny Duo.

Guotai's face turned black with anger. "Didn't the whole world see you making eyes at each other onstage? Do you think everybody is blind? Damn your impudence!"

"Let them think what they want! I don't care a whit for their opinion!"

"Well, I care. I can't stand there and see people bringing shame on their ancestors."

"My body and my heart are my own! I don't need other people's meddling."

"I must and will interfere!" Guotai stood up suddenly.

"It's none of your business!"

"You're shameless!"

"You're a hypocrite."

"Harlot!"

"Bully!"

Guotai's face changed from white to crimson and then to purple. Nobody had dared speak back at him, not to mention abusing him to his face. This was not to be tolerated! A vicious stream of choler shot up to his head. He picked up a piece of firewood and hit out at Granny Duo.

Granny hurled herself at the old man and laid her nails into his face. Guotai was now furious beyond bounds; the end of firewood in his hand beat like hail on Granny Duo's body and hands. Granny Duo continued to curse him, and even though it brought more blows on herself, she kept on cursing.

Grandpa Duo, at first frozen in shock, finally thrust himself between the two. With tears streaming down his face, he implored Guotai, "Hit me! Hit me instead!"

Guotai gave him a contemptuous look, then stamped his feet in exasperation. Throwing away the stick, he left.

That same night Ergeze came back from working

in the fields. He saw the bruises on Granny Duo, but didn't say a word. He just sat silently on the steps, unmoving, until the cock began to crow. Then he glided away like a ghost to his own bed in the hut near the threshing ground.

The next morning we heard that Ergeze had given Guotai a severe beating. He broke two of Guotai's ribs.

Of course, the incident was reported to the district. The authorities were very angry. They held that Ergeze had already committed an offense by flirting with the wife of his master, and now to beat the village chief! Ergeze must be punished severely! But Ergeze was nowhere to be found. It was said he had run far away.

With Ergeze gone, Granny Duo pined away. She began to look quite haggard. I seldom heard her talk, much less laugh. On moonlit nights, she would sit on a grindstone by the threshing ground and sew a pair of thick soles, stitch by stitch; her hands worked with loving care while her eyes brimmed with tears.

Once, she took out the raft and drifted on the river; she laid heaps of crab apples on the raft. As she steered the raft hither and thither, she dropped the apples one by one into the water. Suddenly it flashed upon me that it was exactly one year ago that we made that trip on the raft. The words of her song floated across the water:

> "The curved moon has risen.
> A thousand stars are twinkling.
> If my love is living, send a sign.
> If my love is dead, send a dream."

Her song broke my heart.

*   *   *

One afternoon, as I walked by their home, Granny Duo beckoned to me. In fact, she had been on the lookout for me and hastily drew me inside her kitchen, saying to me very affectionately, "Oh, Little Sheng, Granny has a special word for you. Little Sheng, do you miss Ergeze?" I noticed that Granny's face was alight with excitement as she looked at me.

"Oh, yes," I said, without even having to think. "Is he back?"

"Yes, he's back." She nodded to me and whispered into my ear, "He's in hiding in the mountain canal."

"Why there?"

"They still want to arrest him."

At that she pushed a little basket into my hands. In it was a heap of pancakes covered with leaves. "Take this to Ergeze, but be careful. If you meet anybody, just say you're collecting pig's feed."

I took the basket, walked to the door, and turned around. "Does Grandpa Duo know?"

She nodded vigorously.

The mountain canal she alluded to is to the west of the village, running parallel to the Yellow River. That section of the river runs close to the mountain cliffs. The water lifted through the water cart runs right through this canal—actually a deep cave cutting through the mountain. The cave was a good two *li* deep and very spacious and very forbidding.

Now, for the sake of Ergeze, I puffed up my courage and crept inside the cave. It was very dark and the farther I went, the darker it became, until finally I could barely see a thing. My heart began to beat wildly, so I called out timidly, "Ergeze, Ergeze."

Suddenly a hand stretched out and caught me. There was a burst of laughter. Ergeze was right in front of me, a sly twinkle in his eye. He looked much thinner, with an untidy growth of stubble over his lips.

I collected my wits and looked about me. On the
dry bank overlooking the running water was a bundle of hay. And a stone, evidently used by Ergeze for
a pillow. So this was his retreat. He seemed glad to
see me and asked, while gulping down the pancakes,
"Little Sheng, how's your family?"

"Well, thank you," I said. "And where have you
been the last six months?"

"Why, I've been to the Flower and Fruit Mountain."

"And where is that?" I asked, never having heard
of such a place.

"Near the Water Curtain Cave."

"And where is the Water Curtain Cave?"

"Little brother, don't you even know that?" He
looked at me pityingly. "They're all in 'The Monkey
King.' "

He chuckled and passed his hand over my head.
"You've never heard of 'The Monkey King'?"

"No," I admitted.

"You poor country child. All right, then, I'll tell you
the story of 'The Monkey King.' "

So he told me of the Monkey King taking over the
Cave of the Water Curtain. It was a wonderful story.

"And how did you know all this?" I asked when he
had finished.

"I read."

"Do you mean to say you've been to school?"

"Yes. But, look, Little Sheng, it's late now. It's time
for you to go home."

He saw me off to the mouth of the cave and stood
under the water cart and watched me walk away. I
looked back. He was still there, standing in the moonlight. His long shadow flickered upon the water.

After that I was sent several more times to take food
to Ergeze. Each time he told me a new story: "Making Havoc in Heaven," "The Princess with the Iron

Fan," "The Cow Monster," and "The Flaming
Mountain." Oh, what indescribable joy these stories
brought to me, a poor boy who had seen nothing
except the Yellow River. They opened to me a marvelous new world; they enabled my imagination to
soar. I could neither sleep nor drink for thinking of
the Monkey King and of his somersault leap over one-
hundred-thousand-and-eight *li*.

Then for several days running, Granny Duo did not
send me. One night I lay alone under the grapevine,
looking into the starry sky and wondering about all
the wonderful things that happened up there. I couldn't
sleep any longer, so I got up, dressed, and slipped out
the gate and made straight for the mountain canal.

I entered the cave and walked to Ergeze's hiding
place. He was lying on the hay, covered with a new
jacket that Granny Duo had made for him. He slept
soundly. I wanted to wake him, but then I reconsidered. So I sat by his side, and before long I fell asleep
myself.

I don't know how long I slept, but I was suddenly
wakened by a rustling sound. In the darkness somebody was moving furtively. My hair stood on end. I
thought it was Guotai. I squeezed myself against the
wall, hoping Ergeze would wake up and run away. The
shadow had made its way over.

"Ergeze, my love, I am here."

"Is it you?"

"Yes. Nothing can stop me!"

Two pairs of eyes searched each other in the darkness. Granny Duo bent down; her long hair fell over
Ergeze's face. Their lips crushed against each other.

I crept away silently, stealing out by another opening
in the cave. Once out of the cave, I began to run.
My heart was beating madly, my whole body burning.

★   ★   ★

Evidently Guotai had smelled trouble. One day he brought over a contingent of searchers and invaded the cave. Luckily the cave was so deep, they walked a long way without finding anything and finally retreated.

Every day I prayed that Granny Duo would send me into the cave with food for Ergeze, but she never did. One night I was restless; I crept in on my own.

There was nobody there. Ergeze was gone, and all his belongings with him. Only the bundle of hay was left behind, and the stone he had used for a pillow. I felt the hay. It was still warm. Ergeze had just left. I came out of the cave and looked. Under the glimmering moonlight I searched for him, under bushes speckled with dew, in the shadow of willow trees, by the water cart. As I searched, I called his name softly.

Not a sound, not an echo.

The ancient water cart continued its never-ending revolution. One circle, then another. My eyes watered. I felt something wet and salty running down my cheeks.

I started back, keeping alongside the riverbank. Suddenly I saw a little raft floating silently on the turgid waters, heading out where night was thickest. Under the glimmer of the moon I could make out that the figure in red steering the raft was none other than Granny Duo. Ergeze was crouched behind her. Suddenly I understood. I shot off after them, running along the bank of the river. I wanted to shout but I dared not. I waved my hands, crying in my heart: "Granny Duo, stop! stop! Let me say goodbye, I want to wish you . . ."

I stumbled and fell into the mud. When I raised my head again, the raft had become a speck and then it disappeared from view. The tears welled up in my eyes and I was blinded.

★   ★   ★

Thirty years have passed since that night. I have been to school, settled in the city. The peasant boy survived all the intervening years of upheaval and he has metamorphosed into a wage earner.

Looking back, indeed, what have I not passed through? But everything has gone by like whirling clouds. Only the Yellow River, the glimmering moonlight, Granny Duo persecuted by the likes of Guotai, and the wanderer Ergeze—only they have stayed on in my memory. These long years I have been to many places, seen a lot of life, met all kinds of men and women—but the minute I close my eyes, the image of Granny Duo rises before me: her bright eyes, her light figure, her pink palms. And with her arises the image of Ergeze, his big strong body and the firm expression on his handsome face.

Thirty years ago . . . and here I was back in my home village, during the festival in commemoration of Souls of the Dead.

I went to the grave of my parents. The yellow sands of the plateau were steeped in the warmth and tender green of spring. The peasants came out in families; the young, supporting the old, went to the graves of their ancestors, bringing food and wine. At the grave site, the villagers performed the memorial rites to their respective ancestors, and then gathered together to eat the food they brought, enjoying a simple comradeship, as in a primitive community.

After the villagers left, I stood on the top of a knoll, contemplating the mountains and rivers of my native land, which I had not seen for so many years. In the gloaming I walked to Granny Duo's grave.

That night Granny Duo and Ergeze were discovered very soon after they sailed away. Guotai brought out a contingent of men who raced after them on four

rafts. Around midnight, Guotai and his cohorts overtook and surrounded their raft. Ergeze slipped into
the water and disappeared. Granny Duo, in trying to
make her way out on the raft, caused it to overturn.

When they fished her out of the water, she had
stopped breathing.

The day of the burial, the townspeople turned out
to bid a last farewell to the woman so many of them
had considered evil. When the coffin was lowered into
the open grave, a last rite was performed: the opening of the coffin for people to have a last look at the
departed. Right at that moment there was a distur-
bance in the crowd. Ergeze appeared, very thin and
worn, his face completely expressionless, his eyes calm
and steady.

The people watched him silently. He leapt down into
the open grave, bent over the coffin, and looked long
and hard at the face of Granny Duo. She was dressed
in white; her face was calm, as if asleep. Only her
eyes, once so expressive, were parted slightly. Ergeze
stretched out his hand and closed her eyes with the
long lashes. A tear dropped on Granny Duo's pink
palms.

Then he stood up and people made way for him au-
tomatically. He made a slight acknowledgment, then
walked away in big strides, never looking back.

At the insistence of Guotai, Granny Duo was buried in an isolated spot, away from the burial site of
her ancestors. Grandpa Duo had loved her deeply. It
was a very special kind of love he had for this woman
twenty-five years younger than himself, something
of an elder's tolerance for a beautiful and capricious
young woman. He had carried with him a burden
of guilt for his seniority. Whenever he saw Granny busy
brewing his medicine, sending for doctors, and look-

ing after him so carefully, his heart would swell with
gratitude. Thus when he realized what was going
on between his wife and Ergeze, he was not jealous;
he forgave them with the understanding of an elder.
After Granny Duo's death, he was heartbroken; what
with loneliness and illness, he died soon after. The
villagers buried him next to his wife, according to his
last wishes.

I was shocked to see these two graves so forsaken.
Nobody had come to put new soil over their graves;
nobody had come to perform memorial rites. It was
true, Granny Duo had no children, and their closest
relative, Guotai, would not allow anybody to add so
much as a spadeful of new earth over their graves. I
stood and looked at that desolate scene, unable to check
my tears.

A flock of sheep climbed up the slope, nibbling the
tender grass as they shook their big fat tails. Following them was an old shepherd in a short fur jacket,
with a spade under his arm. His calmness betrayed a
trace of sadness. He walked to the two graves and
started to pile new earth onto the gravetops—until
they were higher than the surrounding graves. At last
he covered them with a layer of turf. Then he squatted down in front of the graves while his bleary eyes
welled with tears.

I recognized him as the scene brought back that
moonlit night of thirty years ago. He also recognized me. He stretched out a rough palm and held me
tightly, shaking my hand up and down as the tears
ran down his face.

He was not at all the image of Ergeze that I remembered. He seemed to have shrunk. His brows
were furrowed with wrinkles. His hair was gray, as was
his ragged beard, and he was stooped. He was every
inch an old old man.

We sat down and talked about old days. He told me that after Granny Duo's death he went back to his native village. Soon land reform was implemented, and with his land allotment, he settled down. For the last thirty years, during every festival commemorating the dead, he would come and add some new earth to the graves of Granny Duo and Grandpa Duo. Sometimes, if the hour was late, he would curl himself up near the graves and spend the night there. With that admission his eyes gave forth a strange light. In that one instant I saw again the young raftsman of the old days.

The lingering rays of the sun finally melted away into the flowing river. I said goodbye to Ergeze and walked down the slope with a heavy heart.

It was dark as I descended. Ergeze had already spread his fur jacket on the ground beside the graves. He said it was too late to go back; he would spend the night there.

I looked back again at the grave of Granny Duo. On the outer border of the grave, the young grass bent slightly in the wind, full of the vigor of life.

Glossary

fen:

smallest unit of renminbi (RMB), the Chinese currency; equivalent to an American penny.

grain coupon:

coupon for buying grain, issued on a monthly basis according to each person's ration.

huar:

a tune to which words can be improvised; popular among peasants of the Northwest.

jiao:

a unit of renminbi (RMB), the Chinese currency, that is one-tenth of a *yuan;* the current rate of exchange is about 3.6 RMB = $1.00.

jin:

a measure of weight, equivalent to half a kilogram.

kang:

rectangular, elevated platform-bed used by peasants; it often takes up half of a room and can be heated from within by a pipe extending from a stove in the same or an adjacent room.

li:	a measure of distance, equivalent to half a kilometer.
Liu Shaoqi:	formerly China's head of state; overturned by Mao during the Cultural Revolution.
mu:	a unit of acreage, equivalent to 0.1644 acre.
Pan An:	literary man who lived around B.C. 247–300.
pebble bread:	baked bread made with rough corn or wheat flour; carried along on long journeys because it does not spoil easily.
production brigade:	unit for collective farming under the commune, usually consisting of one village or several small villages.
production team:	a unit for collective farming within the brigade, usually consisting of around ten families.
Sung Yu:	writer who lived around B.C. 200.
work-point:	a unit for reckoning the amount of work done in collective farming, ranging from four (for half labor) up to ten (for full-time skilled labor). Its absolute value is determined by the total value of agricultural output of each individual brigade.

yuan:	the basic monetary unit of renminbi (RMB); equivalent to a dollar.
Zhou Yang:	formerly head of the propaganda department of the Central Committee of the Communist Party; attacked during the Cultural Revolution for his liberal views.

TITLES OF THE AVAILABLE PRESS
in order of publication

THE CENTAUR IN THE GARDEN, a novel by Moacyr Scliar*
EL ANGEL'S LAST CONQUEST, a novel by Elvira Orphée
A STRANGE VIRUS OF UNKNOWN ORIGIN, a study by Dr. Jacques Leibowitch
THE TALES OF PATRICK MERLA, short stories by Patrick Merla
ELSEWHERE, a novel by Jonathan Strong*
THE AVAILABLE PRESS/PEN SHORT STORY COLLECTION
CAUGHT, a novel by Jane Schwartz*
THE ONE-MAN ARMY, a novel by Moacyr Scliar
THE CARNIVAL OF THE ANIMALS, short stories by Moacyr Scliar
LAST WORDS AND OTHER POEMS, poetry by Antler
O'CLOCK, short stories by Quim Monzó
MURDER BY REMOTE CONTROL, a novel in pictures
       by Janwillem van de Wetering and Paul Kirchner
VIC HOLYFIELD AND THE CLASS OF 1957, a novel by William Heyen*
AIR, a novel by Michael Upchurch
THE GODS OF RAQUEL, a novel by Moacyr Scliar*
SUTERISMS, pictures by David Suter
DOCTOR WOOREDDY'S PRESCRIPTION FOR ENDURING
       THE END OF THE WORLD, a novel by Colin Johnson
THE CHESTNUT RAIN, a poem by William Heyen
THE MAN IN THE MONKEY SUIT, a novel by Oswaldo França, Júnior
KIDDO, a novel by David Handler*
COD STREUTH, a novel by Bamber Gascoigne
LUNACY & CAPRICE, a novel by Henry Van Dyke
HE DIED WITH HIS EYES OPEN, a mystery by Derek Raymond
DUSTSHIP GLORY, a novel by Andreas Schroeder
FOR LOVE, ONLY FOR LOVE, a novel by Pasquale Festa Campanile
'BUCKINGHAM PALACE,' DISTRICT SIX, a novel by Richard Rive
THE SONG OF THE FOREST, a novel by Colin Mackay
BE-BOP, RE-BOP, a novel by Xam Wilson Cartier
THE BALLAD OF THE FALSE MESSIAH, a novel by Moacyr Scliar
little pictures, short stories by andrew ramer
THE IMMIGRANT: A Hamilton County Album, a play by Mark Harelik
HOW THE DEAD LIVE, a mystery by Derek Raymond
BOSS, a novel by David Handler
THE TUNNEL, a novel by Ernesto Sabato
THE FOREIGN STUDENT, a novel by Philippe Labro, translated by William R. Byron
ARLISS, a novel by Llyla Allen

*Available in a Ballantine Mass Market Edition